Books by Sarah Graves

The Death by Chocolate Mysteries

Death by Chocolate Cherry Cheesecake
Death by Chocolate Malted Milkshake
Death by Chocolate Frosted Doughnut
Death by Chocolate Snickerdoodle
Death by Chocolate Chip Cupcake
Death by Chocolate Marshmallow Pie
Death by Chocolate Raspberry Scone
Death by Chocolate Pumpkin Muffin
Death by Chocolate Ladyfingers

The Home Repair is Homicide Mysteries

The Dead Cat Bounce
Triple Witch
Wicked Fix
Repair to Her Grave
Wreck the Halls
Unhinged
Mallets Aforethought
Tool and Die
Nail Biter
Trap Door
The Book of Old Houses
A Face at the Window
Crawlspace
Knockdown
Dead Level
A Bat in the Belfry

Death by Chocolate Ladyfingers

SARAH GRAVES

KENSINGTON PUBLISHING CORP.
kensingtonbooks.com

KENSINGTON BOOKS are published by

Kensington Publishing Corp.
900 Third Ave.
New York, NY 10022

All Kensington titles, imprints, and distributed lines are available at special quantity discounts for bulk purchases for sales promotion, premiums, fund-raising, educational, or institutional use. Special book excerpts or customized printings can also be created to fit specific needs. For details, write or phone the office of the Kensington Special Sales Manager: Attn. Special Sales Department, Kensington Publishing Corp., 900 Third Ave., New York, NY 10022. Phone: 1-800-221-2647.

Library of Congress Control Number: On file

ISBN: 978-1-4967-4417-3
First Kensington Hardcover Edition: May 2026

ISBN: 978-1-4967-4419-7 (ebook)

10 9 8 7 6 5 4 3 2 1

Printed in the United States of America

The authorized representative in the EU for product safety and compliance
is eucomply OU, Parnu mnt 139b-14, Apt 123
Tallinn, Berlin 11317, hello@eucompliancepartner.com

One

Grrr.

At the sound, I shot out of bed so fast that my feet hit the floor before my eyes were even all the way open.

Grrr. Beside me in the darkness, a large, unhappy German shepherd dog growled again, in full alert mode and ready to roll out a complete set of sharp choppers.

"Wait," I breathed, still working on figuring out what woke her while also trying to slow my heart rate. It felt like a hamster was running on an exercise wheel in there.

The dog whined anxiously. "It's okay," I murmured, hoping the next few moments wouldn't make a liar out of me, as I tiptoed toward the bedroom doorway and peeked out. Thin bluish light from the streetlamp outside seeped through the gauzy curtains at the hall window.

Peering past me down the stairs, Fala growled again. This time it was no more than a throat clearing, but from the hairs stiffly raised on her neck, I knew she'd moved on to the lemme-at-'em portion of the program.

"Easy," I cautioned. The banister was cold under my hand.

Fala came down the first few steps with me, then squinted again into the velvety darkness of the downstairs hall.

"Wuff," she said. I wanted to think that she'd startled awake at the sounds of a raccoon plundering a trash can in the alley.

But in the island village of Eastport, Maine, three hours from Bangor and light-years, it often seemed, from anywhere else, we had wild animals galore. Deer, the occasional moose, foxes, and coyotes—even a bear that swam over from the mainland once, and none of them had ever woken her.

"Okay," I told her again, as we padded toward the kitchen. When I snapped the wall switch, the fluorescent ceiling fixture flickered on, revealing its beadboard wainscoting, the tin ceiling pressed in an acorns-and-grape-leaves pattern, and the scuffed hardwood floor with bright rag rugs scattered across it.

On the table were a green glass jug full of orange-berried bittersweet twigs, a frog-shaped cup stuffed with pencils and pens, and this week's *Quoddy Tides*, the "*Most Easterly Published Newspaper in the US.*"

All just as usual, in other words. By now, Fala's neck hairs had smoothed, and my internal alarm bells had quieted, too. Or almost: my big old house on Key Street—twelve rooms, four chimneys, forty-eight old double-hung windows with green wooden shutters—was ordinarily so loud, busy, and overfull, you'd think a hostel for noisy and hyperactive persons was being run here.

But now, it was very quiet. "False alarm," I told the dog. "Thanks a lot, I really needed a midnight wake-up call."

Now that we were up, though, I thought I might as well take her outside again real quick. A couple of steps from the porch to the lawn ought to do it; I turned to the row of hooks in the back hall for her leash and stopped abruptly, staring at the back door.

Which stood open. But I'd locked it, I'd definitely . . .

My husband, Wade Sorenson, was away for two weeks,

working. My elderly dad and stepmother were enjoying a rare trip on their own, a bus tour of northern Maine. My son, Sam, his wife, Mika, and their three little kids were in Portland having the baby's ears looked at: in the matter of my youngest grandson's possible deafness, the jury was still out.

All of which meant I'd been nervously alone in the house for three days now, and as a result, there was no way I'd left that door open. So how . . . ?

I stepped out onto the porch, where the sharp smells of saltwater and fallen leaves rode a chilly breeze. A foghorn moaned somewhere, and it was very dark. Fala whined for me to come back in, but then a new thought hit me: whoever had opened that door might still be in the house.

So, there I stood, barefoot and shivering in a flannel nightgown and nothing else. The breeze stiffened, scattering more leaves. Bell buoys clanked in the distance, and that foghorn sounded again while I hesitated.

But then Fala yelped, and suddenly I forgot all about being scared—so there *was* someone in there.

"Oh, no, you don't," I grated out, yanking the door open. No dog was in sight; no one else, either. "Fala?"

Don't you dare hurt my dog . . . I grabbed up a stick of firewood from the basket by the stove. "Oh, Mis-ter *Prow*-ler," I sang out a little wildly, "I'm coming to *clobber* you!"

In the dining room I snapped the lights on. "Fala?" The old gold-medallion wallpaper glimmered in the glow of the cranberry-glass lamps on the tables. I yanked the draperies back: no one.

Next came the front parlor, with its comfy upholstered chairs, tiled hearth, and grated fireplace; then the sun room, full of wicker and potted greenery: nope and nope.

Finally, I started upstairs. "All right, whoever you are, get out of my house this instant or I'll set the dog on you and then I'll beat you to death."

Which I wouldn't have, of course, but given the chance, I'd

have gotten a few good licks in—by then, I was pretty mad. "I'm *warning* you . . ."

Fala appeared suddenly, shot up the stairs past me, swung left, and ran for my office, a tiny cubbyhole with a desk, a chair, a space heater, and a lamp. The shuffling sounds coming from in there stopped abruptly as I paused outside the door.

"Shh," I told Fala quietly, putting a finger to my lips. The room held tax records, insurance papers, the household checkbook, and so on, along with some rarely used items that I nevertheless found indispensable when I did use them: Night-vision glasses. Camouflage jacket. A Swiss Army knife and a set of lock-picking tools, including several that I'd made myself. And secured out of sight in a gun safe on the top shelf—we had children in the house, after all—a .38-caliber Police Special semiautomatic pistol, loaded and ready.

I opened the office door. Fala lunged past me as something moved in the gloom. I swung the stove wood, feeling a jolt of glee in the moment before impact. Gotcha!

But then there wasn't one—an impact, I mean. Instead, the shape did a weave-and-a-bobble worthy of a Hollywood stunt man and slipped right by me.

"Fala, stay," I said sharply, as footsteps pounded down the stairs and along the downstairs hall before slamming out the door. From the upstairs hall window, I caught a brief glimpse of a dark figure running away down the street.

And I know I should have called the cops right then—of course I should have. But it was so late, I was tired, and they would insist on coming over just to have a look around, even though the intruder had already vamoosed.

Tomorrow. I would tell them tomorrow, I thought, a decision made easier by the untouched state of the tiny office once I got the lamp turned on: nothing taken or disturbed.

A file drawer opened, that was all. And no one hurt, which reminded me. "Fala?"

Her head popped up alertly. By some blessing, she'd stayed

by me the way I asked instead of racing after the intruder. Even now she could probably have caught him—eaten him, too. But that would've exposed me to the Lawsuit That Ate Chicago, dog-bite edition. German shepherd dogs were like catnip to personal injury lawyers, even ones representing burglars.

So, I didn't let her out after him, and I didn't call the cops, either. Instead, with all that high-test adrenaline draining suddenly from my system, I felt as if all the blood had been let out of me.

Woozily, I put a hand out, found the end of the old cast-iron radiator, and clung to it. It seemed clear that I could either (a) sit down, pronto, or (b) throw up and pass out cold, ideally in that order.

Fala looked up at me as if to say, *Couldn't we just get back into bed?* Because she was pretty confident that the trouble was over now—and could she also bring her toy?

A pink knitted snake with a bell in its tail dangled from her mouth. "Yeah, come on," I told her. "That's a great idea."

Back in the warm, dark bedroom, I padded to the window and stood by it for a long moment, looking out, but nothing budged. I was turning away when the dark-green shrubbery across the street started moving, its branches waving this way and that.

The old white-clapboard house over there was nearly the twin of mine: three floors plus an attic, lots of chimneys and windows, built for a sea captain back in the early 1800s. Now a figure crept stealthily from the yard's untidy greenery, up onto the porch steps. Watching, I was just about to reverse my not-calling-the-cops stance when whoever it was dug in his pocket, produced a key, examined it carefully under the porch light, and let himself in, closing the door behind him.

I let my breath out. It was only our longtime neighbor, Wally Bean, entering his own home late at night. Sneaking in, actually, or so it seemed to me—but that was none of my beeswax.

Wally wasn't the sharpest hook in the tackle box, and he

wasn't good at keeping those shrubberies trimmed, either. But he was certainly no brazen home invader, and by the time I got back into bed I'd forgotten all about him.

Settled beside me, soon Fala snored peacefully while I lay wondering: An intruder had gotten in just now, but how, and why? If the reason was burglary, easy pickings were plainly in view downstairs—my dad's framed silver-dollar collection, the spare change jar.

So maybe my intruder was after something specific, or—a less comforting thought—wasn't here to steal anything at all.

Maybe something else motivated him, though I couldn't think what. The people who once might've wished me harm were all in my past, and most of them were dead.

Finally, after a few hours of dozing, I got up again and dragged myself back to the window. To the east, the sun's red edge peeped over the watery horizon, flooding the sky with pink. Gritty-eyed and now too wide awake to bother trying for more sleep, I hauled some clothes on and went downstairs, with Fala galloping ahead of me.

I'd set up the coffeemaker the night before. Now I inhaled the hot brew's intoxicating fragrance like a vampire smelling blood. But the woodstove was cold, no Top 40 radio blared, and no little children still in pajamas slopped spoons into bowls half-full of milky cereal, bored with eating and ready to romp.

Somehow mornings just weren't the same when the kitchen didn't resemble a circus train arriving at a Red Cross feeding station. Then the phone rang and it was my friend and business partner, Ellie White.

"What's wrong?" were her first words when I'd answered. To anyone else I'd have sounded fine, but she knew me pretty well.

"Interesting night," I said. "Okay now, though." I could practically hear her eyebrows rising. "I'll tell you all about it when I get there."

Ellie and I owned a small chocolate-themed bakery called

the Chocolate Moose, on Water Street, across from Eastport's busy fishing harbor. Today, as on most days, we'd be there together.

"You're okay, though? You sound—I don't know."

Funny how a person can get used to other people being in the house 24/7. I looked around the empty, quiet kitchen, where the only sound was Fala crunching her kibble.

"I'm fine," I lied. In the background Ellie's husband, George Valentine, said, "Tell her she can come over here."

Ellie's guest room was private and pleasant, and Fala was welcome. But no way was I going to be driven from my own place by a case of nerves, especially since in the worst-case scenario I did have that .38.

"Tell George thanks," I said. "But they'll all be home soon. And Fala's here. She's good company."

I looked down at the dog, who by now had nearly separated the bell from the snake's tail. Crouching, I grabbed the snake, yanked off the bell, gave back the snake and pocketed the bell.

"If you say so." Ellie didn't sound convinced. "But listen, remember to bring the tote boxes when you come down, will you?"

We used the big plastic boxes for transporting finished baked goods, and today we had plenty to transport. I said I'd bring them, and then, carrying the phone, I unlocked and opened the brand-new breezeway door that led out to the backyard.

We'd installed the door weeks earlier, specifically to make putting dogs outside easier. Now Fala hurled herself through it and made a beeline for the orange rubber ball she'd spent the summer disemboweling.

Even though we still used a collar and leash when it was dark out (see *wildlife*, above), fencing the yard, I thought, as I watched her cavorting out there, was the best thing we'd ever done. Then I looked down.

"We'll need them first thing," Ellie was saying into my ear, "for the class reunion's pastry order."

"Right," I said distractedly. The four dozen chocolate eclairs we'd prepared the day before would just about fill those totes, I guessed as I bent to squint at the breezeway door's new brass hardware, glinting in the early sunshine.

It was a standard exterior-door lockset, put in a few weeks earlier along with the door itself. Now the lock surface bore scratches fine as hairs, made, I was pretty sure, by a tool like the ones I kept with the gun, the goggles, and the camo jacket.

Fascinating. "Jake?" said Ellie. "You still there?

"Uh-huh." I touched the scratches. "Yeah, I'm here."

The marks hadn't been on it when the lock was installed. I knew because I'd installed it. I knew, too, that my visitor had come in by the porch door and exited the same way. I'd seen it standing open, heard it slam when he went out.

But now with the new lock hardware scratched in a way that I recognized too well, I understood that last night wasn't the first time someone had tried getting into the house.

Just the first time they'd succeeded.

My name is Jacobia Tiptree—Jake to my friends—and when I first came to Maine, I had a twelve-year-old son, a car trunk full of cash, an awful soon-to-be-ex-husband, and a price on my head, courtesy of some thoroughly villainous New York City guys who didn't want me ratting them out.

I'd worked for these guys, counting their ill-gotten gains and investing them in all the right places. Also, I knew where the money had come from—the gory details, in other words, all of which I could be made to reveal if the cops grabbed me up.

And they were about to. Thus, my hasty departure. The cash in the trunk, at least, was mine. I'd earned it, and the wages of sin back then were pretty good. But I'd never get to spend it if I didn't vamoose out of Manhattan, like toot sweet.

So I did, ending up a few days later in Eastport, Maine, near the Canadian border. Tiny, remote Eastport was a good place to be when the world ended, I soon learned, since if you lived here, you wouldn't even hear about it for another ten years.

Now, nearly two decades later, I had a grown son with a wife and children of his own, my awful ex-husband was not only my ex; he was also dead, and as far as I knew, there was nobody looking to blow my head off.

La dolce vita, in other words, the occasional housebreaker notwithstanding. After Ellie and I hung up, I opened the kitchen woodstove, built a tepee of newspaper and kindling inside it, and lit it. Yellow flames went up with a *whoosh* and a puff of warmth, and suddenly the house didn't feel so empty anymore.

Next, I went around checking windows and wedging a chair under the knob of the door to the backyard, sliding the deadbolt on the cellar door, and making sure the front door key was not in fact under the doormat where Sam often left it.

Maybe I was overdoing it, but *better safe than sorry* is my motto in all housebreaking and lock-picking situations. By the time I had all the plastic totes carried out to the driveway and loaded into the car, that old house was locked up tighter than the air hatch on the International Space Station.

The car was an old Fiat 124 Sport Spider, with five speeds forward, rack-and-pinion steering, double overhead cams, and a radiator that spewed hot water all over the inside of the engine compartment for no good reason. With an apricot paint job, wire wheels, and a black cloth convertible top now latched in the open position, the car looked expensive, impractical, and as if its rubber timing belt might snap regularly and without warning.

Which it did. I kept spares in the glove box.

Fala leapt in and settled. I clipped her harness to one of the seat belts I'd had put in, fastened mine, and turned the ignition key.

The engine coughed once as I finagled the touchy gearbox into reverse, then settled to a throaty grumble as we backed out onto Key Street. Downhill toward the bay, the blacktop steamed where sunshine warmed the wet pavement. Fog remnants floated in the shade of yellow-leaved maples and sparkled in the grass.

As we turned onto Water Street, the bay came into view, busy with foam-topped waves. Past the Peavey Library, Eastport's two-story brick or wood-framed commercial buildings stood with their OPEN banners snapping and display windows glittering.

We pulled into a parking space in front of the Chocolate Moose. This early, only a few other cars dotted the street.

"So, doggy, do you want to sit here or come in?" I asked.

The Moose was a small brick-fronted shop set between a candy store and an antiques emporium, with a big bay window looking out onto the street and a few black cast-iron chairs and café tables on the sidewalk out front.

Fala leapt from the car, then sat waiting for me on the sidewalk under the sign featuring our shop's mascot, a googly-eyed moose with massive antlers, buck teeth, and a goofy grin.

The little silver bell over the door rang as we went inside, where we found the floor swept, the counters wiped, and the glass-fronted display case sparkling and already full of goodies. From the high tin ceiling two wide-paddled fans stirred the intoxicating aroma of chocolate morsels melting in a pan with butter.

Ellie's blond head rose from behind the counter. "Hi. You, too, Fala-dog. Jake, I was hoping you'd get here soon. When you get settled, could you go down to the cellar?"

Danger, danger. "Uh, sure," I said, coming around the counter for my apron. "Any particular reason?"

I knew the reason. We'd set a rat trap down there after Ellie saw something rodentlike skitter along the wall and vanish behind the water heater. She must've heard it snap.

Luckily, just then the little silver bell over the door jingled and Hetty Bailey bustled in, pink-cheeked and all excited about her latest cause.

"Tunnels!" she said now. "Dark, spooky, mysterious tunnels. Historical ones! Can you imagine the tourists they'll bring?"

Hetty wore a polyester pantsuit in cooked-shrimp orange and a pair of Asics running shoes. She carried her literature—in this case, the handout was a single photocopied page entitled "Save The Tunnels!"—in a white patent-leather pocketbook, as usual.

She was perhaps the most persistent woman I'd ever met. "Now, you don't have to give money," she assured us in her brisk rat-a-tat voice. "Just sign the petition"—she shoved a clipboard in front of me—"we can get a committee started—"

I looked up from signing the petition. Hetty had gotten a dialysis clinic for Eastport so people didn't have to drive 150 miles round-trip. She'd persuaded the city council to put a blinking red light on the stop sign at the foot of Washington Street, so people wouldn't sail right on through the buildings and into the water beyond. But—

"What tunnels? I never heard of any—"

"Oh, that old story," said Ellie. "Hetts, how did you ever get involved in—?"

"I beg to differ." Hetty drew herself up. You could see how she got that clinic built. "My own grandfather saw them. He wrote about them, if I could only find—well, the point is, smugglers built them. Hacked them out of granite."

I didn't quite see how a cold, dark, stone tunnel would attract tourists, but then, I didn't have to. Ellie gave the clipboard back after signing, and Hetty turned away satisfied.

But she stopped in the doorway. "Oh, by the way, if you go out South Meadow Road at night, watch out for the harassers."

"Harassers? Is that like boogeymen, only they pester you?"

Hetty looked exasperatedly at me. "Smart aleck. No, it was on the news. Boys driving around on the back roads at night, coming up on people and scaring them. Menacing, the news said."

Ellie looked over at me. News to us, that was for sure.

"They'd better catch them soon," Hetty said, as she finished going out. "It gets to be icy in winter. You scare someone, they could slide right off the road."

"Absolutely correct," Ellie told her, as the little bell rang once again. Then she turned to me. "Now, about that trip to the cellar. Please, Jake."

"What, go down there and find a little animal with a broken neck? Pick it up by the tail, maybe?"

Ellie had been a friend since almost the minute I arrived in Eastport, first blinking at the large, decrepit old house that I'd bought only a few hours after first setting foot here and then, seeing how hopeless I was at anything even halfway resembling normal life, practically moving in to it with me.

The trouble being that I'd come here straight from a luxury Manhattan apartment where if you needed a lightbulb changed, you called the building superintendent. Meanwhile the house I'd just bought needed a new roof, a new furnace, a new foundation, and a new everything else, including wiring and plumbing.

But Ellie was patient with me. "Okay," I said now. "But you'll have to do it sometime, you know."

I was halfway down the cellar stairs. She peered through the doorway at me, smiling sweetly, looking like a cross between a bright fresh daisy and the nymph off the Canada Dry bottle.

"No, I won't," she predicted, her eyes twinkling.

And you know what? She was right.

"Here," she said, tossing me an opened package of cheddar cheese.

With it I continued down a set of steps so narrow and winding, it was all I could do to untwist my legs at the bottom. Ducking under a pipe, easing between the boiler and the old coal bin, I ducked at last into the four-foot crawlspace that I guessed must be directly under the shop's front bay window.

The unshaded hanging light bulb showed a dirt floor, a clutter of rubble—a two-by-four, some fallen bricks, a litter of drainage tile pieces . . . and a rat trap minus the cheese bait, on its side on the far side of the small, low-ceilinged chamber.

"Oh, so that's the way you want to play it, huh?" I pressed a new piece of cheese into the bait tray's metal prongs. Not that I had anything personal against rats, they're very cute when they run around in those little wheels, but these weighed ten pounds and had teeth like the tines on barbecue forks. And we couldn't have them in the shop. So, as long as I couldn't stop their getting in, I'd have to kill them one at a time.

Thinking this, I set the trap. It was a simple process that involved pulling back the trap's heavy wire bale and holding it down with one thumb—did I mention that the bale is on a spring as big as the ones under tractor seats?—maneuvering the trigger plate squarely under the trigger wire, then relaxing the thumb to let the bale down so it all . . . just . . . balances.

And any movement will spring it. I got up slowly; sometimes a breeze was all it took. But this time the trap remained poised on the edge of springing, delicate as a held breath.

I backed away. He'd never know what hit him. Upstairs I washed my hands very thoroughly, not sure if it was because I'd handled the trap or because I'd set it.

"So what happened overnight?" Ellie asked again, her eyes on the napkin holders she was filling.

I got the feeling something else besides my mysterious midnight visitor was preying on her mind. But she was looking at me expectantly.

"Not much," I said, except . . ." My voice trailed off at a sudden memory of the open porch door. "Well, except for this one strange thing," I said.

Then, while we loaded the chocolate eclairs into the carrying totes, I told her the rest of it. Her thick-lashed, violet-blue eyes widened at the part about the intruder actually getting upstairs.

"Could it've been a mistake? Somebody just broke into the wrong—" She saw my face.

It was possible for a person to break into the wrong house.

But not twice. That was too dumb even for a burglar. I told her about the new door's scratched lock.

"Yeah, that is suggestive." As usual, she was the mistress of understatement. "Makes you think last night was a second attempt."

Bingo. "Why didn't you call me?" she wanted to know. "And have you reported it yet?"

She could see I was still a little shaken. Having a .38 Special in the closet had in no way made up for not having one in my hand during the actual event. The trouble was, I was coming to dislike having it in my hand, so much so that it hardly seemed worth carrying it, lately.

Fortunately, I hadn't needed it, but that also kept me from going to the trouble of lugging it around.

"No sense both of us being awake," I excused myself for not calling her. True but irrelevant, her face said. "And as for the cops," I went on, "besides taking a report, what was there for them to do?"

Believe me, nobody was going to dust for fingerprints or do any DNA analysis. This was Eastport we were talking about here, not *Law & Order.* I'd call the police department today, probably. Civic duty, reporting a crime and all that.

But right now, I was too busy. As we talked, I'd been gathering up the last few eclairs while Ellie took the pan of melting chocolate off the stove.

Finally, we got the totes outside and into Ellie's car. The Fiat Spider was emphatically not a cargo vehicle—heck, it could barely fit passengers. We dropped a squeezed-into-the-car Fala off at home before going on with our errand.

"It's somebody getting past the locked porch door at all that bothers me," Ellie said, as we drove up Washington Street.

Along the way, orange and black banners hanging from the lampposts proclaimed WELCOME CLASS OF '97! The reunions had begun in June, gotten postponed by a massive nor'easter, and were just now finishing up in September.

We turned onto High Street past the Presbyterian church, now at last having its ugly asphalt siding removed. Old black tarpaper strips and ragged sections of dusty, shinglelike siding material clattered down a metal chute into a dumpster.

A whiff of creosote, like tar mixed with mothballs, wafted over us as we drove by. Moments later we crested the hill and pulled into the parking lot behind the high school, a two-story, yellow brick structure, hexagon shaped, with windowed corridors and a courtyard at the center.

Pale sunshine and the smells of dried grasses and autumn wildflowers hit me when I got out of the car: honeysuckle, purple asters, and the flat, greenish-white blooms of Queen Anne's lace. Beyond the parking lot's weedy verge, evergreens grown together and clipped flat edged the blacktopped surface.

Ellie got out and slammed the car door, the sound echoing off the school's muddy-yellow brick. "Listen," she said, turning to face me. "There's something else we need to talk about."

Uh-oh. The blue sky overhead seemed to stretch on forever, a lone hawk circling high in it.

"I hate having to tell you this," she said. Double uh-oh. "But for one thing, they'll probably be talking about it inside."

I waited. By "they" she meant fortysomething men and women nervously greeting old classmates and side-eyeing old enemies, intent on showing off how much thinner and more successful they were now than the last time they'd seen one another.

"Ellie, what could these people possibly talk about that might bother me? I don't even know any of them."

She took a deep breath. "A dead woman. Right here in the parking lot, late last night."

Now I noticed the small white evidence markers stuck into the grass at the lot's far end, near the hedges.

"They think it happened late, during the dinner or while the dancing happened afterwards," Ellie said. "Lizzie told me."

Eastport's chief of police, Lizzie Snow, stopped in at the

Chocolate Moose each morning for coffee and a doughnut. She was the one I'd end up reporting my break-in to. Other than two deputies, who each looked to be well over fourteen years old, Lizzie was the only real everyday law enforcement we had way out here at the back end of beyond.

"So now what?" I peered at Ellie over the totes full of chocolate eclairs that she'd stacked in my arms.

"Now we put these in the cafeteria's cooler the way we said we would," she replied firmly. "Darn it, I knew you'd be upset."

"I'm not upset." I followed her up the concrete steps to the gymnasium's side door and across the polished floor toward a short hall lined with student lockers.

Okay, so I was a little upset. After a summer of murderous mayhem involving a supposedly haunted house and a guy whose fall from one of its balconies was not quite kosher, I'd hoped for no funny business for a while.

"I'm just wondering why you thought I *would* be—"

Plaques, trophies, and framed athletic awards covered the hallway's beige-painted concrete-block walls. A cooler filled with bottled water and juices stood in an alcove between more lockers and wooden benches.

It all made me feel as if someone would appear any minute and shoo me into a classroom, threatening detention. At last, we pushed through a pair of swinging doors into a small brightly lit institutional kitchen with steam tables, a hooded grill, a monster dishwasher, and brushed steel sinks.

It was all neat and clean, but it still smelled exactly like all institutional kitchens everywhere: boiled vegetables, powdered dish soap, and a hint of spoiled milk.

"—upset," I finished, as Ellie opened the cooler and began taking the totes from my arms, stacking them on the shelves. I quickly rearranged the eclairs in the final tote to hide the bare spot where I'd filched one.

"I mean, are we supposed to be doing anything about her? The dead woman?"

It wouldn't be the first time we'd had to do something about the recently deceased (see *haunted house*, above). Ellie handed me a bottled water from the cooler. "Nothing," she said firmly. "We're doing nothing about the dead woman."

Doing nothing about unexpected dead women was not at all our standard method of operation. Somehow or another, over the past few years, we'd become Eastport's premier amateur snoopers into unsolved murder.

Well, maybe not *somehow.* Possibly a natural interest in the affairs of other human beings—snoopiness, in other words—got us going. But that combined with my own bonehead stubbornness and Ellie's burning sympathy for underdogs kept our noses alert for deadly news.

It seemed obvious why we might not get involved this time, though. Right now, I realized as we stepped out into the sunshine, the school parking lot showed no hint of last night's police presence except for those evidence flags planted in the grass.

"So, no foul play?" I said. It would explain the peaceful scene now: no cops or crime techs. Although that didn't make sense either, because then why tell me about it at all?

"Oh, it was foul, all right." We started across the parking lot. "The victim and her ex-husband came to the dinner dance together. They'd been high school sweethearts, and supposedly they were still on good terms even after the divorce."

A laugh escaped me as we got back into Ellie's car. Until shortly before he died, if my ex-husband and I had ever had a reunion, grenades would've been involved.

"Later in the evening, he lost track of her," Ellie went on, pulling out onto High Street. "The ex-husband did, I mean."

In a wide field on the other side of High Street, a dozen

teenagers were flying small remote-controlled drones, their buzz filling the air like a swarm of bees.

"So, he came out to his car looking for her and found her dead in the front seat," Ellie finished. "Strangled."

We headed downhill toward Water Street. Passing the breakwater and the harbor I spotted Ellie's boat, a blue-and-white fiberglass Bayliner with a black bimini, floating prettily in its slip. At the foot of the hill, we turned onto Washington Street, where the shops' banners and flags snapped like whips in a rising breeze off the water, then we pulled smartly into her usual parking space in front of the Moose.

"Anyway, the dead woman's name was Cindy Munson," she said, "and it turns out that she and her ex weren't on such good terms after all. She was suing him for custody of their daughter."

"Huh." That did make things more interesting. Probably the police thought so, too. "And now," I hazarded a guess, "the ex is having a bad morning?"

We got out of the car. "Oh, you betcha," said Ellie. "Lizzie said the two of them had argued at the dance, got pretty loud. State homicide police detectives are talking to him now," she added as she unlocked the shop door.

"So how come Lizzie told you all that? It's not really like her," I asked.

Lizzie didn't often tell random cop stories. Ellie switched the lights and the overhead fans on, and I turned the sign in the door to OPEN and got the music going: *The Art of Fugue* seemed appropriate, since increasing complexity seemed to be the theme of the day.

"She told me about it because there's a little girl involved," Ellie said, wiping some imaginary fingerprints off the glass-fronted display case.

"She's six. Name's Ivy." Wipe, wipe. "Her dad—he's the ex-husband we're talking about—brought her to the reunion dinner to meet up with her mom. It seems Ivy wasn't in the car, but she was right nearby somewhere when everything that happened, happened.

"Not in the car," said Ellie. "But nearby."

"Okay," I said, "let me get this straight. The kid's dad is the dead woman's ex-husband and her mom's the dead woman." I took a breath. "They went to the event together, brought the kid along, got into an argument, and not much later he found his ex-wife in his car, dead."

Outside the shop's front bay window, an old red Ford pickup truck loaded with lobster traps rattled past. I stepped behind the counter to neaten a toothpick jar that didn't need it.

"And now Lizzie wants us to babysit," I said, because of course that had to be it. "She needs a place to stash the poor kid."

I fussed with the toothpicks some more, suddenly aware of the tears brimming in my eyes. Angrily, I blinked them back.

"So I imagine the ex-husband's getting looked at pretty hard?" I asked. This was all starting to sound way too familiar.

Ellie grimaced. "He's the obvious suspect, wouldn't you think?"

Sad but true. If you want to know who hated someone enough to kill them, check their nearest and dearest.

"So the kid's alone," I said. "And her father's suspected of murder." Like mine had been.

It was funny, but not ha-ha funny, how it all just hung on and how clearly I saw it, that time back when I was even younger than Ivy was now. That particular brand of drowning terror, like the sky is about to open and suck you up into it, didn't go away easily.

Or at all, maybe. So it came as no surprise to me that I didn't want to experience any of it again, not even by proxy. That I didn't want to be anywhere near it, in fact, not even if it made me look like a jerk to my friends.

What I couldn't escape, though, was what it made me look like to me.

* * *

The rest of the morning was blessedly ordinary; cookies and croissants, chocolate-chip muffins, and a fresh cherry pie in a chocolate crumb crust came out of the ovens. Then we started on something completely different, a bittersweet chocolate sauce for a venison roast.

The whole dish took three days to make. Meanwhile, this year's deer season opened soon, and we figured that by the time somebody bagged one we'd have perfected the sauce and learned to lard a venison roast, too, with something called lardoons.

Soon enough, though, the little bell over the door jingled and Lizzie Snow came in. She was a black-haired beauty with dark eyes, red lips, and the taut muscular build of your average top-ties gymnast. For her workday as Eastport's top cop today, Lizzie wore black slacks, a navy dress shirt, and black utility shoes. A black leather bomber jacket hugged her shoulders and a holster with a .45-caliber revolver in it hung on her hip.

She was accompanied by a little girl about six years old.

"Family court just signed an emergency order," Lizzie said.

The little girl was about four feet tall, wearing blue jeans, a blue-striped cotton T-shirt, and red P.F. Flyers. Her straight black hair was blunt-cut at the chin line and her eyes were the pale green of a stormy sea.

A sailboat was embroidered in blue on her little pink ball cap. She looked up at me. I could see her lower lip trembling, but she kept it together. "Hi. I'm Ivy," she said.

"I was hoping you could maybe help me out, here," I said, gesturing at Ivy.

"Terrific. Sounds like tons of fun." Just what I needed—inconvenience mingled with dredged-up emotional baggage.

"Jake," she said. "Come on. The kid just lost her mom."

A thunderclap of unwanted memory and emotion boomed in my head. "Yeah, I'll take her," I said.

Standing behind the child, Lizzie Snow looked harried. In Maine, state cops handled homicides everywhere except in Portland and Bangor, but that didn't mean Lizzie wasn't involved. For her, murder in Eastport still meant emails, phone calls, texts, reports, and a ton of media requests, plus interacting with the state people.

"Great. These ladies are really nice," she told Ivy, and then to us, "I've got to go," she said, and rushed off again to do, I supposed, more of the above.

"Hello, Ivy." Ellie crouched in front of the child. "I'm Ellie."

"Nice to meet you," Ivy said, though clearly it wasn't. Those green eyes signaled storm warnings.

I tried to remember what I'd felt once I was old enough to know that my mom had been killed and the police thought my dad had done it.

"Ivy, you'll be staying with us for a day or so while your dad takes care of some things," I said.

She looked at me as if trying to figure out just how dumb I thought she was. "Is he going to jail?"

I blinked, not knowing what to say.

Luckily, Ellie stepped in to save me. "Ivy, have you had any lunch?"

The dad-in-trouble thing wasn't for us to discuss with Ivy, nor anything else last-night-related, either. Lizzie hadn't had to tell us that it could screw up the kid's testimony, if there ever was any—we weren't exactly newbies at the whole murder-in-Eastport thing. Over the years, we'd gotten a reputation for snooping into them, on account of there'd been a few, and we were nosy.

Instead, Ellie sat Ivy down at one of the café tables and brought her a glass of milk. "Thank you," said Ivy when she'd finished it, putting down her emptied glass and folding her napkin primly. But her small sneakered foot kept kicking a table leg rhythmically, her gaze darting around anxiously.

Which didn't surprise me. She'd just lost her mother, her dad was in bad trouble, and she was about to be bedded down with strangers whether she liked it or not.

"So!" Ellie said brightly. "How about if now you and Ms. Tiptree, here—"

"I'm Jake," I told the child.

"Yes, ma'am," said Ivy, who'd been taught nice manners. She regarded me gravely, with her hands folded in her lap.

"You don't need to call me ma'am, either," I added. "We're just new friends, Ellie and me, keeping you company while your dad's busy."

Ivy's sharp look said she didn't need company, or want it, either. Her sneaker went on monotonously bumping the table leg, until suddenly it stopped and her gaze went blank.

"Ivy?" I prodded, but she didn't respond.

Ellie hurried over. "Whoa," she said, eyeing Ivy's pallid face and blank expression. "Is she going into shock?"

Maybe not physically, but emotionally. It sure looked as if Ivy was going bye-bye. "I don't know. Let's get her some fresh air."

What she really needed, I thought, was a distraction, however temporary, from the past twelve hours' events. But what could possibly distract a child who'd just lost her mother? Helplessly, I cast around for anything big and impressive enough to get her attention, and then it hit me.

"Ivy," I said, "I see there's a sailboat on your cap. Do you like boats?"

Saying this, I shot a brief look at Ellie, and she shot it back with an approving nod, while Ivy's green eyes regarded me.

"I don't know," she said doubtfully, at last. But curious, definitely curious.

Ellie hurried to the kitchen to snap off lights and shut down stove burners. Returning, she pulled on her jacket, grabbed up her purse, and thrust my heavy wool pullover sweater into my hands. We'd have to find warm things for Ivy to wear on the way.

"Let's go," said Ellie.

Two

Twenty minutes after closing up the Moose (we'd stopped at Wadsworth's Hardware Store for a nice fleece-lined windbreaker for Ivy), we were at the harbor, where Ellie's boat was tied up.

A long metal gangway descended from the breakwater parking lot to the docks below. The gangway leading down was steep but safe, with a slip-proof metal ramp and metal railings to grab in case you wanted to slow your descent.

My problem was that I didn't want to descend at all. The ramp got steeper or flatter as the tide fell and rose, and right now with the tide at dead low it resembled a ladder aimed nearly straight down.

"Um, Ellie?" I said. I'd been on the gangway many times, but not when it looked like this.

Ivy glanced up at me, noticed my discomfort, and scampered away, stopping at the gangway's entrance to look back defiantly at me before flinging herself down it.

"Ivy, wait!" I ran after her, reaching the gangway moments before Ellie did. It wasn't surprising that a traumatized kid might suddenly start acting out. But looking down now, I wished she'd chosen a different venue.

Because she was already in trouble. Too far down the metal gangway for us to grab hands, she'd gotten scared, but the railings were too high for her to hang onto. So she'd grabbed the chain-link fencing stretched tautly beneath them and now she was stuck, too afraid to let go.

A boat ride, I thought, as I surveyed the situation, *was a terrible idea, actually.* But clearly the only way through this was to do this, and guess who the next lucky contestant was?

Gripping the round metal railings so hard that I thought they might bend, I started down, battling gravity and my own stark fright on a ramp so steep it was like walking down the side of a building. The laws of physics kept suggesting that I let go and fall, and then of course my nervous system got into the act: vertigo, anyone?

Finally, though, I reached the kid. "Okay," I said, crouching above her on the sharply slanting metal ramp.

But it was not okay. "Ivy," I said. Her lips trembled. Her eyes stared at nothing. "Ivy, look at me."

Her small fingers clutching the chain-link whitened with the effort of hanging on. If she let go, she'd slide away from me, thirty feet nearly straight down to the wooden dock below.

I seized a fistful of Ivy's new windbreaker. "Okay, now, I've got you. But you've got to help. Grab on to me, too."

Desperation flattened Ivy's face as one of her hands lost its grip entirely, flailing in thin air. Then Ellie was there, scrambling down the ramp until she had the child firmly in hand.

But now Ivy wouldn't let go of the chain-link. Or couldn't.

We coaxed and pulled, but to no avail, and now we were getting attention from people on the dock. Probably they thought we were brazen kidnappers or something.

Finally, *Nuts to this*, I thought. Bracing myself, I seized one of Ivy's stubbornly clenched-on hands; Ellie grabbed the other, and then—*two minds with a single thought*—we pulled hard. We weren't rough, but we weren't having further arguments about this. Ivy yelled and started to struggle but she stopped once she got another look straight down that steep ramp.

I felt a moment of triumph when she gave in, but then gravity presented me with a choice: fall or sit. Like, immediately.

I sat. "Hey," Ivy said. Ellie had already turned away and started back up again, thinking that we were right behind her. But we weren't. Instead, all at once we were sliding down the ramp's steep incline as if we were on a sled. At the bottom I just kept going, sliding off the ramp and across a wooden dock slick with seawater and slippery with god only knew what—fish guts and seagull poop, most likely.

Also, I'd crashed into a tall stack of lobster traps and now they were piled on me, stinking of lobster bait. Ivy stood over me, her hands planted on her nonexistent hips.

"You hurt me," she accused, as I climbed to my feet and began taking stock of my injuries, meanwhile wondering if she'd always been an infuriating little brat or if this was just a result of her unfortunate recent history.

"Didn't you hear me?" she demanded petulantly, stomping a small sneakered foot. "I said you hurt me!"

The ramp we'd just slid down had serrated ridges so your shoes didn't slip, but I hadn't been on my feet so my tail end now felt like Swiss steak.

"Not yet I haven't," I told her, and walked away from her. I wasn't proud of it, and I didn't enjoy doing it, but it gave her a little something to think about. For one thing, the scowl slipped off her face almost at once.

"How's it look?" I asked Ellie when I reached the wooden finger pier where the Bayliner was tied up. The boat had a nice open deck area, a cuddy that slept three, and with the repairs she'd done on the engine recently, more power than a locomotive.

"All shipshape," Ellie reported, as if a boat of hers would ever be anything else. Behind me, Ivy took a few tentative steps along the dock and stopped, gazing wide-eyed at the whole other world down here: seagulls swooping, the big, bulky hulls of the fishing vessels towering on either side, the intoxicating smells of fish, diesel fumes, and cold saltwater.

That low tide right now, though. "Is there enough water to get out?" I eyed the many exposed rocks doubtfully. If the tide was too low, we'd run aground just trying to leave the dock.

Ellie hopped nimbly from the pier to the boat's deck. No scraping sound came from below, which meant the boat's keel wasn't hitting bottom.

"Yeah, probably enough," she judged, squinting. "Tide's rising, too. Come on, you can come aboard," she told Ivy, who'd joined us at last and was looking very doubtful as she neared the boat's port rail.

Then with no fuss she climbed over it onto the boat as if she'd done it a million times. Ellie plunged her arm into the aft hatch to turn on the battery, then went around pushing buttons and flipping switches for radio, GPS navigation, and bilge pumps while I got lifejackets onto all of us.

"Nice work hopping onto the boat like that," I said, as I fastened the straps on Ivy's jacket.

She smiled slightly, accepting the compliment. I got the sense that she'd like to forget our earlier episode, and for different reasons I wanted to, also; I could just about imagine what I'd looked like, rocketing down that ramp.

Finally, Ellie turned the key and the outboard fired up with a guttural roar. Nowadays, the old engine had every bit of its original horsepower and few if any of its original parts, a condition it seemed to enjoy. Going fast on the water is not my favorite pastime, but even I knew that engine was a beast and it ran like a bat out of hell.

Ivy climbed up into the mate's chair beside Ellie at the helm while I untied the lines. Then as we drifted away from the pier I jumped aboard again and hauled in the bumpers, air-filled anti-scuff cushions that hang between the boat and the dock.

At last Ellie backed us out of the slip very slowly. The channel here was deep enough for the boat to move in, but its sides were still jagged granite that could scuttle us.

The engine's transmission shifted with a gentle thunk, and we motored out between the fish pier and the dolphin, a massive, oddly-named concrete and steel block where the really big boats tied up—the freighters and cruise ships and so on.

As we glided toward open water the Eastport waterfront slid by, the shops and restaurants, gift shops flying SALE! flags, the Tides Museum with the horse-trough water fountain out front, and the fish pier itself, with the white solar-powered weather station's aerometer whirling at the end of it.

"Hang on," Ellie advised when we reached open water, the breakwater and the fish pier suddenly behind us. She pushed the throttle and the boat surged up onto the waves' bright surface, skimming their tops and only scaring my wits out a little bit.

Spray flew, sunlight glinted, and ahead of us porpoises arced up one after another, black as ink drops. Ivy's lips parted in wonder as Ellie steered us east toward the Bay of Fundy and the Atlantic Ocean beyond.

Gradually a miragelike cluster of small islands called The Wolves appeared, blurry on the horizon. *Now what?* Ellie's look asked me.

The islands seemed to float on a cloudlike bed of haze that looked as white as spun glass. Closer by, Ivy sat by the boat's rail: cormorants, more porpoises . . . a seal's round black eyes regarded us briefly before his gleaming wet head dunked beneath the waves with a liquid *plunk!*

"Why am I here?" she asked suddenly, still watching the water. Our little dustup was history, I gathered.

"Well," I repeated what I'd told her before, "while your dad's busy you'll need— "

"No, *here.*" She waved around at the boat and the water, the birds and the seals so on, with her face creased in puzzlement. "I mean why did you bring me here?"

I thought about whether the truth was a good idea, decided what the heck. At least I'd be able to remember what I'd said.

"So you could see something and be somewhere that's not ruined," I told her. "Something good."

It's what I'd have wanted if only I'd known enough to ask for it back then. Ivy's lips pursed, and I wondered if she was too young, if I'd made a mistake.

But finally, she nodded, her look oddly adult. "I'll be all right," she said softly. "Don't worry about me."

Maybe it should have been reassuring, but instead, a chill went through me. She was six years old, and she'd just lost her mother, but she was being (with only a few brief lapses) a good little soldier about it.

Too good. A Sherman tank wasn't that resilient. Besides, those green eyes of hers were a barometer and the needle was stuck on *Stormy*. I didn't know what, if anything, to do about that.

Eventually Ellie turned us back toward Eastport, the toy-size town on the distant shore. It hadn't seemed to take much time getting out here, but it was a long way back into a rising tide and a stiffening breeze.

The Bayliner's wake churned behind us in a roosterish fan-tail of white churning foam. Sun, wind, spray, and the engine's drone—Ivy sat soaking it all in. Watching her, I thought this might not've been such a bad idea after all.

A good long while later—too long for me—we neared the breakwater, now, at nearly noon, lined with people casting mackerel jigs, their coolers and lawn chairs and umbrellas and fish-cleaning tables set up all around them, along with ice chests for carrying the catch home.

A trio of otters swam curiously up to the boat as we slid between the fish pier and the dolphin. Ivy gazed raptly at the funny-faced animals' agile play but lost interest abruptly when something on the breakwater captured her attention. We were sidling up to the finger pier, Ellie at the helm and me busy throwing a line over a cleat, when the child dropped her life jacket onto the deck and hopped nimbly out of the boat.

"Daddy!" she cried, as her sneakers thumped away down the dock. Leaving Ellie shutting the engine and the electricals down, I jumped out, too, and hurried after the kid.

By the time I got to the gangway's top, gasping and with my knees threatening to quit, she'd reached a man who was standing there waiting for her and thrown her arms around his legs.

"Daddy!" she cried, her high voice carrying even over the breakwater's busy comings and goings: cars, trucks, boats, the early afternoon crowd around Rosie's Hot Dogs stand.

The man was tall and dark-haired with a long, narrow face and a short brown mustache, in gray slacks and a white shirt with a sport jacket hanging open over it. A tie bulged from one jacket pocket.

Bending to one knee, arms opening wide, he caught sight of me and his face went flat. "I'm Terry Lawson. Why is my daughter being kept from me?" he demanded as he hoisted her.

He spoke with the confident air of a man who wants all this straightened out. *Or there'll be consequences*, his look said, and of course I didn't just laugh in his face. I mean, not to overstate my experience with rash actions, but the fact is you could build Mount Everest with the consequences I'd faced in my life.

Behind Lawson, Lizzie Snow came striding toward us, her cop badge glinting in the midday sun. Seeing her, Ivy flung her arms even tighter around her dad's neck.

Her murdering dad, allegedly. He didn't look murderous.

But then, they so rarely do, or at least not until the last minute. His car, whose driver's-side door hung open, didn't look like much, either—brown Chevy station wagons so old that the fake wood is peeling off not being exactly a rarity around here.

"No! Don't let them take me!" Ivy cried, and buried her face again as I approached. Close up, the stubble on Lawson's jaw looked less like style and more like he just hadn't shaved.

Or slept. His brown hound-dog eyes looked so exhausted, I thought they might droop right off his face. Just then Lizzie reached him.

"Mr. Lawson, you're aware your release conditions stipulate no contact with Ivy, correct?"

Ellie stood beside me, frowning at this. "So he can't coach her," I explained. "And so no one can say he might have."

Ivy clung tightly to her dad's shoulder, eyeing us like we meant to steal her and feed her to wolves. Meanwhile Lizzie tried patiently explaining to Lawson that a court order couldn't be ignored, as he was now defiantly proclaiming that he would.

Around us people meandered happily, pleased to be near the water on a bright, unseasonably warm autumn day, many of them eating hot dogs and onion rings and swigging soda or water from go-cups—or the ever-popular double strawberry margarita, one of which I could've used right then, myself.

"Mr. Lawson, I have to ask you to let Ivy stay with these two nice ladies for now," Lizzie said. "Your lawyer can ask the court for a change, but I—"

"What are you, nuts? I'm not leaving her with anyone," he insisted. "This is crazy!"

He looked around as if to solicit help from passersby, but the hot-dog-eating, margarita-guzzling folks on the breakwater weren't up for conflict. It was too nice a day, and whatever had happened was none of their business, anyway.

"Mr. Lawson," Lizzie said patiently again. She knew how to talk people down from ledges, both figurative and literal. It beat hauling them down by brute force, she'd once said, and it made for a lot less report-writing afterward, too.

But this time it didn't work. "Help!" Ivy shouted as Lizzie reached for her. "Help! They're kidnapping me!"

"Mr. Lawson," Lizzie persisted. "Listen to me, now, you don't want this fight, get it? Right now, what you want is to be calm, stay available to the state police, don't say anything to anyone about anything, and most of all— "

Most of all, she was about to finish, stay out of trouble. Suspects who went out and did more bad deeds made criminal court judges want to fine them up the wazoo, and maybe even jail them.

Lawson seemed to realize this, finally. Peeling her arms gently from around his neck with his two hands, he eased Ivy's feet down onto the pavement and knelt before her.

"Don't worry, honey, this'll all be over soon. You go on with the nice ladies, now, okay? That's what'll help me most."

Ivy gave him a dark look of childish betrayal and turned her back on him. But an unhappy daughter was the least of his worries right now, it seemed, as Lizzie took a call on her cell phone, listened briefly, and put the phone away again.

"The state guys would like to talk with you again," she reported to Lawson. Homicide cops, she meant. I didn't know why he wasn't in custody already. "They're on their way now, you can meet in my office when they get here," she said.

His hands clenched. "They think I killed her, don't they? I can't believe it! They actually think I— "

Wow, I thought, look at who just woke up. Next he'd be marveling at the brand-new information about water being wet.

Lawson broke off his rant, looking stricken. "Just don't give these ladies any trouble," he told his daughter. In reply, she stuck her tongue out at him.

"Let's go," she said, taking Ellie's hand in a soft, trusting way that didn't fool me at all. So far, I thought Ivy was a mostly polite, mostly pleasant child who, for whatever reason, was also about as soft and trusting as a poisoned dart.

As she and Ellie turned away, Lizzie stepped in front of Lawson, who at this late date was apparently having some second thoughts.

"Look, don't make me report this or the judge will probably have you taken back into custody."

A thought hit me. "How about if he comes with me? The state cops won't be here for an hour if they're coming from Augusta."

Which they would be. Heavy-duty law enforcement didn't spend a whole lot of time on Moose Island. "We'll take a walk," I said, "maybe get some lunch—"

Lawson looked put-upon. *Too bad*, I thought. *You dump your little girl on me, I dump my curiosity on you.*

Besides, it would keep him out of Ellie's way. "We'll all feel better after something to eat," I finished, as if he were a toddler needing to be eased out of a tantrum.

Which wasn't far wrong. "Oh, all right," he sighed, seeing as Lizzie was eyeing him narrowly. Possibly he was remembering, too, that he hadn't eaten recently.

And I couldn't have looked like a problem to him spilling-the-beans-wise, assuming he had any. In the very few mirrors I bothered looking into anymore I saw medium height, medium build, short, dark hair in no particular style, and a face that didn't scare small children.

Threatening-looking I was not, in other words. So Terry Lawson wouldn't have figured out yet that Ellie and I were so nosy, we could pry secrets out of dead men.

Or women.

"Why'd they cut you loose, anyway?" I asked Lawson when Lizzie and the girls had headed back toward the Chocolate Moose.

A corpse in his car should've been plenty of reason to charge him with something just to keep him in custody. But instead, here he was, strolling with me down Water Street toward a restaurant with a sign out front: BRADY'S BRUNCH.

Lawson shrugged. "Well, see, there's this little thing called evidence. Then they'll need a grand jury and finally an indictment. Also, I had no reason to want Cindy dead," he added. "So there's a motive problem."

He shook his head irritably, striding along beside me. "And it's not like I'm some deadbeat," he went on. "They know I'm not leaving town. I can't walk away from this, it all has to get straightened out."

Yeah, that was one way of putting it. That it could end with him in prison didn't seem to have occurred to him yet.

"I work with a large finance firm in New York," he said. "You probably wouldn't know the name, but— "

"Try me," I interrupted pleasantly. Because sure, I might let him patronize me a little just to get his story out of him faster, but he wasn't going to walk all over me, and he might as well know it right from the start.

"Sorry," he apologized quickly, when he realized what he'd implied, that I was too dumb and/or ill-informed to know how important he was back in the big city. He named the financial firm. Not only had I heard of it, they'd been one of my own regular stops when I was a teenager running bags of money around town for the bad guys.

"It's been a long time since I've been back in Eastport," he said.

A pickup truck with a scallop-dragging harness strapped to it rumbled past in a commotion of rusted-out muffler and springs that had sprung. Most of the truck's body was roughly smeared with Bondo or held together with silver duct tape. A bumper sticker read *Hate logging? Try plastic toilet paper!*

"People here might not look smart on the outside," Lawson

said musingly, when the truck had gone by, "but on the inside they're sharp as tacks."

I hadn't noticed people here looking not smart on the outside. Meanwhile, if this guy got his foot any farther into his mouth, he'd choke on it.

"Not that I've kept in touch with folks here," he added. "Family's all gone, I hardly even know anyone anymore."

He stopped, turning to me. "The thing is, though, I'm sticking around now for my own reasons. Whatever happened last night has to be known for sure, or questions about me are bound to linger. And that," he finished, "will be bad for business."

Fair enough. After all, who wants their high-income clients wondering if their money guy is secretly the midnight strangler?

We were almost to the restaurant. "Ivy doesn't seem too terribly upset, at least," I changed the subject.

"Ivy didn't know her mother well," Lawson said. "She lives with me in the city, has for almost three years, now."

We reached the post office on the corner of Water and High Streets. Then I led him left down a weedy bank to a path behind the Water Street buildings overlooking the bay.

"Anyway," said Lawson impatiently, "my attorney's on his way up from the city right now."

"I imagine he must've warned you not to talk about it to anyone, though?" I asked. Surely, he would have—*shut up* being perhaps the most useful advice an attorney can give to a client.

"I don't care," Lawson replied stubbornly. "I'm his boss, I tell *him* what to do."

Good, I thought. "She a big drinker, your ex-wife?" It was likely why he'd gotten custody—that or some other debilitating drug. In some ways, Eastport was like anywhere else.

Lawson nodded as I led him up a set of wooden stairs to the

enclosed deck outside Brady's Brunch. Here you could get cream cheese and lox on a bagel while gazing at the water where the fish had been swimming recently.

"It's why I sued for custody, and why she didn't fight it," he said, as we stepped onto the deck. "It was better for Ivy."

The outdoor dining area featured picnic tables, hanging ferns, and propane heaters spaced strategically around the gardenlike enclosure. Once we were seated, our orders taken, and had a couple of mimosas in front of us, I started in on him again.

"But Cindy had cleaned up?" I guessed. "That's why Ivy could visit with her on this trip?"

Lawson plucked a silver cigarette lighter with some kind of gemstone set into it from his inside jacket pocket, along with a crumpled pack of smokes, then noticed the absence of ashtrays out here and tucked them all away again.

"Supposedly," he said. "She put on a good show of it, anyway. For a while."

He swallowed some of his drink. "But it all seemed fake to me. I couldn't forget what she'd been like for so long, or that she could be that way again, anytime."

"Still, she's Ivy's mother," I said. "And if she really has gotten clean—"

"Cindy was a pill-popping, powder-sniffing drunk," he said flatly. "When I filed for divorce and sole custody, she didn't even fight, just put Ivy on a bus in clothes that must have come out of a ragbag. Her shoes were too small, for Pete's sake."

He frowned. "She hired a teenager to ride with Ivy. I had to buy the ticket to send the girl home, though, plus snacks and so on. Cindy hadn't given them any expense money."

It sounded bad, but I reminded myself that this was his side of the story, not Cindy's. "But she'd cleaned up?" I asked again. "This time when you saw her, she was—?"

"Yeah," he relented. "She'd straightened out pretty well. She had a job and so on, even bought a house. I came to the reunion to see it for myself and let Ivy visit with her."

Our food came, delivered by Bridget Brady. "Hey, Bridge," I said, "how's Jax?"

"A little brat," she said with a smile. The small mixed-breed puppy she'd adopted recently had turned out to be a perpetual energy machine, but he was also just as cute as a sweet little pup could possibly be, and friendly, too.

"He goes to day care," she said. "That blows some of the steam off. But you know how they are," she added affectionately, "little lovebugs when they're not driving you nuts."

The tall, slim woman in her early fifties had her thick, wheat-pale braids coiled atop her head as usual, like some small-town Valkyrie; her eyes, a pale, innocent blue, always seemed to hide some sad secret, and I happened to know that so far, she'd survived enough tragedy for an opera.

She almost never talked about it, but she'd made an exception for me. I'm not sure why people think they're safe telling me their troubles—maybe it's because something about me says I've had my own.

Anyway, she seemed to know Lawson already, turning a smile on him as she set his plate down, her look lingering on his face as he turned to me.

"Bridget and I were classmates," he explained, "back at good old Eastport High." And then to her: "I'd say I was sorry that you couldn't make the reunion last night, but under the circumstances . . ."

Last night, as every night, she'd been here behind the bar trying to earn a living. "I'm sorry for your trouble, Terry," she said kindly. "I hope things work out all right for you."

The doors leading out to the deck stood wide open. Through them I could see Eastport's small but colorful swarm of habitual barflies, fellows who made Bridget's establishment their de facto morning hangout. Then customers whose blood alcohol wasn't over the limit began arriving and the barflies buzzed off to who knew where.

My across-the-street neighbor, Wally Bean, was in there, too, a fresh boilermaker in front of him and his bottom parked firmly on the barstool as if it meant to take root there. At least his wife always knew where he was, I reflected, as he threw the shot back, followed it with whatever was on tap.

When I turned back to the table, I thought I caught a look passing between Bridget and Lawson, which didn't surprise me. With her strong, angular features, full red lips, and cornflower-blue eyes, she was an attractive woman. It didn't hurt, either, that she was the owner of a functioning business and of a very decent piece of commercial real estate on the water.

But functioning was all it was, and the building—two hundred years old and historically protected—needed major repairs. Even the trio of small private banquet rooms she'd added along one side of the place a few years ago were showing their age, and never mind what the electricals and plumbing were probably like.

In short, it was worth money on paper, but you'd bankrupt yourself fixing it, so she couldn't sell it for anything like what she needed to get out free and clear.

Or to get out at all, really. I'd heard all about this several times when Wade and I would come down here for a drink and a little socializing.

Her smile sweetened as she turned it on Lawson. I recalled that they'd been a romantic pair, once. Now, if I was in her position, he could look like a ticket out of here to me, and I couldn't help wondering if she'd grab it, should the opportunity arise.

Depending on the situation, I can't swear I wouldn't. She smiled at us both again and was gone. Lawson applied himself to his burger. I ate some chicken salad and waited for him to fill the silence, as people do if you give them enough of it.

"Ivy said she wanted to go with me to the reunion dinner

and see her mom there," he said, after draining the last of that mimosa and blotting his lips with a napkin. "So that's what happened, and everything was fine. Cindy was pleasant and completely sober, putting on a good act for our other classmates, and for Ivy, too."

"Act?" I had another sip of my own drink. You might think a sophisticated New York City business guy like Lawson would balk at direct questions from a stranger.

But Lawson was angry, tired, and alone except for his six-year-old daughter, and he was also seriously in danger of being charged in the death of his ex-wife.

And now he was a little drunk, another thing I was fairly sure wasn't normal for him. "What kind of act?" I asked. "Like, in a play or something?"

His eyes flashed anger. "Yeah, the kind that ends when the wicked witch appears." He signaled Bridget for another drink. I put my hand over my glass.

"All through dinner the two of them got along like carrots and peas," Lawson said. "I thought they were making friends, and I was glad for both of them."

"But after you'd taken Ivy back to the car, Cindy dropped the bomb on you—about suing you for custody? Yeah, I know about that," I added at his sharp look.

I saw him deciding whether or not he cared how I'd found out. Knowing that people were already talking about him couldn't have been fun. But then his hand twitched impatiently, waving the thought away.

"Yes," he answered after a moment, finally, "she did tell me then. And we argued about it. Pretty loudly—I suppose we made a scene. But it wasn't about the custody, though that was bad enough." He drank some of his fresh mimosa. "All the while the two of them had their heads together over dinner, Cindy was telling Ivy all about how she wouldn't be going home to New York with me, that I didn't want her anymore."

"But that's awful! What a cruel thing to say to—"

He nodded. "Ivy told me about it when we went to the car. She was upset—what Cindy had said scared her—so I said let's just leave, that we could go back to the motel and watch a movie together, maybe microwave some popcorn."

He made a face of distaste, and I laughed. That microwave popcorn smells like a dumpster fire and sleeping in a motel room with it is the worst was an opinion we shared, apparently.

He washed the last of his burger down with the last of his drink. "Really. What kind of mother terrorizes a kid like that? Besides, it wasn't even true, it wasn't discussed, and I wouldn't have agreed if it was. But Ivy was nearly hysterical about it."

His voice rose, a pink flush climbing up out of his collar. A few of the customers at other tables glanced over curiously.

"Calm down. Let's not put on a show for the people," I said quietly. On the other hand, I wasn't about to waste the moment, heightened emotion being a well-known exposer of interesting information. "So in the end, though, you took Ivy out to the car and left her there? She was okay with that?"

Suddenly he looked suspicious. Maybe I'd pushed too far. Or maybe I should've ordered him another one of those tasty tongue-looseners that Bridget made in the bar.

"What's your interest in this, anyway?" he wanted to know suddenly. "Are you a police detective or something? Aren't you supposed to tell me that, identify yourself?"

He was halfway up off his bench. I raised my hands, palms out. "Wait, wait. You've got it wrong, I'm not the police. Not anything like that."

I got up, too, caught the check on the way out and paid it, then followed Lawson to the sidewalk where he was walking fast, already halfway down the street.

"I'm fifty percent of the team that'll be caring for your daughter," I said when I'd caught up to him.

He didn't look at me, just kept walking. "While," I added, "you're being questioned about a murder."

No one had officially said the word yet, at least not in front of me, but I figured it was a pretty good bet that Cindy Munson hadn't strangled herself.

Lawson's step slowed. "Ah, forget it. It's not going to make any difference to anyone. I've told the police all the same things I told you. I'm not hiding anything."

Ouch. No wonder he'd been so forthcoming. "I didn't know they let fools near any financial businesses. Didn't you say you had a lawyer?"

Said lawyer was going to skin this guy limb from limb, as Sam would say, for not keeping his big mouth shut. But that was Lawson's problem; all I cared about was Ivy, albeit reluctantly. For one thing, kids with dead moms don't win many prizes in the Most Easygoing contests—hey, I ought to know.

"Anyway, those cops from Augusta should be getting here around now," I said.

We passed Bridget's car in the fish pier lot. It was a rusty broken-down old jalopy, a Studebaker with tires so bare you could've used them for ice skates and one rear window replaced with an inadequately attached piece of cloudy plastic tarp, the whole barely running mess yet another result of her shaky money situation.

Lawson regarded it silently as we went by, as if drawing some information from it. Crossing the street ahead of me, he wobbled slightly, I guessed from the mimosas. Even fifty percent less buzzed than he was, I felt the pleasant warm sensation that comes from a drink at lunch.

But the feeling only lasted until we neared the Chocolate Moose. Ellie stood outside on the doorstep watching Ivy jump hilariously up and down atop one of the black cast-iron-filigree café tables on the sidewalk.

The table's legs teetered dangerously. Lawson started toward the child. "Don't let her see you," I said, putting a hand on his arm, "or she'll get upset all over again."

Although she looked plenty upset already. Her brief bursts of brattiness earlier came back to me as Ellie, no stranger to childhood meltdowns, reached up and seized the girl's waist with both hands. Then, in a thoroughly no-nonsense manner, she swept the child down off the table and onto the sidewalk.

"And that, folks, is how you do it," I said, watching Ellie herd the little girl inside amid howls of protest.

Lawson gazed after them as the shop door swung shut. "She's a spunky one," he said of his offspring.

Right, and she was staying at my house. "She sure is," I agreed with Lawson, hearing more yells from inside the Moose and wondering again what I'd gotten myself into.

Spunky. Yeah, that was a nice word for it.

After giving me a card with his cell phone number on it in case I needed it for something about Ivy, Lawson walked on up Water Street toward his chat with the state homicide police. I went into the Moose, where Ivy was telling Ellie that she was a great big poopy-head, and Ivy hated her.

She's angry and scared, I reminded myself. *Like you were.*

"Hey, Ivy," I said, "I just had lunch with your dad." She quit spouting bathroom words and ran to the door to go out.

I got there first, pried her fingers off the knob. "He told me to say he loves you, that he's fine, and that you should be a good, brave girl and wait for him."

She looked up doubtfully. "Did he really say that?"

I knelt before her. "Every word," I lied. "And especially about how much he loves you."

Her wide eyes regarded me. Even I knew it didn't sound like him, and I was pretty sure she didn't believe me.

But: "Okay," she whispered shakily, at last, and my heart broke a little for her. Turning away, she returned to the café table and climbed onto a chair, where ten minutes later I found her with her head down on her arms, asleep.

The shop was quiet except for a Brian Eno piece playing on the sound system and the soft hum of the display case's compressor. Ellie was in the kitchen reading yet another recipe for a pastry we wanted to try, kolacky, featuring a richly sweet and eggy dough plus fruit or sweetened cheese or both.

We thought chocolate-filled ones would probably be a pretty good variation. While Ellie went on plotting our first attempt at creating these novel delicacies, I poured coffee from a fresh pot she'd started and stood by the door with a cup.

Up and down the street, the day's business went on: the mail truck, another trailer (this one loaded with firewood), two dogs being walked by a woman whose arm stuck straight out in front of her and whose shoulder looked half pulled out of its socket.

Peace at last, I thought, turning away, but moments later the little silver bell over the door jingled briskly and my elderly housekeeper-slash-stepmother, Bella Diamond, came in.

"You're back!" I said. Five feet tall and weighing about ninety-two pounds, Bella had big grape-green eyes, corn-kernel teeth, and a face like a hatchet with frizzy, henna-red hair on top, a stubborn chin jutting on the bottom.

Casting her sharp gaze over the shop's interior, she spied Ivy, now awake, and moved purposefully toward her.

"Sit up, child," she said kindly, producing a wad of clean tissues from the pocket of her blue sweater, worn over jeans and a pair of sneakers. "Use these," said Bella, then stood by patiently while the child dabbed her eyes and blew her nose.

"Thank you," Ivy murmured, just as Ellie came out from the kitchen.

"Bella! Welcome back!" She looked around. "But why so soon, and where's Jacob?"

Bella had first been my friend, then my housekeeper, and finally, after my father reappeared in my life, my stepmother. Now she and my dad were practically inseparable.

"We got homesick," Bella said, by which she meant bored. At our old house, she and my dad presided over a motley crew of kids and dogs plus variously aged adults, all busy with their own activities, which I guessed made looking out a bus window seem tame by comparison.

"And I finished my book." She held up an Agatha Christie novel. Having fallen in literary love, Bella planned to start with *The Mysterious Affair at Styles* and just read right on through them all, a project that if she kept up at this rate would take her until about next week.

"Anyway, we just got back, we're going up to the house now," she said. "I just wanted to let you know that we're here, before we—what?"

She'd seen my face change. "Uh, listen," I said, trying to think fast and failing as usual. If I told Bella anything about last night's intruder, I might frighten Ivy. Or even Bella: she was a tough old bird but easily spooked. On the other hand, if I let Bella go without a word, she'd be annoyed, and rightly so.

"Jake," Ellie said—and that was Ellie, sensitive as a cat's whisker—"why not go, too? Help everyone get settled?"

I reviewed my mental list: there were cookies left to bake, the batter already chilling in the refrigerator. Cupcakes were on the agenda as well, but they were easy.

"What about Ivy?" The child still sat at the café table, one sneakered foot slowly kicking a table leg again.

"I'm staying with her," she pronounced, indicating Bella with a sideways jerk of her dark head.

That came as no surprise: unlike mine, Bella's face did in fact frighten small children on occasion, but not for long. Soon they caught on to the fact that this old lady was on their side, even if what she was doing or saying right now seemed harsh.

"Get up, child," said Bella. Ivy got up, brushed at her clothes, stared at her shoes. "And look up, for heaven's sake. Don't ever be ashamed to let people see your face."

Ivy peered sideways at Bella's own seriously unglamorous kisser. Bella gazed calmly back at the child, her look sweetly inquisitive and utterly unguarded—that look was her secret power.

"Okay," Ivy said, all the sass gone out of her suddenly. I thought it was probably the calm before another of Ivy's storms, but at least it got us out of the shop and across the sidewalk to Bella's old green Ford Galaxie, parked at the curb.

The car was so ancient that you had to visit junkyards to find parts. It had ashtrays, a lighter, side vents, and windows you rolled down with a crank; if it had been much older you probably would've started it with a crank, too.

"Hello, ladies," said my dad from the passenger seat. His grooved, age-mottled face resembled a walnut shell. He walked with a hickory stick, took multiple heart pills, and wore a pair of Bluetooth-enabled hearing aids so powerful they could pick up messages from outer space.

But even in his nineties, he'd kept his optimism and mental quickness. Now he sized up the little girl who clutched Bella's hand, eyeing him shyly.

Stringy gray hair tied back in a leather thong, a bloodred ruby stud in one earlobe, a fading, too-big denim jacket on his compact frame, which was as skinny as a coat rack—

"Hey, punkin," he greeted her gently. Bella opened the car's rear passenger-side door; Ivy hesitated, her gaze veering doubtfully around to me.

I, after all, had talked with her father, and I'd gotten her first down and then up that damned gangway, too, without her either drowning or breaking her neck. Even the boat ride, which in spite of everything she'd enjoyed, had been my idea.

And I saw those memories in her eyes right now. "Go on with them, Jake," Ellie urged from behind me on the sidewalk. "I'll be fine here."

True, and it wouldn't be kind to leave Ivy alone with Bella and my dad, would it? They'd just gotten home, they were tired and needed to unpack, and besides, I suspected that sooner or later even Bella's super-duper kid-wrangling talents might not be enough to keep the peace back at my big old house.

So we got into the car, me and Ivy in the backseat. "Ivy," I said as Bella drove, "I'm so sorry about all this. About your mom. And I know you'd rather be with your dad right now."

No kidding, her answering look said, but I didn't hold it against her. I wanted to tell her they'd be together soon, her and her dad, but I didn't know if it was true.

"He's doing his best right now to arrange things so he can come and get you," I said, the hollow sound of evasiveness ringing in my ears. Her small shoulders moved minutely under the windbreaker we'd bought her. I wouldn't have been satisfied, either.

Bella slowed and turned left into our driveway: between two ancient lilac bushes, past a shed full of enough lawn and garden equipment to run a small farm, finally onto the wide graveled area where we all parked.

Only the Fiat was there at the moment. Ivy's eyes widened at the sight of the pretty little sports car with its top down and its paint gleaming. I tucked her interest away for future reference as we got out and approached the house.

"Go on, now," said Bella briskly, waving the child ahead of her toward the porch while I stayed back helping my dad.

"Surprise houseguest?" He gripped the knob of his prized hickory walking stick and hoisted himself with it—shakily, but he was up on his feet.

"Uh-huh." I gave him the gist of Ivy's story while we made our way across the gravel, and as usual he caught on fast.

"Murdered mom, suspect dad, kid's all alone," he summed it up neatly, then stopped, leaning on the stick, thinking.

Finally, he lifted a gnarled hand to my shoulder and rested it there. "Take care of yourself," he said. "Be careful."

I understood. We'd gone over this and over this and laid it to rest, finally, our sad, terrible shared history. If he hadn't run after my mother's murder, leaving me to grow up in care homes and on the street, he'd either still be in prison, now, or he'd be dead.

I knew that, knew well enough to admit that it's exactly what I'd have done, myself. "I'll try," I said. "It's just for the rest of today, and maybe overnight."

It was starting to dawn on me that Lawson's absence might not last only for a matter of hours. For his sake, I hoped that lawyer of his showed up soon, because he really seemed to need one.

I got the suitcases from the Galaxie's big trunk, almost as large as the Fiat's passenger compartment, and when I'd hauled them up onto the porch, I realized—

No dog sounds came from inside. Fala should've been at the door barking her head off, hurling herself at it while loudly threatening either to lick you to death in joyous rapture at your homecoming or rip your lungs out.

Now, the silence reminded me again of an important fact about the house: last night's intruder. "Careful," I said as Bella pushed the door open, but she ignored me, sensing something not-quite-right, too.

"Fala?" she called, stepping inside.

Silence, except for the clock ticking loudly in the hall. No doggy toenails clicking, no German shepherd thumping heavily to the floor as she leapt off a bed.

"Fala!" I hurried through the house: laundry room, parlor—a mangled dog toy in the shape of a rag doll sprawled like an accident victim on the carpet—dining room, pantry.

Upstairs was the same. "Fala?" The closets, the bedrooms—all empty, as was my office. But a sound came from behind the closed bathroom door: *Crunch. Crunch-crunch.*

I put my ear to the door. "Hello? Somebody in there?"

In our house the answer was mostly yes. This time, the crunching stopped briefly, then resumed. "All right, now—"

I yanked open the door. Fala looked up from where she lay on the bathroom rug, cheerfully unhurt and with her jaws clamped around an enormous bone.

A real bone, the kind I never allowed, wary as I was of splinters and mad cow disease. It looked like a beef knuckle or maybe a length of femur; she'd gnawed a lot of it away by then.

All I really knew was that I hadn't given it to her.

Three

Bella had already washed up the cups and plates I'd left in the sink by the time I got back downstairs. Now she was wiping off the red-checked vinyl tablecloth with a soapy sponge, her ropy arm moving in long arcs.

"Don't you want to unpack, first?" I asked. I should point out, though, that among Bella's favorite pastimes was polishing the fronts of the appliances until the paint nearly melted; *clean freak* doesn't even begin to describe how she felt about smeary fingerprints.

Of which I'm sorry to say that I had left quite a few. But that wasn't important now.

"It's just laundry from the trip, and if I unpack them now, I'll have to wash them," she said, gathering the crumbs she'd collected and brushing them into her cupped hand.

Another hard-and-fast Bella rule: if the hamper was full, it's off to the washing machine we go. Meanwhile her glance at me said plenty about how I couldn't take care of myself or my surroundings—those dirty dishes—for even a few days, and I probably hadn't drunk any orange juice, either, had I?

She was right: I hadn't. But that wasn't what I had to talk to her about. She'd heard Fala's toenails on the bathroom floor, I supposed, and assumed all was well.

"Bella," I said, and my tone made her look at me again.

Then I told her every single solitary thing that had happened since she'd been gone, including the midnight visitor, the dead woman behind the high school, the bone I'd just found Fala with, finally the unhappy reason why Ivy was here with us right now.

"Where is she, anyway?" I said, looking around, and then I heard the little girl's startled "Oh!" from the front hall. She'd already met Fala once, I gathered, down at the shop, but I rushed out there anyway to make sure she wasn't scared this time. The dog loved kids, but her looks suggested she ate them for breakfast.

Au contraire, however. I found Ivy sitting on the front stairs' bottom step with her arms around Fala's neck, and Fala thought this situation was just ducky, her pink tongue lolling happily. The two of them followed me back out to the kitchen.

Bella eyed the child. "You and I need to visit the Dollar Store, little lady," she said, and Ivy's expression brightened further. So that afternoon we let Ivy pick out the pajamas she wanted, white cotton ones with yellow ducks on them, along with an assortment of other essentials and a new red rubber Nylabone for Fala.

It was a pricey haul, but I thought it was worth it that evening when the kid and the dog lay together in front of the TV, Fala chewing her new rubber bone (I'd 86'd the real one) and Ivy transfixed by a live feed from the International Space Station.

"Anyway, thank heavens for Bella," I told Ellie when she called to see how we were doing. I'd already told her about finding the dog confined in the bathroom. Then a knock came at the back door.

"Hang on a sec." I went to the door and found Lizzie Snow looking tired, dejected, and badly in need of a glass of wine. I let her in and poured her one, went to tell Ellie good night, and when I got back to the kitchen, retired state cop Dylan Hudson had arrived, too, and filled a glass for himself.

"Cheers," he said, not sounding cheerful. His usual heart-stoppingly handsome grin was not on duty tonight, either. Lizzie ran a hand through her short-clipped black curls and looked up at me, her eyes smudgy with fatigue.

"Can you possibly keep Ivy for tonight and tomorrow night, too?" she asked. "I had no idea these older-child placements were so hard to arrange."

Nor had I, but it made sense. Babies at least stayed where you put them. "I know it's a big ask," she finished.

Correctamundo, as Sam would've put it. I loved him and his whole energetic young family, and I adored being around them, but a quiet house was a rare luxury. Still, what was I going to do? The kid in question was asleep right now on my living room rug. Also, I remembered where I'd been sleeping when I was six. "Sure," I said, "we'll be fine."

Of course we would, I told myself firmly. The trouble was, my self didn't believe it. Maybe Ivy was calm and cooperative now, but that could change in a heartbeat, as I'd already seen.

We sat at the kitchen table: Lizzie, me, and Dylan. Then after a few minutes Ellie came in—she'd apparently gone straight from the phone to her car and zoomed right over.

I put out a plate of cookies, then some pieces of fruit and cheese, finally the rest of the bread, assorted cold cuts, and curried squash soup we'd had for supper. Lizzie and Dylan fell upon the feast like a piranha dumped in a neighborhood swimming pool. They seemed to think my house was a haven of comforting domesticity, which was hilarious if you happened to be stepping on an already well gummed teething biscuit in your bare feet.

"So what's Lawson's situation right now?" Ellie asked, as I started a pot of coffee. What the heck, it was turning into a dinner party.

Dylan shrugged. "Stickin' to his story." Dylan had been a state homicide cop himself, retired early due to an on-the-job injury, and still had contacts in the division—not always friendly contacts—Dylan was not always the easiest guy to be around—but they were talkative contacts.

"Lawson says he took the kid to the car, got her settled, then went back inside to find his ex-wife and straighten things out."

Now, there's a phrase that can cover a multitude of sins. "That's what he said? He wanted to straighten things out?" It wasn't the impression I'd gotten.

Dylan shrugged, pushing back a shock of dark hair that had fallen over his forehead. With hooded dark eyes, a lean, angular face, and a smile so devilishly attractive it should've come with a warning sticker, he was also so charming that (according to Bella, who was smitten with him) he could talk the birds out of the trees.

And what a pain in the tail he sometimes was, too. Although not right now: "So Lawson had a last drink," Dylan said, "looked around for his ex one last time, then went back to the car, planning to return to the motel," he said.

The Motel East, he meant, on Water Street, overlooking the bay near where the old steamship terminal once stood. "The rest of Lawson's and Ivy's things are still in the room?" I asked.

Dylan raised a dark eyebrow. "Yes, but don't get any ideas. Other than the kid bunking here, I don't see your connection to any of this."

He was no big fan of amateur snooping. I wondered if what Ivy and I had in common counted as a connection, knowing already that it did.

"Social service people already asked Lawson about any other relatives who might care for Ivy," Lizzie said. "He says no one.

I guess Cindy didn't have much of a family left, either. Or at least nobody's stepped forward."

"Anybody ask him about leaving her alone in the car?" I spoke up. I'd been thinking about this. "It's dark outside, people have been drinking, and did she even have a phone to call him if she got nervous, or if anyone gave her trouble?"

At her age I'd known how to jimmy a car ignition. I could do it so fast that older guys would pay me for it, then speed off in the stolen car. But Ivy wasn't that kind of kid at all; whatever happened, she'd have been largely defenseless.

"No," said Lizzie, confirming my opinion that a screw was loose somewhere in Lawson's daddy act. "She didn't have a phone, and she still doesn't," Lizzie added. "I checked."

The whole idea of keeping the two apart was so Ivy's story remained uncontaminated in case she had to testify about it. "When's she being questioned?" Ellie wanted to know.

Lizzie made a face. "Day after tomorrow in Augusta. A psychologist, a rep from child services, an assistant DA, and an attorney for the child will be sitting in."

A little silence fell over the table, all of us thinking the same thing. Finally, I said it. "Lizzie, they don't really believe that Ivy could've—"

Ellie chimed in. "Oh, come on, she's not big or heavy enough to—" Right. That *strength* and *strangle* are similar words is no coincidence.

Dylan put a hand up. "They've been checking backgrounds on everyone at the dinner dance," he said, "just in case."

"Surely the child doesn't have a criminal record," I said.

Fala walked into the kitchen, drank water, and eyed her food bowl. Behind her came Bella, who gave the German shepherd a dog biscuit, picked up the food bowl, and began scrubbing it at the sink as if it had plague germs in it.

Then again, she scrubbed everything that way. "No," said Dylan, "but it turns out her father does."

Uh-oh. Ellie rolled her eyes at me across the table: What fresh hell was this?

"Seems Lawson and his neighbor in their high-end New York City suburb got into a fistfight over a dustup between their offspring. The neighbor said Ivy had strangled his son that day at school."

"And the little boy, what did he say?" Ellie asked.

Dylan spread his hands. "Nobody asked him. Cop told the dads to knock it off and they did, but after he'd driven away it seems Lawson came back, pretty much knocked the neighbor's block off. Guy pressed charges, Lawson's hotshot lawyer pled it down, and Lawson paid a fine."

Another silence. Fala lay down in her dog bed by the woodstove. "Well," I said finally. "There's a new wrinkle."

The strangling a kid at recess part, I meant. "Have you told them yet about our burglar?" Bella asked while rinsing the dog bowl in steaming hot water from the faucet.

She'd changed from travel clothes into her usual outfit of faded cotton housedress, muddy brown heavy-duty support stockings rolled down to her ankles, and black orthopedic shoes. With a frayed, off-white cardigan over her housedress and her usual gauzy purple hairnet pulled snugly onto her reddish frizz, she looked happy as a clam to be back in her own kitchen again.

I'd told Lizzie about my midnight visitor, but she hadn't told Dylan; I could tell by his sharp glance. "Fala woke me," I began to explain—

Schno-o-onnk! The dog's honking snore interrupted. "—and I must have scared away whoever it was," I said.

I didn't describe the part about coming downstairs with not even a flashlight. They'd have thought it unwise.

Lizzie's sigh said she knew scolding me about it was useless. Still, "Next time call, okay? I'll come right over. Him"—she pointed at Dylan—"too."

Rising dramatically from his chair, Dylan put his hands up palms out and intoned. "Mine is but to do or die," he declaimed, looking tragic, and even Bella had to smile at his performance.

Then she pressed a coffee can into his hands—and have I mentioned that Bella thought Dylan pretty much walked on water? His eyes widened as he hefted the can testingly.

"Could this be . . . fruitcake?" he asked wonderingly. But he knew it was, the can lined with double layers of buttered waxed paper and filled with dark, fruit-and-nut-rich batter. After you baked it, you doused it with brandy every other day for a week, which was part—some said most—of its charm.

"You lay that by until December," she instructed Dylan. "By then it'll be just right."

He looked bereft. "Not even—" His long fingers pulled a few imaginary morsels from the can.

"Not a crumb," she scolded, "If you do, I'll know."

Dylan hugged her shoulders. "I think you might, at that," he conceded, and then he and Lizzie made their way to the door.

"Call me," Lizzie urged again, "if—"

"I will," I lied, and when they'd gone Bella was already going around locking windows and doors.

"Bella," I said, "it's still too nice out there to close things up, don't you think?" Soon enough winter would trap us inside with the windows closed and the storm windows lowered.

Besides, I'd figured it out. The prowler, the bone . . . I was sure I had it all thought through.

"And I'm telling you," I went on, "no one's going to try getting in—"

From the parlor where she'd been sleeping in front of the TV, Ivy screamed.

An hour later, we tried putting Ivy to bed in the small, cozy room next to the parlor fireplace. Hardly bigger than a closet, lined with colorful pillows and quilts, and with a low wooden bed on a braided rag rug tucked into one corner, it was the perfect hideout.

But Ivy was still too upset. “It was *not* a nightmare,” she insisted. “I *saw* someone.”

She could not, however, describe the someone. “I told you,” said Bella, her face saying she wanted those windows not just locked, but boarded over. “Something funny’s going on here.”

“Yeah, you think?” I brushed Ivy’s straight black hair off her face. She jerked away, refusing to be soothed.

Bella rolled her eyes, her hands dropping to her sides in a gesture I knew well: *This calls for the big guns.* Leaning down, she gathered Ivy into her arms.

“Come on, honey, we’ll go read a bedtime story. Out in the kitchen, in the rocking chair by the stove, okay? And Fala can come, too.”

Sniffling, Ivy let herself be guided out of bed. I saw with a pang that someone had painted her toenails, blue with glitter in it. A nanny had done it, maybe, or some other child’s mother. From the kitchen came the woodstove’s heavy cast-iron door clanking shut and the rocker’s familiar creak.

Then I heard Bella’s voice, raspy and harsh but somehow still as comforting as a warm blanket: “Once upon a time, in a land far away . . .”

Once I was sure they were settled, I called Ellie and told her what had happened. “Almost like someone was waiting for the house to quiet down,” she said, when I’d finished.

Which was my idea precisely. The idea that perhaps someone had been in here all along, watching and waiting, made me want to go lock all those windows again.

“What would you do in my situation?” I asked. The situation being that Ivy was majorly freaked out, and who could blame her?

“Could you let her sleep with you?” Ellie asked.

Oh, dear god. Small legs kicking restlessly, a child's unhappy little body tossing and turning . . .

"No," I said. "That won't work. If I don't get some decent shut-eye pretty soon, I won't be responsible for my behavior."

"Hmm," said Ellie, reconsidering. She'd seen me at my sleep-deprived worst. "You could be right." Then: "Listen, it won't get you the responsible mom of the year award, but there's that blackberry cordial that Bella makes."

"Ellie! You mean you'd—"

"Well, not as a rule, of course, but yes, I'd give Ivy a shot glass full of the stuff. Knock her right out, I'll bet."

Bella's cordials, made from Eastport fruit—mostly wild blackberries, but also grapes, dandelion blossoms, even rose hips—were sweet, tasty, and as potent as rocket fuel. In fact, the stuff was very much like rocket fuel in that it didn't take much of it to get you really high.

In short, it was a great idea. "I could use some, too," I said, meaning the cordial. "Later, though."

Ellie's tone changed. "Why? Are you planning something?" By something she meant snooping.

"Tonight's probably the only night Lawson's room will still have his stuff in it," I reminded her. By tomorrow he'd likely be in custody, his things stuffed in a canvas bag with his name on it and tossed into a locker.

"I just can't help thinking there's more here than meets the eye," I said. "The thing about Ivy being right nearby when it happened—but not in the car—is very weird. If she was," I amended. "And if she wasn't, where was she?"

I took a breath. Where Ivy was during the deadly event, what she saw or heard—those were just the things we weren't to talk with her about.

"And now I've got a prowler or whatever. Ivy thinks someone was in the house." I still hoped she'd been dreaming, but what if she hadn't been? "I mean what's with all this, anyway?"

I heard my voice rising and shut my mouth. "Jake," Ellie said after a moment, "did you think you'd have to persuade me?"

Into trying to find out, she meant, and it was true that I'd never had to coax her into a snooping trip.

"I've got my hat on my head and my car keys in hand," she said. "But if we're going, we should probably get a move on."

Correct. Eastport evenings were lively pretty late until around mid-September, but after that, the nights got dark early, and the sidewalks practically rolled up all by themselves.

So unless he had somewhere else to go—and I doubted that he did; he'd said he hardly knew anyone here—Lawson would likely be returning to his room at the Motel East within, say, the next hour or two.

Assuming he wasn't in it already.

"Oof," Ellie muttered from the darkness ahead of me half an hour later. Early sunsets made sneaking around easier, but more dangerous.

"You okay?" I worked my way through the overgrown azaleas to the rear corner of the Motel East, facing the water.

"No," came her reply. "Put your gloves on, there's poison ivy up here, it looks like. And barberry bushes."

Fabulous. Poison ivy was the worst enemy—I didn't just itch, I caught fire, meanwhile wheezing and eye-watering—but barberry thorns are the cruelest weapons the vegetable kingdom has yet developed.

So, I pulled the gloves on and pulled the bill of the baseball cap I wore farther down to shield my eyes. Then I shoved, ducked, sidestepped, and scrambled through those barberry bushes, red-leafed and heavy with small red fruits that hid the thorns.

Another hot jab stung me—those thorns were deliberately targeting me, I decided. Then I froze at the muffled crack of a stepped-on stick, followed by the silence of a held breath.

"Jake?" Ellie whispered from somewhere ahead of me. "What's going on?"

I waited, listening. "Nothing," I whispered back finally, hoping it was true as we crept on toward the long row of motel rooms, each with a railed concrete patio equipped with tables, chairs, and a gas grill.

At last, I emerged from the stabby shrubberies, just in time to see Ellie vaulting lightly over the railing surrounding the first room's patio.

The plan, we'd decided, was to *look* in, not go in. But I'd only managed to fling one leg over the railing she'd jumped when she began trying the room's sliding glass door.

Inside, the drapes were fully drawn. Alarm pierced me as the glass door slid open an inch. "Ellie!" I whispered. This hadn't been in the plan.

She glanced back, slid the door open a little farther, and slipped into the room, easing sideways between the curtains and the glass until she reached the place where the drapes parted at the middle. Then she sidestepped her way swiftly back; a moment later and she was outside again.

"Well?" I whispered, still halfway over the patio railing. One foot in, one foot out—stuck that way, actually.

Thoroughly stuck. "Wow," Ellie said, seeing my predicament, somehow managing to keep a straight face. "Can you sort of hop, maybe get one foot high enough to swing it over?"

"You mean over the rail?" I shot her a glance. In some other universe, maybe; in this one, no way. Meanwhile, behind us the bay spread coal-black, the lights of Campobello twinkling distantly on the other side. The tide was out, and small waves slopped the exposed shore distantly.

Downhill from the motel under a single streetlight, an unpaved road ran along the water. Sooner or later, someone was going to come along and—

"Duck!" Ellie whispered urgently. Footsteps sounded from

the darkness beyond the old canning factory at the water's edge. The defunct cannery's black, yawning window holes watched down silently; then a flashlight's yellow cone appeared, moving steadily back and forth on the road.

Moments later the smell of patchouli oil reached me, like a sharp stick being poked repeatedly up one nostril. I stifled a sneeze, since believe me, sneezing is not what a person perched the wrong way on a metal railing wants to do.

The flashlight's owner stepped into the thin patch of lamp-glow from the motel.

"Lawson," I said, half turning to Ellie—a full turn would've meant amputating one of my legs at the hip.

"Darn, sooner than we expected. He doesn't seem to be coming up here, though," Ellie whispered. Then, "Hey, he fell."

I squinted into the gloom near the water. The shoreline rocks, jagged and weed-slimed, were treacherous even at low tide, slippery wet and determined to break your leg.

But he seemed unhurt as he struggled up. "Seems to know right where he's going," said Ellie.

His flashlight brightened a patch of sand with rocks encircling it. I watched for a moment longer, until I was sure.

"Hiding something," I said. He finished tucking a smallish package under a rock that lay high enough on the shoreline's embankment to be safe from the tide.

Or so he thought. "Huh," said Ellie when he'd returned to the road. I fixed my gaze on the rock where he'd hidden whatever it was, trying to memorize anything that might help me locate it again.

Meanwhile he'd reached the shadowy end of the dirt road where it entered Sea Street Park. I let out a relieved breath. But another problem was worsening. "Ellie," I said, keeping my voice calm with an effort. Lawson went on into the park without looking back again.

"Ellie, certain limits are being reached with regard to my anatomy," I said. "I can only stand on tiptoe for so long."

Time, pressure . . . I was in the process of being bisected was the truth of the matter.

"Okay," said Ellie, grabbing a low footstool from the patio furniture behind us. As she placed it under my left foot, it hit me that we were still right smack in front of the room she'd sneaked into. If someone was in there, any minute they might come out of there, and—

Ellie slid the patio's other footstool under my right foot, distracting me. "Oh, thank you," I breathed, and got ready at last to swing my inside leg out over the patio rail.

Just then the motel room's tenant approached the glass door's nearly drawn curtains, his shadow moving behind them. As I'd feared, he must've returned while we were focused on Lawson; now we were in trouble.

Fingers appeared on the edge of one curtain panel as if ready to pull it back. *Caught . . .* Desperately I tried to come up with a halfway believable story to cover this situation. But instead, the shadow in there changed its mind, moving away from the curtain.

Instantly I leapt off the footstools and over the railing, lost my balance, and landed in more barberry bushes. "Jake!" Ellie hissed, as I scrambled up.

"Okay," I gasped, plucking a dozen needle-tipped thorns from my pants. She was already moving away down the row of motel rooms.

"Come on," she advised over her shoulder at me.

Easy for her to say. I pushed through more shrubbery, this time, thankfully, not of the backside-stabbing variety. Instead, landscapers had placed large granite boulders among the bushes here; for variety, I supposed.

And I only collided with one of them, but one was plenty. Warm dark blackness descended over me, stars whirled and Ellie's hands gripped my arms, guiding me . . . When my head cleared at last, we'd reached the last patio in the row.

Puzzled, I peered back at the rooms we'd passed by without looking into them. "But how do we know it's—?"

Turning away, she hopped over the end room's patio railing. It held the same kind of table, chairs, footstools, and gas grill as the others had. Plucking up a small, shiny object from the table, she held it out to me. "This."

On a good day, Ellie could pick out the birds in the trees on Campobello. But this was astonishing even for her.

Seeing my expression, she pulled a small pair of binoculars from her pocket. "Don't worry, I'm not developing superpowers," she said. "I found these a while ago at a tag sale."

Small, silver, finely crafted, the maker's name delicately engraved on one of the barrels. Then I turned my attention to the other item she held, a silver-painted cigarette lighter with a gemstone set into it.

The last time I'd seen it I was seated across from Lawson in Brady's Brunch's outdoor dining area. I felt a smile spread on my lips.

"Oh, well done," I told Ellie. She was a genius at having the right gadget handy, but this time she'd really nailed it: this was Lawson's room, all right. But next came disappointment: unlike the first one she'd tried, the curtains were open here but the sliding glass door itself was locked.

So, we could see in. We just couldn't get in. "Drat," I said. Because you can't just go breaking into places like this, you know? The police—and there will be some, I guarantee—will emphasize the "breaking in" part of the episode and never mind your so-called reasons.

Still, Ellie waited stubbornly for me. "Oh, all right," I gave in finally, "let's get me over that damned railing, first."

After all, what's a little felony breaking and entering among friends? Besides, there was something really sketchy about him hiding that package. I'd been hoping for Ivy's sake that he wasn't a bad guy and that all of this would get straightened out, but the package thing was . . . strange.

By the way, did you know you can open those sliding-glass-door locks with a credit card?

It was your usual basic motel room: nightstands, beds, TV, closet, the usual small fridge and terrible-coffee setup.

A suitcase lay open on one of the beds. The desk held a few sheets of paper, a pen, and a list of area dining and activities.

On the other bed lay a small backpack; I resisted the urge to rummage. Beside it was an open spiral notebook full of crayon drawings: one of a fish with green gills and a sappy grin, another a pink, frilly fairy with gold hair and a magic wand.

I turned a page, felt my eyebrows go up. "Yeeks."

Ellie looked up. "Wow," she agreed.

The drawing was of a broad-winged, green-scaled monster whose red eyes spat jagged yellow bolts. Its teeth dripped long slime strings while its claws scrabbled furiously at the air, which was also full of smoke and fire.

"You know," Ellie said, "this is actually pretty good. She can draw."

"Mm-hmm." Better than that insipid fairy creature, anyway. I set the notebook aside and we ventured into the bathroom: shaving cream, an electric toothbrush, and a paper cup with a child's toothbrush leaning in it.

"Jake, look at this." I glanced into the sink where Ellie pointed and felt a chill up my spine; there was a hair in the sink, and it wasn't Lawson's.

Not Ivy's, either. It was long, wavy, and way too red to have grown that way out of anyone's head: Cindy Munson's, in other words.

"Oh, my stars and garters," Ellie murmured. Suddenly it occurred to me that the evidence techs hadn't been in here yet.

"Okay, let's finish up and get out," she said finally, and I was already eager for that latter part, so we made it quick, lifting pillows, peering under beds and behind standard motel-room paintings, feeling around under the tissues and towels and flipping through the old Gideon Bible in the nightstand—

"Nothing," I said, straightening from inspecting the spaces behind the bureau and its mirror.

"Me, neither," Ellie replied, peering into the coffeemaker. In the end the lighter, the notebook, and the long, wavy strand of red hair were our total haul of cluelike items.

I glanced around to be sure nothing in the room was left out of place. "We should go before he comes back."

The room's front door led out to a paved parking lot, bright with the kind of lighting typically used for nighttime sporting events. The glass sliding door we'd come in through, by contrast, led only to thorn-infested darkness.

Before I could decide which one I liked less, footsteps approached across the parking lot. A split second later, after I'd hurled myself out through the sliding glass door and yanked the curtain shut behind me, a faint beep from the room's key-card reader was followed by the click of the front door opening.

On the patio I stumbled into a chair, grabbed at and nearly overturned the table, and nearly hamstrung myself again on that damned patio railing, which by now I was looking forward to dismantling with my bare hands, someday.

That is, if I ever got out of jail . . . but finally I escaped the patio. Ahead, Ellie scampered down to the dirt road running along the water. I followed, picking my way while also picking wood bits out of my hands; ahead, the rising moon shone whitely onto waves the color of crumpled aluminum foil.

Stumps of old dock pilings studded the beach, remnants of a nineteenth-century steamboat terminal from which Eastporters could depart for anywhere in the world. Now the expanse stretched to a barely visible line of foam at the tide's distant edge.

"I found it," she said when I reached her. She was staring toward the beach and the rocks lining the embankment near where Lawson had been earlier.

Where he'd been hiding something. She put the binoculars in her pocket. "But I don't want to take my eyes off the spot in case I can't find it again," she said.

Then she started off across the rocks that lay between us and the place where she'd been aiming the binoculars. And by rocks, I mean quarried granite chunks, each the size of the mobility scooter you'd be needing if you fell from one.

They'd been dropped here years ago to slow erosion—and to slow me, apparently. Ellie danced along like one of those angels on the pins everyone's always arguing about, but on anything but a flat floor I'm—well, I'm unpredictable, to put it nicely.

At least these particular rocks weren't too slippery, I thought, jinxing myself completely as my sneakered foot hit a patch of seaweed that the tide had left behind. That foot flew forward while the other went up in the air; the next thing I knew I was wedged in. And have I mentioned that it was dark out here?

The only illumination came from the motel's lights and from that streetlamp on shore. Ahead of me, Ellie moved steadily from one rock to the next. I could hear her talking things over with herself as she went.

"He's not from here, he doesn't realize he could've been seen . . ."

Yeah, that was an understatement. In Eastport, if you stub your toe at one end of the island, five minutes later somebody is filling a foot basin with hot water and epsom salts at the other end. "Hey, Ellie, could you give me a hand, here?"

A series of unsuccessful squirms had convinced me that my leg was truly stuck, pinned between the two-ton chunk of granite I'd slipped from and one of those old, rotted, and slimy dock pilings from the steamship era, rounded and shortened by time and water, but still firm.

And now the tide was turning, icy water seeping beneath me where moments before it had been merely damp. Coming in fast, as usual, that tide. Soon the water here would be deep.

"Ellie!" See, the thing about the tide is that it just keeps rising—right over your head if that's what happens to be in the way. It was an indefensibly stupid way to die, and it could happen to me real soon, now, if she didn't hear me.

Or if she couldn't get me unwedged. A small puddle appeared by my left thigh. Then somewhere above and behind me something moved on the rock that I'd fallen from; oh, great, I thought in what I figured were probably the last instants of my life, some night-hunting wild animal is about to start nibbling.

But these things never end with just nibbling, do they? Clenching my fists, gritting my teeth, meaning to get in a few punches, at least, and—

"Jake! Oh, for Pete's sake." It was Ellie behind me on the rock, but when she grabbed my hands and pulled it was no go.

Damn. "What makes you so sure you've found whatever he put there, anyway?" I groused.

Hey, it was better than contemplating my probable fate: glub-glub.

"Never mind that," said Ellie, eyeing the incoming tide's foamy edge. It had come a lot closer.

"Can you get out of the jeans somehow?" she wanted to know, her voice newly tinged with anxiety.

"That would mean getting my foot up through the cuff," I said, "and the foot is . . ."

I tried wiggling it again but it didn't budge, and the boulder definitely didn't; meanwhile the tide's incoming edge crept stealthily nearer still.

"Okay," said Ellie, "this is maybe a little crazy, but—"

From the satchel still over her shoulder she pulled a spray bottle whose unusual shape I recognized even in the gloom.

"Ew, why are you carrying that around?"

It was a pint of the food-grade lubricant we used at the Moose for oiling the moving parts of the coffee grinder, the blender, the food processor, and the cooler's compressor.

"Ordered it online, I was bringing it in to the shop," she explained as she twisted the spray top off the bottle.

"When you feel it in your shoe, start pulling." To get my foot out of it, she meant, and then she began pouring.

I supposed there must be worse things than having food-grade motor oil squirted out of a bottle into your shoe. But the stuff seeped down into my sock, oozed in between my toes, and made them slide greasily in ways almost guaranteed to bring on a foot cramp.

Which it also did. "Yeagghh," I uttered shudderingly, my foot jerking reflexively away from the horrid sensation. But then: "Hey."

Suddenly I was looking at my bare foot, fishbelly-white against the dark granite. Retrieving my wet, oil-soaked sneaker and putting it back on was no barrel of laughs, but being alive to do it consoled me a lot.

"Jake," said Ellie, who'd climbed up onto the rocks and was poking around, aiming a flashlight into the crevices—because of course she had a flashlight. Ellie always had a flashlight.

I slogged toward shore across weed-strewn sand that looked solid but was in fact mostly water; with the tide halfway in, now, and rising fast, it would soon be completely flooded.

With that tide still uncomfortably in mind, I climbed up to where Ellie now crouched on a wide flat rock. "This seemed like such a good idea," I said, "back before we started doing it."

She just laughed. "And that's different from our usual expeditions?"

"Yeah, yeah." I sat. "Ellie, we should regroup, get warmer clothes and some gloves that will stand up to these rocks—"An autumn night in Eastport can be balmy enough to sleep out on the porch, or it could be the kind of weather we were having tonight: breezy, chilly, and damp in a way that goes right to your sciatic nerve and settles there with a vicious twinge.

"Hey, Jake?" Ellie tried interrupting, but after my near-death experience I was on a roll.

"—and come back here when we're equipped for—"

"Jake, *look.*" She took my chin firmly between her fingers and turned my head toward what she held in her other hand. In the distant glow from the motel and the streetlamp I could just make it out: Money.

Lots of it, all in hundreds; ten thousand dollars, I guessed, or more.

"Hey, you know what would be funny?" I asked.

Cold saltwater soaked my pants, my feet squished yuckily in my wet shoes, and the boulder-bonk on my forehead from earlier felt swollen to melon size.

"If we replaced this with Monopoly money and put it back in its hiding place," I said, feeling a giggle rise from somewhere inside me. Not drowning had made me cheerful.

Even in the dark, I could see Ellie's eye roll as she shoved the money into her inside jacket pocket; then we made our way back to land, jumping from rock to rock ahead of the tide until we reached the embankment.

Across the bay, distant headlights moved along the shore road on Campobello. I was cold, wet, bruised, thorn-scratched, and stinging like fire wherever salt water had touched broken skin. But I was still breathing, which for a little while there I hadn't expected to be.

So that was good. Ellie plunked herself down in the dry grass and gravel of the embankment, unwrapping the layers of plastic wrap that were wound around the cash, setting aside the small electronic tag that she'd predicted would be there.

She finished counting, looked up. "Jake, there's fifty thousand dollars here."

I glanced around. There was no one nearby that I could see,

but that didn't satisfy me, suddenly. If Lawson had indeed gone around to the motel's parking lot and entered his room via the front door, he might be inside right now, watching us from in there.

The idea must've struck Ellie at the same moment. Keeping low, we made our way toward the remains of an ancient pier, now mostly collapsed planks plus a few dangling crosspieces dangling from rusted spikes. Seaweed swathes draped like aging curtains from the wet, wormholed dock pilings, dripping in the gloom.

"Where"—I ripped a clammy sheet of weed away from my face—"are we going?" I croaked out, spitting seaweed bits. We'd reached the old cannery, a now-decaying brick building where sardine trimmings got turned into cat food, back in the days when Eastport had a booming sardine fishery.

"Around the water side of the building." she said. "It's the only way to get to the street without being seen."

"Ah." Because we didn't *know* Lawson was in his room, did we? And if he wasn't, and he spied us lurking around in the same vicinity as where he'd hidden all that money—

Resignedly, I trudged toward the short, rickety wooden ladder leading from the partly collapsed dock: ten or twelve aging, dilapidated rungs up to street level. Ellie scampered up like a little monkey and waited.

I put my foot on the ladder's first rung. The damp, rotted wood broke the rusted nails holding it in place, and the next rung just fell off by itself. Fortunately, I'd been expecting this. The evening hadn't exactly been a run of good luck so far, had it? Flinging my hand up defiantly I grabbed onto the third rung, and I got about halfway up the ladder before the whole thing collapsed.

On my way down I glimpsed a short length of rusted rebar sticking out of the old structure, sharp-ended and all ready to remove my appendix. Instead, I swerved, flailed out wildly, and caught the sharpest, rustiest section in my bare hand. Then something below me grazed my foot very tenderly and slurpily, as if wondering what I might taste like, and the next thing I know I was all the way up on the building's dock.

Here was where waste sardine bits destined for cat food bowls arrived by barge, and it was not a delicate business, this cat food making. A ghostly whiff of stewed fish innards seemed to float on the damp night air as I went along in near-darkness, trying not to trip over a chunk of concrete or skid through a patch of engine oil leaked from who knew where.

Then came an old set of concrete steps leading down past a pile of fallen pieces of fire escape to a bit of waste ground and an alley. The lights on Water Street were only a hundred yards distant but seemed miles away, here in the near dark. I stepped over what had once been a seagull that got turned into something's lunch and now was a messy, bad-omenish pile of feathers and gore. Next came the remains of a fast-food breakfast, finally a short, thoroughly annoying length of barbed wire.

"Wonderful," I said irritably to no one, unwrapping the wire from around my ankle while wondering how a quick, simple snooping trip had deteriorated into such a fiasco.

That's when I heard the footsteps coming up behind me—and that did it. So far tonight I'd been stabbed, bashed, allergied, and perched on a rail more uncomfortably than I can even describe, not to mention grossed out by that seagull corpse. So by the time I spun around to face whoever it was, my roughed-up body parts and way too busy fight-or-flight system had overridden my common sense.

What little I had. "All right, dammit," I snarled at the dark figure that had stopped a few yards from me.

A flashlight beam blinded me. Footsteps approached. Ellie came back to stand beside me, raising a hand to shield her eyes from the glare.

The flashlight beam fell, and I made out a face. Dark hair,

dark eyes, red lipstick nearly black in the gloom. "Hello, girls." It was Lizzie Snow.

Darn, I thought, suddenly conscious of the fifty thousand dollars in Ellie's jacket.

Not to mention all the other things we'd been up to. The barberries, for instance, and that bonk that my noggin took.

"Looks like you could use a little assistance," Lizzie said, her voice suddenly seeming to come from far away.

"Maybe," I said uncertainly, frowning at the way my knees felt, i.e., watery, and then not there at all. An odd sensation came over me, ears roaring and my head spinning.

Lizzie eyed me narrowly. I put a hand out. Someone grabbed it; someone else got a shoulder under my arm, holding me up.

"I don't feel so good," I managed to say through lips that felt thick, prickly and numbish—*that poison ivy*, I realized—and all that plus the hooting and clanking of foghorns and bell buoys out on the dark water are the last things I remember before lights-out.

Four

The Eastport police station was located in the old A&P grocery building, across from the post office on the corner of Washington Street. The low, yellow-brick structure was dark and silent as we crossed the empty blacktop parking lot; the inside smelled like carpet adhesive, sweeping compound, and coffee left to stew until the brew was like squid ink.

Lizzie unlocked her office and sat us down. Besides us, it held her desk and office chair, two straight chairs, and a set of file drawers. On the desk were several short stacks of paperwork, a to-do list with only about half the stuff crossed off, and a half-eaten Hershey bar.

Outside, through the room's one window, I could see a man walking an Irish setter in and out of the light of the streetlamps on Washington Street. His pipe sent pale smoke puffs in the shapes of small question marks into the night sky.

"Are you sure you don't need medical attention?" Lizzie asked me sternly. Once I'd proved I wasn't dead by waking up and complaining bitterly about those thorn wounds—I'd seen my reflection in the rearview of Lizzie's squad car, and I looked like I'd been dragged behind a truck for a while—she'd administered first aid swiftly and correctly: a Benadryl shot plus now a cup of that thick black squid ink.

With, dear god, powdered creamer. She leaned across the desktop at us. "So, you want to tell me about it? Or should we waste time letting me ask questions until I hit on the right one?"

She lifted the plastic-wrapped cash that Ellie had produced from her jacket pocket after Lizzie had noticed it bulging out like a tumor. "This is going in the safe right here for now. I'll see tomorrow what the state cops want to do about it."

"We do know it's Lawson's money, though," Ellie said. "We saw him hide it."

"Yeah, I'll tell them," Lizzie replied. "I'm sure they'll be impressed."

So much for our evening's heroics. Then she turned to my other problem. "The family services team should be here by noon tomorrow," she told me, "to do Ivy's interview and take her into care while her dad's thing plays out."

While Lawson got either arrested for murder or not, she meant. Then the rest of what she'd said sank in and I sat up straight. "Wait, what?"

"Well, like I said this morning, by tomorrow they'll have an already approved foster family for her." Lizzie eyed me strangely. "You sure you're okay? We talked about this."

"Uh, yeah. I mean, not about the okay part. I think the truck that hit me might've left a few sharp parts stuck in me, but otherwise—yeah, no, that's fine."

I nodded as well as I could without making my bruised brain bump the inside of my skull. "Tomorrow," I said. "We'll be ready."

"Kid's already traumatized, it's a shame to move her. It's a rotten situation," Lizzie said. She glanced at her watch. "It's late. Jake, you're sure about not getting checked out?"

"Yup," I muttered. The squid ink woke me up, all right, but

mostly by eating its way into my stomach like battery acid. Only the bright lights and brisk bossiness of an emergency room could have made me feel worse.

"I'd give a lot to know Lawson's reaction, though, when he finds that money's missing," she said as we got up to leave.

I felt my eyebrows rising, which was good since it meant the benadryl had worked and some of the swelling was fading.

"What are you suggesting," I asked as we stepped outside and started walking across the parking lot, "—that we follow him around?"

In black slacks and a dark-blue uniform shirt, carrying a holstered Glock and with her short black ringlets clinging tightly to her head, she looked slim as a switchblade and twice as deadly.

"Why would I do that?" she inquired innocently. "Nothing you've told me connects the money to any crime."

"But," Ellie objected, before she caught on and her trap snapped shut.

"He'll check to make sure it's still there," Lizzie said, as we reached her squad car. "When it's not, he'll be upset, and then you never know. He might do something . . . unwise."

On Water Street nothing moved but a cat slinking furtively into an alleyway, heading for the breakwater and the bounty of dock-dwelling rats who spent their lives among the dock pilings.

The car was a 2011 Crown Vic with the standard police package: lights, sirens, radio, etc. The backseat behind the perp screen smelled like Lysol and some other things the Lysol didn't quite cover. Lizzie glanced at me in the rearview.

"Hear anything more from your prowler?" she asked.

The seat's upholstery was a patchwork of silver duct tape slapped over rips and tears, the result of a thousand or so drunk drivers, barroom gun wavers, fistfight instigators, wife-clobberers, and juvenile runaways. Those being the crimes most common around here . . .

"Jake?" Lizzie eyed me acutely. "You still with us?"

Had I passed out again, she meant. It was what I felt like doing—atop the night's various frights and exertions, that Benadryl was like a tranquilizer dart.

"Yeah, I'm here. I don't know what's going on in the prowler department," I said. "But probably nothing."

In the back of my mind I wondered whether Lawson might've sneaked in and Ivy caught sight of him. It seemed even more the kind of thing he might do now that I knew money was involved in all this somehow.

People will do all kinds of things when money is at stake. "I don't know what happened," I added, "or who it was. But it hasn't happened again, and there aren't any fresh scratches on that door lock, either."

And Ivy's visitor could've been a bad dream. Not that I'd hallucinated the figure in my office: "Some poor intoxicated person wandered up to the wrong house and found a door I forgot to lock or something."

I'd locked them. I'd definitely locked them. But it was the only explanation I could think of that made any sense at all, and each day that passed with no further developments on the topic made it harder to keep worrying about.

The Crown Vic rolled slowly down Water Street, Lizzie's practiced eyes scanning the shadowy gaps between buildings. The lit-up display windows in the shop fronts went by in a smear of bright colors. We passed the old redbrick Peavey Library with the cupola on top and the cannon bolted to the lawn out front.

Then she turned right, and moments later she pulled the squad car to the curb in front of my big old house. The porch light was on, but the rest of house was dark—it was long past midnight. With an effort I heaved myself forward and climbed painfully from the backseat. Once I got myself upright on the sidewalk, all I wanted to do was sit right back down again.

Ellie took my arm, waved to Lizzie, and helped me toward

the house. The porch steps were especially challenging since I kept falling asleep in between them. Inside, she helped me off with my jacket while Fala danced around me unhappily, whining and bumping me with her nose to make sure I was all right.

Which I was not. I felt just exactly like somebody was hitting me with a rubber baton. Ellie sat me down at the kitchen table and began making coffee. It was too late for it, but I thought I might die without it.

"Who's still up watching TV?" she wondered aloud as she pushed the coffeemaker button. "The light's on in there."

My dad and Bella would ordinarily have been in their own private part of the house at this hour. I hauled myself up.

In the hall, a low night-light threw shadows that climbed to the pressed-tin ceiling. I followed the TV's blue glow into the parlor, where the murmur of Weather Channel voices excitedly described a low-pressure system over Louisiana.

My dad lay asleep on the carpet with a pillow under his head. Nearby in the recliner, Bella dozed with Ivy tucked in close beside her, also asleep.

"Dad?" I crouched next to him. "Do you want to go to bed?"

His eyes opened, focusing swiftly on me. "Why, I think that's a fine idea." Gripping his hand, I helped him to his feet and we made our way past the hall clock, through the kitchen, and into the old folks' private suite.

"Poor child," Bella said quietly when I got back to the parlor. Ivy had meanwhile crawled all the way into her lap and popped her thumb into her mouth.

"Don't bother about us, I'll put her to bed," said Bella quietly.

I hesitated. "Isn't she heavy?" But Bella just shook her head, and she was an old lady who knew what she wanted, so I let them be.

Then I went around checking windows and doors, all locked

up *tight as ticks*, as my dad would've put it. But as I rattled the doorknobs and wiggled the latches once more, I couldn't help peering out through the dark windowpanes into a night that might have anything in it, even a murderer.

Soon Ellie went home, and shortly afterward, I decided that bed was the only rational option for me, too. My thorn-scratched face felt like needlepoint canvas, my head pulsed steadily with dull pain, and the rest of me was just a wrung-out dishrag.

At the foot of the stairs, I looked into the parlor once more and found Bella asleep again, but Ivy's bright eyes were wide open and watching me.

"Ivy, do you want to get in bed?" She had her new pj's on, and the fuzzy yellow slippers we'd gotten for her.

I leaned over. Bella snored softly, her bony old hands spread in her lap. "Ivy?" I whispered.

"She's dead, isn't she?" The words hung in the air. "My mom—she's really dead?"

Oh, hell. I sat down on the footstool next to the recliner. "Yeah," I said. "She is. I'm really sorry, Ivy."

A tear leaked down her face. "I woke up and thought she wasn't, that it was all a bad dream."

She looked at me through eyes that knew more than any kid should. I wondered again what she'd seen or hadn't seen the night before, and after that I led her to the bathroom, to the kitchen for a glass of milk, and finally to the tiny bedroom tucked in beside the parlor fireplace.

With a low, slanted ceiling, a small brass-shaded lamp mounted on the wall, and a white-painted iron bedstead heaped with colorful quilts, it was the perfect hideout for a child, all sweet and snug.

"Or," I pivoted smoothly when she hesitated, "you could stay in one of the bedrooms upstairs and I'd be next door."

Maybe she didn't want to be alone down here, even though

Bella and my dad were so nearby. "Would you like that better?" I asked. But Ivy just shook her head, marching forward with an air of stoic bravery that wrung my heart.

Fala maneuvered her big furry body into the room with me. Eyes alert, ears pointed, the dog looked at me and then at the little girl and lay down very deliberately beside the bed.

"Good doggy," she whispered. I'd given her a small frog-shaped clicker that made a harsh "ribbit!" sound when you squeezed it; she could use it if she wanted one of us to come, I'd told her. Now she fingered it as if reassuring herself with it, then reached up and turned off the light all by herself.

A night-light burned low in the parlor, and I left Ivy's door ajar. Bella had gone to bed. As I climbed the hall stairs, the whole house seemed to yawn emptily around me. My own room was going to be lonesome without Fala, I thought.

It was.

Ladyfingers are sweet, airy biscuits shaped like—well, you'll figure it out. They're used in desserts like tiramisu and in trifle, a bread pudding with fruit, custard, and cream that is to die for.

Or you can dunk them in coffee and then in chocolate syrup, the way I was doing the next morning at the Chocolate Moose when the little bell over the door jingled and Ellie hurried in.

"Gosh, I'm running late this morning," she breathed, flinging her satchel one way and her jacket the other. "Not a great morning to oversleep."

By which she meant that she hadn't been up at her usual crack-of-dawn hour. Now it was 7 AM, and it always amazed me how her wild tosses always landed her belongings on their hooks, while mine always landed nearby, sort of.

"What are you—?" She took in my swollen, scratched face, puffy eyes, and the bruise on my forehead, now turning a lovely shade of greenish purple. Then she surveyed the nonstandard morning meal I was enjoying.

"Jake, you need vitamins and—"

"Yes, and minerals. I know." I plucked up another fresh, warm ladyfinger, dunked it, and held it out. "Here, have one."

So she did. "Wow," she managed through the sudden tide of chocolate-fueled feel-good chemicals flooding her brain.

"Eat a good breakfast," I intoned serenely, "feel better all day."

I'd put on a new pair of earrings, turquoise sea glass on silver loops, for good luck—the way I'd felt, I figured I needed all I could get. I'd left Ivy spooning up a bowlful of oatmeal with a few chocolate chips melting into it and Fala lying contentedly on the kitchen floor beside her.

Now I got up, ready to leap tall buildings and so on. "Okay, so what besides a million more of these"—I waved at the plateful of ladyfingers I'd been demolishing—"is on our agenda for today?"

Actually, it *was* about a million more. We were making chocolate-cherry trifles for the high school reunion's closing ceremony, about thirty-six hours from now, not a terrible task overall since we'd prepared very thoroughly for it.

Those ladyfingers, though. Fruit trifles took a lot of them—you need plenty for the fruit's juice to soak into—and these had to be finished and chilling in the cooler before tomorrow night's event. So today would be a marathon baking day, and not much else would get—

Yeah, I was trying not to think about Ivy leaving, was what I was doing. "Well, there is one thing," Ellie said.

Uh-oh.

"I ran into Lizzie just now on my way here," she went on. "She asked for a favor."

"And?" I asked cautiously. It could be anything from a doughnut and coffee delivered at lunchtime to a request for some unofficial surveillance—snooping, in other words.

That last part, especially. "Well, she didn't say it flat out, but I got the strong sense that she'd like us to find out a little more about Cindy Munson. Just, you know, asking around a little. And keeping our eyes open."

Not traipsing around in the dark getting thorn-scratched and running our heads into rocks, in other words, but that was fine with me; my head still ached. "Sure, we can do that."

Hey, the sooner this all got straightened out, the better for everyone. Also, it might distract me from the idea of Ivy getting into a car with strangers and driving away.

In the kitchen, more ladyfinger ingredients were laid out: eggs, sugar, flour, baking powder, and cocoa powder, plus two large mixing bowls and two wire whisks. I'd been keeping myself busy.

"She also mentioned that the state cops have finished with Cindy's house," Ellie said.

Meanwhile, she was bustling around shutting down the kitchen lights, the sound system, the credit card reader, and the heat under a pan of chocolate chunks and butter I'd set to warming on the stove.

"Huh," I said, catching on. So that's where we were going, and right now, too, apparently. "We're going to what—just waltz right in and rummage around?"

Pawing through a recently deceased person's belongings was among my least favorite parts of snooping into murder, right up there with tripping unexpectedly over the victim's body and getting chased by the killer.

"Well," said Ellie, drawing the word out. "Maybe not quite *waltz* in."

Five minutes later we were in Ellie's car, headed for the address Lizzie had given her. The sky overhead was a clear hard blue, the color of winter; crows and blue jays flocked in the yellow-leafed maples, yelling insults at each other as we went by.

"What do you suppose he was doing with all that money?" Ellie asked as we crossed the culvert at the end of Middle Street and started uphill.

"No idea," I said. "I'll bet some cop will be asking him about it soon, though."

I wasn't sure why I was doing this—something about Ivy leaving today, maybe, plus Lizzie's request for information and a growing feeling that way more was going on here than met the eye.

"Before you ask," said Ellie, out of the blue, "we're doing this now so you don't decide to do it alone, later."

"Why in the world would I do that?" Why, the whole idea was completely—

Slowing, she turned left onto a short, narrow lane lined on both sides with more of those dreadful barberry bushes, their branches positively clogged with small orange-red fruits and the adjacent poison-tipped daggers.

"Oh, I know you," Ellie said. "You'll get thinking about it and take a notion."

"Hmm." Just looking at those barberry bushes made my face hurt. I changed the subject. "I wonder if he already knows the money is gone."

Ellie shrugged. "High tide was at 4 AM. Anytime after 5 or so, he could've gotten to it and checked. Would've been light enough to see, then, too."

She pulled the car into a gravel driveway between two cedar trees and a mailbox: MUNSON. The house was a small, one-story ranch with gray siding, an aging shingled roof, and a concrete front step with a couple of Dollar Store lawn chairs on it.

We got out. Yellow police tape across the driveway had been taken down, but a few torn lengths had snagged in the untrimmed box hedge shielding the house from the street. The car door's loud slam shocked the birds into silence.

"He could've been meaning to offer it to Cindy, to pay her to drop the custody suit," I theorized.

"Maybe." Ellie stopped short as something occurred to her suddenly. "Stay right here," she said, hopping back into the car and starting it again.

"Don't go anywhere without me," she added from behind

the wheel, possibly remembering similar trips when I'd gone in somewhere alone. Recalling the calamities that followed, too, probably, but never mind. Soon she returned on foot, having stashed the car somewhere nearby, I gathered, and we went on up the driveway and along a brick path leading out back.

There, more tall box hedges created a Zenlike stillness, the only sound a small fountain trickling at the center of it all. A bench by the fountain completed the peaceful scene, while a breeze set a quartet of wind chimes to plunking and clunking.

Wind chimes usually remind me of broken glass falling out of the headlights after a car wreck, but listening to these I could feel my blood pressure dropping. "Nice spot," I said.

"Mm. A refuge." Regret tinged Ellie's voice. Whatever peace this serene spot had brought Cindy Munson, it hadn't been enough to save her life.

We scanned around for places from which we might be seen: neighbors' windows, kids' tree houses, drones taking scenic videos. You never know when someone might call the cops when you're nosing around somewhere you don't belong. But the untidy hedge was like a green wall, blocking the view of Cindy Munson's green yard and the small wooden deck overlooking it.

"You take the deck, and I'll try that window," I said. Of course, Lizzie wouldn't have said straight out that we should try to get inside. But she knew our methods, and otherwise why tell Ellie that the state cops were done with the place?

Ellie strode across the lawn toward the deck and its sliding glass doors. I marched over to the window, which was low to the ground and handily furnished with a sturdy windowsill.

A whiff of ammonia tickled my nose; the window had been washed recently. That's why—yes!—a step stool still stood nearby. Gratefully I positioned the stool under the window, stepped up onto it, and looked in past freshly washed white curtains to a bright, pleasant, aggressively neat bedroom.

Tightly made bed, uncluttered bureau, nightstand with book, tissues, hand cream . . . A small wooden block propped the window open a crack. I stuck my fingers into the space and pulled upward, expecting resistance. Instead, the window flew up as if it were weightless, knocking me off-balance.

"Ack!" The stool toppled one way, I tumbled the other, and while the ground was soft and there were no barberry bushes here, there were ants boiling up out of the anthill that I'd just disturbed by landing on it.

Red ants—and boy, were they mad. "Ellie!" I gestured frantically at the garden hose looped over the spigot near the deck steps. Amid wild brushing-off gestures I yanked off my shoes and socks, then shirt and pants, while angry ants rained out of them by the dozens.

Then a hard stream of cold water hit me, fire-hosing more of the horrid little buggers off my skin while also turning my internal organs to frozen slush.

"Oh, jeez," I grated out through chattering teeth. "And I can't even put my clothes back on."

Wrapping my arms around my shuddering-cold self didn't do much good, either. Meanwhile, though, Ellie had dropped the hose, hopped onto the step stool, shoved the window all the way up, and disappeared through it without visible difficulty.

And if she could do it . . . With visions of a hot shower dancing gloriously in my head, I jumped up onto the stool again, too, whereupon a big, red *Now What?* sign replaced the visions.

Ellie excelled in the wiry-and-agile department; I, on the other hand, couldn't walk and chew gum at the same time. But there wasn't much choice right now, so I just imitated her: Placing my hands flat on the windowsill, I pushed down hard on it. The idea was to hop and hoist myself up over the sill and sail headfirst through the window, just as Ellie had.

But when I tried it, nothing hoisted. My feet remained firmly on the stool; it was the hopping part that stumped me. Then

Ellie appeared behind me, outside again on the deck, which was when I realized I could've just waited for her to open the sliding glass door.

Ten seconds later we were both inside. "Here." Ellie shoved towels at me. "From the linen closet."

It felt kind of creepy, but—what the heck, Cindy wouldn't be needing them anymore. I wrapped one of the towels around my waist and dried my chilled, goose-bumped legs with the other, scratching at the blooming ant bites, which already felt fiery.

The silence in the house felt enormous, like time had simply stopped in here. "Okay, let's just look the place over," Ellie said.

She crossed to the kitchen, a sunny, pleasant nook with open shelves and a window looking out to the backyard. The curtains, place mats, towels, and pot holders all featured the same wide-open-beaked rooster, crowing up a storm.

But the most obvious feature of Cindy Munson's kitchen was that absolutely, positively nothing was out of place in it. I ran a finger behind the toaster on the spotless Formica counter: pristine, and I smelled fresh floor wax in here, too.

"We can tell Lizzie one thing, this Cindy person was a neat freak." The kitchen opened into the living room and dining area; to the right, a hall led to the bath and bedroom. I headed to the bedroom where, heaven forgive me, I was about to ransack a dead woman's wardrobe for something dry to put on.

Along one bedroom wall was a closet behind sliding doors. I shoved hangers aside—slacks, a few blouses, a couple of skirts—until I found an ordinary pair of jeans that sort of fit me.

Ellie came down the hall. I zipped up the pants, pulled on a sweatshirt I'd found. "Reporting for duty, ma'am."

"Great. You do the front, I'll take back here?"

"Fine by me." I returned to the kitchen and started opening drawers, bins, and cupboards, teetering on a kitchen chair to peer behind the boxes and jars on the pantry shelves. The beady gaze of all those roosters seemed to follow me. Even the shelf paper inside the pantry was covered with them.

"Oh, go cluck yourselves," I muttered crossly at them. as I started on the living area. It was nothing fancy: tan carpet, beige walls, green curtains, plus two upholstered armchairs and an old, comfy-looking leather sofa in front of a TV.

Again, not a speck of dust anywhere, not a stray sock or a crumpled tissue or a book left facedown on the pristine carpet. I crossed to the desk in the corner, where bills for utilities lay open beside a personal checkbook and a book of stamps.

Nothing in the checkbook seemed unusual, no big amounts written to cash, no overdrafts, no odd-looking expenditures. A forensic accountant would've died of boredom looking at it, and the same went for the file folders of old tax papers and rubber-banded bundles of canceled checks.

"Ellie?" I could hear her back there opening and closing drawers, a medicine cabinet, finally something big and zippered—a dress bag, maybe, or a blanket box from under the bed.

She came to the doorway, looking around again at Cindy Munson's clean, orderly home. The space outside was decently cared for as well, the untrimmed hedges more a privacy feature, I thought now, than from neglect.

"I thought Lawson was dead set against Cindy having custody," Ellie said, "even after she quit her old habits." She gestured around. "I thought he meant he still had reasons not to trust her with Ivy. This isn't what I expected."

Me, neither. Even the philodendron in the clay pot on the windowsill was well-groomed, not a dead leaf on it.

I didn't suppose being a neat freak necessarily made you a good parent, though, and I was about to say so when the sound of a car came from out in the lane beyond the box hedges.

"Lawson," Ellie whispered, peering out. Through the gap at the driveway's end, I saw the old Chevy station wagon with the fake wood paneling and the rain flaps.

"Darn," I said. "You hid our car?"

Ellie nodded. "Next street over behind the Carsons' garage. They've already left for the winter," she confirmed.

The station wagon pulled away, then went by again in the other direction, and just as I thought it was finally gone, the car returned, pulling into the driveway this time. I ran to close and lock the sliding glass doors while Ellie rushed back to the bedroom to straighten it up after her search.

"Ellie! He's—" Right outside, I wanted to finish, but the sound of someone trying the front doorknob stopped the words in my throat.

Don't have a key, I commanded him silently, though why he would have one was beyond me. On the other hand, this was the guy who'd hidden a whole bucketload of money under a rock that would soon be underwater, and I hadn't expected that, either.

"Let's get out of here," Ellie said, and it was definitely the most sensible thing I'd heard all morning, so I dropped to all fours and began creeping across the beige carpet, staying low so as not to be seen from outside.

But the carpet was made from some roughly abrasive nylon-polyester stuff; by the time I reached the hall, my hands felt like I needed skin transplants. Not that the rest of me felt any better: my thorn-scratched face was radiantly hot and tender, and my arms were still a road map of red, puffy scratches.

Also, I was pretty sure that head-bumping boulder had given me brain damage—otherwise, what was I doing here, crouched in a dead woman's house, trying to get out?

The sliding glass doors rattled violently. "Yikes," Ellie breathed from behind me.

"No kidding." But he wasn't quite ready to break anything yet, apparently, and when I peeked again toward where he still stood outside on the deck, I saw why.

I'd picked up a bit of that yellow police tape earlier, then dropped it without thinking much about it. Now it was in his hand. As I watched, he looked from it to the bedroom window.

The window was closed but the step stool still positioned under it pretty much gave the game away, I figured.

"Okay, look," Ellie said quietly, "the minute he gives up on the bedroom window, we're out through it."

Excellent plan, but: "Why will he give up? Why not just move the footstool, climb up onto it, and raise the window the way you did?"

"Because I locked it," Ellie said, eyeing me with the calm patience that a kind person might show to a confused puppy.

"Oh," I said, and then as a new idea hit me: "The house has a basement, doesn't it? And we haven't looked down there yet. On top of which, there must be a cellar door leading out, wouldn't you think?"

The small windows set low in the concrete-block foundation suggested that it did. Lawson had gone away from the sliding doors, now, although not for long, I figured. He didn't behave like a man who was getting ready to surrender.

But in his probably temporary absence we found the steps leading to the cellar, a plain cement-floored area with a furnace, a washer and dryer, and enough metal shelving lined up against the concrete-block walls to stock an auto parts store.

But no auto parts. The shelves held plastic storage boxes; I opened several and found them full of garments out of season: winter boots, jackets, and hats and so on all neatly arranged in some, summer stuff the same way in others.

Of course: this was Cindy's place. From the way she kept it, I could feel her imposing order on everything in her life, replacing the old disorder. Except . . . back in one corner of the cellar where barely any light reached from the high windows, a heap of rumpled old blankets and pillows loomed uninvitingly.

Discards, I thought, remembering unhappily the amount of bed linens I'd thrown out when Sam was still drinking. Then a set of rough concrete steps leading up to a pair of slanting metal Bilco doors distracted me.

"Found 'em!" I called out to Ellie. They were our way out,

and now only one thing stood between us and escape: the thick, hideously layered draperies of spiderweb massed heavily in front of them. Mold-gray and riddled with tunnels and holes, alive with small bodies of all shapes and sizes, the webs rippled with thousands of skin-crawlingly active arachnids.

"You first," I told Ellie as she peered over my shoulder at them. Oh, yeah, those cobwebs were moving, all right . . . But why had an obvious neatnik like Cindy Munson left them here? Why not call an exterminator?

Then I spotted the cans of insecticide spray on the floor near the steps; so maybe she'd had a plan, just not the time to put it into action before someone killed her.

"Hang on a sec," said Ellie, and turned back to the wall lined with metal shelves. "I know I saw it somewhere . . ."

She scanned the plastic boxes, opened one and then another. "They're not all clothes . . . here!" She came back with something gunlike in her hand—that is, if guns came in orange plastic.

"Stand back," she uttered, and pulled the orange trigger. A blast of hot yellow flame shot from the barbecue lighter.

At least the webs burned fast. Probably the tiny screams were only in my imagination. Next, she grabbed a broom leaning against the cellar wall and swept briskly at the ashy remains; foolishly sentimental she is not, unlike myself.

Finally I hustled up the steps to the Bilco doors and reached for the heavy-duty slide bar that held them shut.

"Wait!" Ellie whispered, then passed me a small metal can with a plastic nozzle tip, and may I just say right here that if you have a friend who carries WD-40 in her purse, stick with her. She's the one who'll get you out of a jam.

"Thanks," I whispered back, then sprayed the oily, squeak-preventing stuff onto the metal slide bar holding the doors shut. Now no metal-on-metal shriek would alert the whole neighborhood.

"Are we clear, do you think?" Of Lawson, I meant. We didn't

want him standing out there when we emerged, which he still could be if he was quiet about it.

"I think he's gone." Ellie stood on a plastic milk crate to peek through the cellar window. Just then a car out front pulled away with a roar of old Chevrolet engine and a tire squeal.

"Ooh, he mad," said Ellie. Maybe because he couldn't find a way in that didn't involve breaking in.

"Uh-huh," I said. "Too bad. Can we go now?" Hey, we'd just sent a legion of eight-legged souls to whatever they had for a heaven; I figured we should at least use the exit they'd died for. So I reached for the metal slide, still slightly warm from the flamethrower's attentions, and pulled on it.

The bar worked easily, but next came the doors: not so much. WD-40 to the rescue yet again, however . . . squirt-squirt-squirt on all the hinges. Then I put my shoulder to them and pushed once more.

But those doors didn't budge, and it was clear they weren't going to. Sitting back on my heels on the dim, cremated-spider-smelling concrete, I thought glumly about the only reason that made sense: those doors weren't just locked on the inside, they were secured from the outside somehow, too.

Then it hit me: With Lawson gone, we could simply go back upstairs and walk out, no problem. In fact, Ellie was already on her way to do just that, standing at the top of the cellar steps in front of the door we'd used to come down here in the first place.

But now it didn't open, either.

Five

If you've never climbed up the metal shelves in an auto parts store as if they were a big, shaky piece of gymnasium equipment, crept across the top, and finally shimmied headfirst out a window barely big enough to force your hips through, you've lived a charmed life.

I was the one who'd pulled the door shut without checking the button lock in the knob, trapping us down here. So, after we'd emptied and maneuvered one of the tall metal shelves over to the aforementioned window, it fell to me to go first.

Besides, without Ellie behind me I'd never get out of here. *Just do it*, I told myself firmly, and got my feet onto the first shelf without too much difficulty. But the next one was a lot higher than the first—to get my foot up that high, I'd have to disconnect certain important ligaments in my leg.

"Wait a minute." Ellie scurried away, came back swiftly with something dangling from her thumb and forefinger. It was black and yellow, and about the size of a half-dollar.

Somehow escaped from the fiery inferno that consumed its pals, it was the biggest, fattest, juiciest-looking garden spider

I'd ever seen in my life, and although my mind knew it was harmless, the rest of me yelled, "Gah!"

The next thing I knew I was halfway out the cellar window, where I immediately encountered a choice: straight down from the window was about a three-foot drop to a bed of pea gravel. That was my landing zone, and directly at the center of it lay a dog's recent calling card.

Very recent. So, should I land on my face or my hands was my big question. Contemplating this while also wondering if my hips were going to fit through the cellar window, I felt my choice being made for me by a hard shove from behind.

The result was the first and probably the only handstand of my life, my hands planted in the pea gravel on either side of the dog's poorly timed but thematically appropriate contribution to the situation.

Then my legs began toppling backward—and no, I didn't flip up and land on my feet, what are you, a wise guy or something? But I landed on grass, which by then felt like great good luck, and Ellie was out, too, already fitting the window screen back into the opening.

I'd pretty well mangled it, punching straight through it on my way out, but hey, it looked okay from a distance as we made our way hurriedly through the neighborhood's backyards to where she'd stashed the car.

But that was about the only thing that had gone right. "We didn't even find anything useful," I griped.

"Sure, we did. We found out that Lawson had some reason to show up at Cindy's house. Thought he might find a way in."

We got into the car. "I'll bet he looked for the money, found that it was gone, and came straight here," she said.

"Huh. You know what? That sounds right." Or at least very possible, so our question was still why, but now I wondered something else suddenly.

"But what ever made him think he could find it again in the first place? Those rocks all look alike, you know?"

It was an understatement. The difference between a big granite chunk and a tiny chunk is their size and nothing else. Line them up, try to pick one out and remember it.

Then try to pick it out again, I dare you.

Ellie backed the car out and aimed it toward town while I kept trying to come up with an answer and not succeeding. Ellie, too, and finally, as we came down Battery Street, she spoke. "Air tag."

Of course I'd seen the small tracking device. "Are they waterproof?"

"With the amount of duct tape and plastic wrap Lawson used on it, you could probably build a submarine."

We crossed the culverts over Abner's Cove, where the brine-soaked staves of an old ship's hull stuck up out of the water like the rib cage of an ancient whale.

"Well, that's a new wrinkle," I said. I didn't like it that he'd picked up the scrap of police tape I'd dropped and eyed it so curiously.

And I especially didn't like it when I reached up to push my hair absently back from my face and discovered that I was missing an earring.

"Hi! Hi!" cried my six-year-old grandson, Ephraim, jumping up and down in excitement when he spotted me arriving at the Chocolate Moose in Ellie's car. His four-year-old sister, Nadine, stood behind him, smiling around the thumb in her mouth.

I got out of the car and swept her into my arms, and she giggled. "Mom!" My daughter-in-law, Mika, threw me a side hug. With the other arm, she hoisted a sleeping two-year-old whom we all still called Baby Lawrence, settling his weight more securely up onto her narrow hip.

Her straight black hair smelled like vanilla. I looked past her. “Where’s Sam? And what did the doctors say?”

Their stay at a small seaside resort near Portland while the baby had his ear examinations was my son’s idea. He and Mika traded time at the hospital with Ephraim-and-Nadine time at the resort’s indoor pool and outdoor playground.

“We swam and swam!” Ephraim enthused, throwing his arms around his mother’s legs while Nadine ran to meet Ellie.

“Sam’s dropping our laundry at the laundromat. Back in a minute.” She looked expectantly down Water Street. “As for the baby, they still don’t know. Some tests, he scores perfect. On others, it’s like he’s not hearing anything at all.”

Oh, dear. “So they want us to come back in six months,” she went on tiredly, “and see if there’s any change.”

Just then Sam pulled up to the curb in the van he’d finally given in and bought. Mika herded the kids into the backseat and got into the front. I waved as they pulled off, realizing with mixed feelings that my few days of peace and quiet were over.

Then I went in—those chocolate ladyfingers weren’t going to bake themselves. Also on the Moose menu for tomorrow, we had chocolate cinnamon rolls, triple threat cookies (chocolate batter, chips, and frosting plus a sliver of white chocolate in the top), and the strange little soft doodads we called hotsy-totsies (chocolate, coconut, sugar, mango, hot peppers).

Only one still remained in the display case; I popped half of it into my mouth and bit down, whereupon a sort of chocolate bomb went off on my tongue. Fire spread over my tonsils and up into my sinuses, and I could feel my eyes poaching gently in the hot tears springing to them.

Then the dark chocolate kicked in: mellow, soothing, and equipped with a pepper-powered kick that put the flavor into overdrive. Licking my fingers, I set the remainder of the hotsy-totsy aside for later—I already knew what I would have to do about that missing earring, and I would need blast-off levels of pure hotsy-totsiness to do it—I joined Ellie in the kitchen.

She was already busy cutting ladyfinger shapes from a sheet of dough she'd rolled out on our marble pastry slab. The warmth of the kids' hugs still clung to me.

"Well," I said, "at least nobody broke any bones falling off the playground equipment or got poison ivy at the resort."

Then I stopped. Ellie was staring at me. "We didn't tell them. We didn't tell them Ivy's there," she said.

The kids would be meeting her right about now, in fact. I imagined Nadine's eyes narrowing while Ephraim demanded to know who *that* was, anyway. They'd relax soon enough, I felt sure, but I hoped Bella was managing the introductions okay.

"So what was Lawson doing at his ex's house?" Ellie asked. His appearance there was our day's main takeaway so far.

"Oh, God, I have no idea. Especially if he'd just found out his money was missing—why would he look at her place for it?"

Ellie cut another plump, shapely ladyfinger and deposited it on the cookie sheet. I fetched another chilled ball of dough from the cooler and grabbed a rolling pin.

"I'm guessing he went to check the money as soon it was light enough and the tide was low enough to do it," I said. "So when he went to talk to the cops, he already knew it was gone."

"And then they started asking him about it," she agreed with my timeline so far. "That must've surprised him."

"You think?" I applied the rolling pin very gently to the ball of chilled dough. It's a tricky business: press too hard and they break into dry, uncooperative fragments; not hard enough and the stuff sticks to the rolling pin, which—trust me—you do not want.

I turned the dough ball one quarter of a rotation on the floured pastry stone and pressed again, this time rolling back and forth gently. You don't want to handle the dough much or the cookies will be tough. This time it flattened without breaking, and soon I had it rolled flat, ready for Ellie to cut.

After that, we worked in silence for a while, me moving on to beat a bowlful of cinnamon roll dough into shape and Ellie baking ladyfingers en masse, four sheets at a time.

"So now what?" she asked finally. She'd perched herself on a stool in front of the oven's glass window. A properly baked ladyfinger is the faintest bit brown around the edges, no more, and the chocolate dough made this condition harder to diagnose.

"You got me there," I said. I did know, but I didn't want to say it any more than I wanted to tell her about the missing earring, and now as I watched her carefully loosening the baked ladyfingers from the pan with a spatula, I decided not to.

The bell over the door jingled, and Dylan Hudson came in, his lean, sharp-cheekboned face creased with annoyance. "Have you seen Lizzie?"

He eyed me from under dark, frowning eyebrows, as if I might be hiding her behind the counter. "Half an hour ago she told me she'd meet me at the station in ten minutes," he said.

He took a second look at my face, which after last night's thorns still felt as if I'd been in a prizefight. "Looks like you've been doing something interesting in your spare time," he remarked drily, but the concern in his eyes was real.

Then Ellie came out, drying her hands on a dish towel. "Have you tried calling Lizzie?"

He looked flatly at Ellie. "Gee, why didn't I think of that? I've tried a dozen times, it goes straight to voicemail, and her car's gone. Her own car, I mean."

A trickle of unease chilled the back of my neck. She hated that car, a dinky sedan that did zero to sixty in five minutes. I tried her myself, but my call went to voicemail, too.

I put the phone away. "Look, she's gotten a cop call and gone to handle it," I said. "I'll bet she's back any minute."

Dylan shook his head. "I don't like this. We talked a few minutes ago, she was out on County Road, had some kids in a car pulled over. She'd have told me if—"

"Hey, Dylan?" Ellie said. "She's not the most vulnerable woman on the planet, you know?"

I saw the truth of this strike him. Besides having a lot of firepower stashed regularly on her person, Lizzie could take him down two times out of three; I'd seen her do it.

"True," he conceded. "It's not like anyone could just grab her and carry her off."

And especially not teenagers. Lizzie was not a large person, but she could levitate you right off the ground with just her voice—I'd watched her put big men behind the perp screen in her squad car like she was popping a large angry genie back into a bottle: Look, ma, no hands!

"Okay," said Dylan, giving in. "But if you hear from her, let her know I'm looking for her."

Yeah, yeah, I thought as he went out. I liked Dylan a lot, but interrupting myself to help him find his missing fiancée was not on my to-do list. "Now, where was I?" I said when he'd gone.

"Getting ready to leave," said Ellie, handing me my jacket. "The kids are home, Ivy's still there, it's getting near dinner time, and by the way your face looks awful, do you know that?"

I hadn't, but now when I looked in the mirror behind the counter I found out. The barberry scratches of last night were red and puffy; my eyes looked like raisins pressed deeply into risen dough.

"Go on home," said Ellie, "and take care of things there. I'll finish up."

It was a generous offer—a pan of cinnamon rolls was still rising on the shelf over the oven, and a dozen more hotsy-totsies had still to be completed—but I took it, because seeing my face just now had reminded me: I really wasn't feeling so good, and I hadn't been for several hours.

Ellie squinted hard at me and walked me toward the door. "Yeah," she said, "any redder and you'll get mistaken for a fire truck."

Right now, I was being mistaken for someone who could stand up and put one foot in front of the other. But once I got going, I did make it home, walking very slowly and telling myself that I'd be fine, absolutely fine.

The damp, sea-smelling air wafting in off the bay was cool in my throat and on my feverish-feeling face. Still, by the time I reached my house, I was nearly staggering. Seeing the old place was like glimpsing the gates of heaven.

The only problem was the strange car in the driveway.

From inside I heard Sam's voice, then Mika calling a reply from upstairs. Meanwhile, little Nadine banged on, it sounded like, a saucepan while Ephraim tootled on a kazoo.

"Everyone quiet down!" Bella's rusty-screen-door voice rose over the din, whereupon silence descended just as I opened the door and went in.

Bella was at the stove, where it looked like she was trying yet again to re-create her friend Pearl Wilson's curried carrot-and-turnip soup. She was sure that Pearl had deliberately left out some secret ingredient, the one small element that made the whole thing work. But she looked furious, her forehead furrowed and her thin lips clamped tightly together, and I had a strong feeling that it wasn't the soup she was upset about.

Lizzie Snow glanced up at me from the kitchen table. Seated there with her was a woman I didn't recognize—it was her car in the driveway, of course.

"Jake, I was just going to call you," said Lizzie. "Deanna Wright"—she turned to the other woman—"Jake Tiptree."

Deanna had a thin manila folder open in front of her and a pleasant look on her round, heavily made-up face. "Deanna is Ivy's Family Services caseworker," Lizzie said.

"Good to meet you." I offered my hand. She took it, smiled in a way that looked genuine, and met my gaze evenly.

"I have to apologize, it turns out the psychologist we had expected today got called to testify in a court case," she said.

Her highly processed hair was teased and sprayed into a blond pouf, her nails were pale pink with tiny sequins glued to them, and her eyelashes were tarry with black mascara.

One glance into those ice-blue peepers of hers, though, and I knew she was no fool. Suddenly I was sure that she'd noticed the torn wallpaper where Ephraim had tried climbing the lattice in the pattern, and the cracked kitchen windowpane I'd been promising to fix since last spring. Proper foster homes, I felt sure, did not have such flaws.

"I've been explaining to Lizzie and Bella that the rules are pretty strict," Deanna told me. "We can't very well just leave kids with people we don't know much about."

"Damned fools want to yank her out of here," Bella grumbled audibly, standing at the stove with her back to us.

Deanna's look was clear: *I don't make the rules.* "A family has gotten approval to be fosters," she went on. "It's a very thorough process, everyone in the house gets a background check, gives references, has a home evaluation—"

So Ivy would be safe, Deanna meant. "Funny," I said. "Yesterday I was all for sending her off with you immediately."

But today was different: for one thing, I had this sudden lump in my throat. Deanna's eyes said I wasn't the first person to trip over her own heart in regard to a foster kid.

She leaned across the table and put her soft, beautifully and carefully manicured hand atop mine. "You could always start the application process," she said gently.

Right, us and our model household: my dad, the ex-federal fugitive; my son, who'd been in police custody so many times before he got sober that they kept a coffee cup for him at the jail; and of course my own not-always-minor misdeeds, from back in the bad old days when I managed ill-gotten gains for a no-kidding evil empire. "But I'd still be placing Ivy with this new family," Deanna added.

"Of course," I said, forcing the words past the lump. We'd never see Ivy again, probably; on the other hand, her departure would mean one fewer human being in a house that was already way too full of them.

As if to prove this, just then little Nadine marched theatrically into the kitchen, stomped twice around the kitchen table, and high-kicked her way out again while blowing loudly and tunelessly on a green plastic penny whistle.

Deanna smiled bravely through it. "Believe me, if it were up to me, I'd—"

"It is up to you," Bella said, turning sharply from the stove. "Write a report, say she can't go anywhere, she's too upset to be moved around like this, that it would even risk her mental health—"

"*. . . but of course there are always exceptions,*" Deanna raised her voice, and when what she was saying sank in, Bella stopped talking.

Then a new voice piped up unexpectedly: "I don't care what you say, I'm not going anywhere, and you can't make me."

It was Ivy, standing there eavesdropping in the hall with her jaw thrust out mulishly and her arms folded disapprovingly across her chest. Fala stood beside her, looking as staunchly protective as only a German shepherd can.

Deanna smiled sweetly, crooking a sequin-tipped finger. "C'mere, honey." The kid, she meant, not the dog.

Ivy hesitated, looked wary, but then Deanna opened her large black leather purse, dug up a small, gold-wrapped piece of candy, and held it out. Ivy stepped forward, took the candy, stepped back.

"I was telling your friends here that it's hard to find places for kids who are probably only staying a short while," Deanna told the little girl kindly.

Ivy's eyes narrowed at the sound of that "probably," but she went on listening. "So I was about to ask Jake to let you stay here with her a little longer," said Deanna.

I blinked, startled by the sudden about-face. Somehow, I had the idea that Nadine's penny whistle had something to do with it. "Doesn't Ivy's father have some say in this?" I asked.

Because Deanna was right about background checks, at least in principle; for all the Maine Family Services people knew, we could be ax murderers. "I mean, surely he gets some input?"

Lizzie shook her head. "Court order says Ivy and her dad can't have contact until their statements have been taken. Maybe not afterward, either. It depends."

Ivy looked mutinous. Suddenly all I could see was a little kid trying to keep some tiny bit of control over something. Anything.

"They'll get here around noon," said Deanna, "the psychologist and the lawyers for the witness interview—which has to be videoed, so they'll do it at the police station. They're very nice and they just want to ask you a few things," she added to Ivy, who'd begun looking alarmed.

"There'll be another custody order after the interviews," the caseworker said, turning to me, and that was that. She was waiting for my answer about whether or not Ivy could stay. They all were, I saw, even Fala, who tipped her big head inquisitively at me.

"How about until after the interview is completed we just leave everything the way it is?" I said. "Ivy stays for now, and afterward, we'll see what the custody order looks like?"

That seemed to sound reasonable to everyone. Lizzie's phone buzzed. With a glance at it, she got up to go, throwing us all a farewell salute on her way out.

"Go on, now," I told Ivy. "Go find Ephraim, have him show you his Power Rangers."

The child ran off as Deanna closed her purse and got up. "I can easily say it's too soon, she's just too upset to be moved," Deanna said. "What child wouldn't be?"

Moving toward the door, she trailed a nearly visible cloud of some pungently fruit-flavored cologne. "But don't make me regret this," she cautioned.

The sun slanting in the west ignited the pair of yellow-leafed maple trees in the dooryard. "I won't," I said with a confidence I didn't quite feel.

Then Deanna crossed the lawn to the driveway, got into her car, and drove away, leaving me there wondering if I might be the one who would end up regretting it.

For the rest of the day Ellie and I baked ladyfingers, pan after pan of the sweet dainty digits, and talked about why in the world Terry Lawson reacted the way he had to losing all that money: by going to his dead—his murdered—ex-wife's house.

"He couldn't very well have thought she took it," I pointed out unnecessarily, sifting yet another four cups of flour into the glass mixing bowl. I'd have done more at a time, but bigger batches didn't come out right.

"Maybe he thought someone else took it?" Ellie poured powdered sugar into a measuring cup, ran a knife-edge over the top to level it, and set it aside to start on the eggs.

I cracked and separated them, handing the bowl of whites to Ellie and pouring the powdered sugar into the yolks. "And this someone would've taken it to Cindy's house because why, again?"

"No idea," said Ellie, then fired up the electric eggbeater and applied it to the egg whites until they formed stiff peaks. After that, it was all ladyfingers, all the time, until we went home, bone-tired but with the baking marathon completed. Now I could concentrate on the other thing that had been worrying me all day: that dratted earring.

Not until later that evening, though, when dinner was eaten, the dishes done, and the children were starting to be herded upstairs for baths, did I go upstairs, too.

From down the hall I heard Nadine and Ivy whispering and

giggling together. Ivy had already merged almost seamlessly into the household routine, I thought while selecting the night's outfit: black pants and sweatshirt, dark socks, black sneakers. I'd have put on a black ski mask and gloves, too, but my sore face and hands wouldn't tolerate it.

Then I went back downstairs where my dad sat in the parlor with his wrinkly old eyelids dropped like curtains over his eyes, listening to the Yankees outplay the Red Sox. My husband was hearing it, too, I imagined, lying in his bunk or hanging out with the other guys down in the mess room of a freighter transiting between Newfoundland and St. John, New Brunswick.

A quick mental snapshot of the ocean out there, cold, dark, and furnished with all kinds of watery dangers—rogue waves and fuel leaks and sharks' jaws, oh my!—flashed in my head. I banished it firmly, hoping urgently instead to find my missing earring before someone else did.

Because I didn't want to look dumb, that's why—now I knew how Sam felt about losing his keys.

I figured it had fallen out while I was wiggling through Cindy Munson's cellar window, so tight it was like being squeezed from a tube of toothpaste. But knowing me—I could lose a pair of shoes while they were on my feet, Bella always said—I should have checked myself for lost or forgotten items before I left, and now I just wanted the thing back before I had to tell anyone else about it. Ellie, especially.

"Where are you going?" Turning with my hand on the screen door, I found Ivy looking up at me, barefoot and in her pajamas.

"None of your business, and what are you doing down here, anyway? You're supposed to be getting ready for bed."

Hands firmly on hips, she looked me up and down. "I'm coming with you."

"No, you are not—"

"I'll make a fuss," she threatened. She would, too, I could see it in her eyes. But one yell out of her, and tonight's secret mission wouldn't be so secret anymore.

"Ivy, why do you want to— " Any minute now Bella would be down here to capture her little escaped bathtime mischief-maker. And if, in the process, Bella learned that I was going out, there'd be a whole big thing about why I was going, where I was going, couldn't I go tomorrow, and when would I be back, plus general fussing and tut-tutting.

Familiar footsteps creaked on the hall stairs. But I couldn't take the kid with me; between the possible psychological damage it could do her and the damage that Lizzie would do to me if she found out, it was out of the question.

Also, I was pretty sure the social worker wouldn't let Ivy stay here any longer if she found out I took Ivy for a visit to her murdered mother's house. "You march out into that parlor and sit down in front of the TV," I told her sternly, "and that's that."

She turned and walked away, surprisingly obedient, and then of course I needed an excuse for Bella as to where I was going and why, so I made one up on the spot.

"Just a little drive to clear my head," I told her, and she accepted it with a skeptical look at me, but she let me go. I shoved Ivy's jacket at her with one hand, opened the door and went out through it, then pulled it firmly shut.

Outside, the fog had come in, and the September sky was thickly hazy with it, the streetlamps balls of white mist shining down on black pavement gleaming with damp. In the driveway, the Fiat sat with its convertible top conveniently up and latched. I mentally thanked Ellie for nagging me into the habit of always leaving it that way.

I opened the Fiat's passenger-side door and from the gloom inside a dog poked its head up between the seat backs. Big, white choppers, thick, black-and-tan coat . . . after I finished nearly having a heart attack, I recognized Fala.

"I put her in," said Ivy, her little head popping up beside the dog's. Then she climbed through into the passenger-side bucket seat and fastened her seat belt all by herself.

Apparently, she'd used the time I'd spent mollifying Bella to sneak out here. Turning from behind the wheel, I regarded her. "So you decided you were coming along with me no matter what, and—"

Ivy nodded. "And you were so sure of yourself that you went ahead and put the dog in the car?" I finished.

Fala stuck her head in between us. From the grin on her wolflike face, she clearly thought this was a great adventure. Yeah, right.

"I cannot believe I'm doing this," I muttered as we pulled out of the driveway into the fog-streaming night. It was reckless, it was crazy—

"Me, neither," Ivy said happily from beside me, her eyes shining as if we were headed for an amusement park instead of to the scene of the crime I was about to commit.

Six

Cindy Munson's neighborhood at night was a tangle of dark twisty streets made narrower by encroaching lilac and forsythia shrubs. Widely spaced streetlamps shed dim light on evergreen boughs bending heavily under the mist.

I'd called Bella to let her know where Ivy was, of course, then explained that I'd explain later.

"But why— " she began.

But by that time, I was backing the Fiat into Cindy Munson's dark, silent driveway. "Gotta go," I told Bella.

Few lights burned in neighboring houses; this lane was a tiny enclave for mostly summer residents, and a lot of them had already gone south. On the Fiat's benchlike backseat, Fala sat up alertly, pointed ears erect, eyes laser-focused.

Like wolf eyes. She was a sweet, gentle animal, but if anyone tried anything with Ivy or me, she would have them for a snack, picking her teeth with a sliver of bone afterward.

I swear, it warmed the cockles of my heart just to see her there. "I'm going around behind the house for a minute," I told Ivy. "You two stay right here."

Too bad she'd already let the dog out of the car, not that Fala might run off. GSDs are hard to lose: you might not always know where they are, but they always know where you are.

Now she and Ivy went ahead of me up the driveway. If I could just keep them reasonably quiet and near me, I told myself, this could all still be okay. Gripping the flashlight I'd miraculously remembered to bring along—smart things like that were usually Ellie's job, for obvious reasons—I followed my unwanted companions in crime into a dead woman's backyard.

Here the fog-reflected gleam of a distant streetlight put the yard in a dim, ghostly glow. In the half dark, the fountain trickled; the benches and lawn chairs were X-ray renditions of themselves. I wondered how Ivy felt about being here, or maybe in the dark she didn't recognize the place.

Or maybe, as with so much else that had happened to her lately, she just wasn't talking about it (which, if you ask me, is a practice more people should adopt).

Besides, I wasn't supposed to talk with her about any of that. It was bad enough that she was here at all; if the social worker learned about it, I'd be in trouble. But there was no help for it now. I picked my way with the flashlight across the deck on the off chance that possibly I'd dropped the earring here, or inside the house.

Through the glass doors, the flashlight's beam caught the edge of an end table, a lampshade's fringe, the corner of an upholstered chair. No blue sea-glass earring was anywhere on the deck—what I'd do if I had to get in there, I still wasn't sure—so I steeled myself next for a search through the grass under the bedroom window.

Before we left, earlier, I'd gotten rid of the dog dirt that had been there, but at night a few garden slugs might lurk there in darkness, huge and squishy, and glistening with slime so sticky they should use it in airplane assembly.

Fala and Ivy were checking the yard's perimeters, a drill Fala insisted on when visiting a new place. I bent to my search, wondering how long I'd be pawing through the wet grass before I either found the earring or gave up.

But then I aimed the flashlight at the white pea-gravel under the window, and there it was: a plain silver hook with a shard of turquoise sea glass on a wire thin as a hair.

When I reached for it, though, my sigh of relief caught in my throat. The earring lay centered on a fallen maple leaf. This wouldn't have worried me if there was even a single maple tree in the yard, or in any of the yards nearby.

But there wasn't. I got up, scanning the gloom for Ivy and Fala. Finally, I spotted them near the yard's rear edge, peering into the unkempt clutter of bushes and saplings that Ellie and I had escaped through earlier that day.

"Hey, you two," I said uneasily into the shadows. Ivy started backing away, hands up as in a warding-off gesture, and Fala dropped to an aggressive crouch.

I wished I'd brought a weapon. I wished we hadn't come here at all. "Ivy! Fala! Run!"

Then a skunk waddled out of the thicket, and it was a *purposeful*-looking waddle. The skunk's fluffy black-and-white tail curled up over its striped back as it trundled toward us.

And turned. "Fala," I said quietly. "Fala, wait."

She did, and I'd have dropped to my knees, relieved, if I wasn't afraid it might trigger the skunk to open fire.

Fala stood motionless. The skunk, too. But after a moment the smaller-brained creature forgot all about us and returned to his thicket, trundling along unhurriedly until he reached it.

Returning to mine was probably a good idea, too, I decided. The newly risen half-moon shone steadily through the thinning mist—we were much less hidden than before.

"Okay," I told Ivy once we got back to the driveway. "In the car, no dawdling. Fala, hop in."

We still hadn't seen or heard anyone. Still, when we were all in the car again, I thought about the snarling sound the Fiat's engine always made, starting up. So instead of turning the ignition key, I pushed in the clutch, let off the hand brake, and let the car roll in first gear—and in silence—down out of the driveway.

When we hit the street, I quickly turned the key, popped the clutch an instant later, and put my foot on the gas. The Fiat's engine caught smoothly and quietly, just as if it had been running all along, then settled into a low grumble.

"Did you find what you were looking for?" Ivy asked as we pulled away.

"Yes." She'd been a pretty decent little shotgun rider on this wild-hair excursion of mine, I had to admit. Now she sat primly, seat belt fastened, as we made our way home through the dark streets.

"Yes," I said as we turned onto Key Street and started uphill, "I certainly did."

The trouble was that someone else had seen it lying there, too, and recognized whose it was.

And used it to send a message. Or maybe the leaf had simply blown there from a long distance and . . .

Puzzling unhappily over this, I turned off the Fiat's ignition and let the car roll silently into the driveway. But I needn't have bothered trying to be vewy, vewy quiet: the porch light was on, its pallid glow turning Ellie's strawberry-blond hair flaming red as she sat on the step waiting for us.

The house was silent, everyone in bed. I'd begged Bella not to wait up and for a wonder, she hadn't. I added a log to the woodstove, set the kettle on top, then began putting Ivy to bed, meeting her predictable resistance with a question: "I took you along earlier, didn't I? At night," I added. "In a no-kidding sports car. With the dog, on a secret mission."

A smile touched her lips as she recalled all this. Nodding slowly, she pried off her sneakers one after the other.

"Which you'll shut up about, right?" She nodded again as Fala smiled up at her from where she lay on the braided rug by the bed. "Why did you want to go along so badly, though?"

She pulled on her pajama top. I waited while she arranged herself under the quilt. "It was my mom's house, wasn't it?"

"Yeah. But how did you know? Had you been there before?"

Her shoulders moved under the blanket. "Yesterday. Me and my dad picked her up from there before the dinner."

Uh-oh, we were getting close to forbidden topics. "Yeah," I said casually, "but don't tell me any more about that, okay?"

Then out of nowhere I realized what I'd been missing at Cindy's: any sort of preparation for a child's presence. There wasn't even a second bedroom in the place.

Yet Cindy was suing for custody, or at least Lawson had said that she was. "Ivy, I'm just trying to help you while you're here. The rest is somebody else's work, right?"

I could've lied to the kid and said I thought her father was a really good guy, and I'd try getting him off the hook. There'd been times when I'd have taken such a lie's comfort gladly, taken it and made it last.

But she'd have known. She was like that, I could already tell. She switched out the light. It had been a long day. I heard Fala jump up onto the bed and settle with a contented groan. Then from the darkness: "You were mad at me today."

On the breakwater's sharply slanting metal gangway, she meant, where she'd nearly sent us both tumbling. Good heavens, but it had been a long day. "Yep," I said.

"Are you sorry?"

"Nope. Are you?" I pictured her in there with Fala settled snugly beside her.

"Nope." Silence, then: "We're okay now, though, right?"

"Yes, Ivy," I said. If she kept talking much longer, I was going to have to pull up a chair. "We're fine, now close those little jellybean eyes of yours and go to sleep."

No answer. I tiptoed away. My face still felt hot, and now it was getting itchy, and up from the ninth rung of hell somebody had dredged a migraine-level headache for me, too.

But when I got back to the kitchen, the last thing in the world that I wanted to see was in it: people. Ellie was making the kind of hot toddies that either kill you or cure you—black tea, plenty of sugar, and enough Irish whiskey to turn you into a leprechaun or just make you feel like one.

Also in the kitchen, however, was Lizzie Snow, sitting at the kitchen table with Dylan Hudson standing behind her, looking severe.

"So you found her," I said to Dylan, and he nodded, rolling his eyes.

"I showed up," she said defensively. "Maybe not right on time, but . . ."

I diagnosed more wedding jitters. Lately, these two were in an ongoing sparring match with Lizzie doing most of the punching, even though she was the one who most needed to be knocked out.

I wondered if a wedding could be held if one of the main participants was heavily sedated. "To what," I asked, looking around, "do we owe the honor so late in the evening?"

I tried to sound wry, but it came out ragged. Also, I'd seen myself in the hall mirror and I looked like a child's drawing of an accident victim.

Dylan ignored all that. "So this break-in you had here the other night."

I'd wondered why he was here. Lizzie, too, for that matter. And why so late? "That you thought was probably just some kid," he went on. "They take anything?"

The more Dylan managed to sound pleasant, I'd learned, the more likely he was to be thinking unpleasant things.

"No. Why?" I took a generous gulp of my hot, boozy drink just on general principles. "What's so interesting about that all of a sudden?"

The whiskey hit me—suddenly, there were two of everyone.

"We're trying to figure out if it is interesting," Lizzie said. "The other thing I needed to talk with you about, though," she went on, "is Cindy Munson's house."

Darn. I took another sizable swallow, hoping to pass out, but no luck.

"I went by the place a little earlier and there was a car in the driveway." She looked hard at me. "Your car."

"Um," I replied. "Yeah, actually I went over and had a look around, that's right."

Dylan smiled: *suspicions confirmed.* Unlike Lizzie, he was always ready to catch Ellie and me poking our noses where we shouldn't, and I'm sorry to say his remarks were often right on point. Also, he'd saved my grandson's life once, and that smile of his didn't hurt, either: half wicked, half wise.

All *gotcha.* But Lizzie looked exasperated. "I asked her and Ellie to pass along anything they happened to learn about Cindy," she said. "Which," she added, looking straight at me, "might've been a mistake."

So that's how I ended up telling them about Ellie and me snooping around in Cindy Munson's house and nearly getting caught there by Lawson, who'd seemed intent on doing the same thing but couldn't get in. I added that the place had been so clean you could do brain surgery in it, and in no way ready for a child to live in.

Making it all sound, meanwhile, as if all these things had been learned just this evening, when Lizzie spotted my car in the driveway, and leaving out all mention of an earlier trip.

It was the only way I wouldn't have to admit (1) losing an earring, (2) going back for it, and (3) taking Ivy with me.

Collectively known as being a *dumkopf*, as my father would have put it, or as "child endangerment," as Deanna might have, and there would go all the rule-bending that Deanna had done for us: *kaput,* as Dad would also say.

"The trouble is, we don't know these people," I said, changing the subject. But it was true: "Cindy, Lawson—we don't know their backstories, what's gone on between them over the years, or even who to ask about them."

I touched the earring in my left earlobe with my fingers, recalling how it had looked in the glow of the flashlight, centered in a perfect yellow maple leaf as if placed there.

Like a message—or a warning.

The next morning came way too soon. "Listen, I never asked you to break into her house," said Lizzie, her voice coming tinnily through my cell phone as the Fiat's headlights probed the chilly mist on Washington Street heading out of town.

"Well, what did you think we'd do, send questionnaires to her neighbors? Who are mostly all in Florida, by the way."

"I don't care, if you'd been caught it would've—"

Yeah, yeah, I knew what it would've. But it hadn't. I rubbed an itchy spot on my cheekbone, then yanked my hand away. My whole body felt like an itchy spot this morning.

"Anyway, sorry to put a crimp in your evening plans." At 7 AM, the dense fog covered the whole island, beading on the Fiat's windshield and making the car's interior feel warm and safe. "But we're trying to help," I added. I touched the dashboard button and NPR's *Morning Edition* theme burbled from the radio.

"Yeah, well, try not to commit more crimes while you're at it," said Lizzie. "I've got a job to hang on to."

"I know, I know." Besides being the town's top cop, she was our friend, which sometimes gave us a bit of extra leeway in the snooping department; still, I took her point.

"Speaking of which, I should've hung on to those kids I pulled over yesterday. I think they're the ones chasing people down on the back roads late at night."

"'Chasing people'? Like, to hit them? For fun?" For a minute the idea seemed almost plausible, given the things I'd been thinking about lately.

"No," she said tiredly. I heard the rustle of the paperwork she was leafing through as she talked. "People in cars, these guys race up behind them, nearly ram them, pull out and crowd them onto the shoulder. Last night some poor lady coming home from a church meeting ended up in the ditch."

Just what we needed, murder *and* mayhem. I made a mental note to send cookies to the church lady's next meeting. "Hey," I said, changing the subject, "poor Dylan was all bent out of shape yesterday. I think he thought those scary teenagers might kill you and stuff you in their car trunk."

But the joke didn't land. "'Poor Dylan' should take a chill pill," she snapped. Then: "Sorry. I know he means well. But—"

The Fiat took the curve around Carrying Place Cove sitting tight on the wet pavement. The car was old, finicky, hard to find parts for, and had a rubber timing belt that liked to snap without warning, preferably in the fast lanes of major highways.

Still—*vroom*. The carburetor growled thrillingly. "—it's like I can't even take a breath sometimes," Lizzie went on. Then: "Don't tell anyone I said that."

Dylan, she meant. "Yeah."

She did love him: truly, madly, deeply. But boy, could he drive her crazy. And she hadn't told me yet where she'd been.

"So, you breaking up with him now, are you? Cancelling the wedding?" I knew she wasn't. We'd been through all this before. Not that there was much to cancel: a justice of the peace and the required two witnesses was absolutely all she wanted, and she would have ditched the witnesses if she could.

A helpless laugh came through the phone. "Shut up," she said, and changed the subject: "Anyway, the other thing I wanted to tell you. The evidence techs are there now, and they've found a hair in the sink in Lawson's motel room. Not Lawson's hair, or Ivy's, either."

If I hadn't been driving, I'd have gotten down on my knees right then and there. In the back of my mind, I'd been worried that the hair might have shifted just from the pressure of me looking at it, and it would've slipped down the drain by the time the evidence technicians finally got there.

But—"Wait a minute, don't they need a warrant to search?"

"Nope. Lawson gave them the okay," Lizzie replied. "Said he had nothing to hide."

Her tone said how not-smart she thought that was, and I agreed. If people would just keep their mouths shut, there'd be fewer of them in jail is my opinion on the matter.

Ahead stretched the causeway, curving whitely across the bay's dark, choppy expanse. "That lawyer of his better get here soon," I said, "or they'll have him writing out a confession."

"Uh-huh. He's on his way is what I heard. Hope he brought a staple gun with him."

For his client's mouth, she meant. People think being frank and forthcoming with the police shows they're innocent, and lots of those people end up hearing their cell doors slamming shut.

Lizzie signed off with another warning about not getting too felonious; I promised I wouldn't—she believed it about as much as she ever did—and we hung up.

No school today, the radio had reported earlier as I blearily confronted a kitchen full of people eating breakfast, drinking coffee, and looking for items they'd need later, like Sam's canvas tool vest and Mika's leather briefcase and Nadine's underpants, the pink ones with little hearts on them.

Boiler explosion, the radio said—not a terrible one, no one hurt, but enough damage to keep the school's radiators cold until the boiler repair guys came over from Bangor to fix it. That had given me an idea.

The first turn off Route 190 ran past the gravel pit, which looked like something had taken a ragged bite out of the cliff. Down on the pit's flat, wide floor, the recently hauled lobster traps stood in tall stacks four deep, waiting for next season.

The old road narrowed and curved onto a dirt track that ended in a shady dooryard surrounded by old spruce trees. I got out of the car into a silence so complete that I could hear my heart hammering.

Sunlight slanted in gold bars between tree trunks crowded up to a low center-chimney Cape with two square front windows and a door between them, like a child's drawing. A massive old copper beech tree, its shaggy, mottled trunk as big around as a Volkswagen, occupied most of the small dooryard.

The brick front walk sported green moss grout. Bolted into the granite-slab front step was an old iron boot scraper cast in the shape of two lumberjacks band-sawing a log. *Macrae*, the heavy brass doorplate read in engraved script.

The brass door knocker's harsh *clack-clack* was loud in the stillness. No sound came from within. But Macrae's car, an old Citroën even more venerable than the Fiat, was here, so I lifted the knocker again.

Just then the big old wooden door opened fast, yanking me in, whereupon I tripped over the threshold, flailed wildly, caught myself by grabbing onto a nearby coat hook, and staggered forward into an entry hall that smelled richly of fresh coffee, funeral flowers, and decades of faithfully applied warm beeswax furniture polish.

"Yes?" the large, athletically built man who'd answered the door inquired politely, not commenting on my doorway acro batics.

Not only that, as it turned out I didn't have to explain much of anything else to him, either. I just told him who I was, and he figured out why I was there all by himself.

"The murder lady. I guess I should've expected you."

There'd been a feature about the Chocolate Moose in the *Bangor Daily News* recently, and of course it had included a few choice references to the proprietors' snooping history.

He looked past me out the door. "Where's the other one?"

"Just me. Ellie couldn't make it." Because she was at the Chocolate Moose, baking the rest of the chocolate ladyfingers as fast as she could. We'd agreed that I'd do the snooping today, and when I'd heard about the boiler explosion, a bang went off in my mind, too, i.e., who met nearly every kid in town, sooner or later?

The high school principal, that's who. His name was Ian Macrae, and I gave him my best "I'm harmless" smile.

He sighed resignedly. "I don't suppose there's a chance this is about your catering work for the class reunion?"

Ian Macrae, who'd been for three decades the principal of Eastport High, was tall, trim, and muscular. I'd have guessed his age at midforties except for his tanned, weathered skin and the silver threads in what remained of his curly, once-coppery hair.

"No," I said. "It's not about the catering. Actually, it's about Cindy Munson and Terry Lawson. I just have a couple of—"

. . . ways to mess up a nice, quiet morning, his face finished for me. But: "Questions. Yes, I'm sure you do. Come along, then. Would you like a cup of coffee?"

I was already caffeinated right up to the eyebrows: getting through my kitchen in the morning unscathed requires a beverage interchangeable with rocket fuel and plenty of it.

"I'm good, thanks." He led me into a bright, airy sitting room and waved me to a green velvet chair.

"Sit down, please." The chair's carved wooden feet were in the shape of lions' paws. Or panthers'; who knew? Everything was vintage or antique, though, I knew that much: the mantel clock, the needlepoint cushions, the hooked rugs, and the very finely made rolltop desk and parquet card table.

"I hear you're caring for Lawson's daughter?" he asked, when we were settled. He'd poured coffee for himself from a warmer on the inlaid mahogany sideboard.

"Yes," I replied, "and the thing is, she's been asking me a lot of questions that I don't know how to answer."

"Uh-huh." It was perfectly obvious that he didn't believe me. "So, these are really her questions, then."

He leaned forward, glancing around at the room full of valuable things. It looked as if he'd been collecting for years; that, or he'd inherited a treasure trove.

"I sympathize with the child, of course. It was a terrible thing. But I'm not sure how I can help."

For his unexpected day off, he wore tan corduroy slacks, a brown plaid shirt over a black T-shirt, black socks, and leather sandals. His physique made him look like a physical fitness enthusiast relaxing after a morning workout, and maybe he was.

A small fire flickered in the sitting room's delft-tiled hearth. "I wonder if you could tell me a little about Cindy and Terry back in the day," I said. "When they were your students. And about anyone else I should talk to about them, maybe?"

I was pushing it with that last bit, but I didn't have a lot of time. In reply, he looked up at me with a directness that signified soul-searing honesty.

Or not. "For the little girl," he repeated, watching me. I wondered how he made the switch every day from cultured aesthete to high school principal, equipped for the everyday rough-and-tumble of school life.

"Yes, to help her," I confirmed, since by now I'd caught on. If anyone ever asked him why he'd told me anything at all about a student who wasn't my own kid—even from thirty years ago—he'd be able to say why he'd done it, to justify it.

That still didn't mean he would talk to me, but he was curious, I could tell by how carefully he listened, and I got the strong sense overall that there was more to him than met the eye.

And hey, if I was going to learn more about Terry Lawson's and Cindy Munson's early years, I had to start somewhere. "Cindy was a high school senior when you became principal here?"

He answered the way I knew he would. "No, a junior," he corrected me. I guessed they must learn that tone of voice in teacher school. But letting people correct you right off the bat helps them feel superior—maybe not a lot, but enough.

Meanwhile, people who feel superior tend to talk more, I've found, and I'll bet he didn't learn that in teacher school.

"I didn't know Cindy well," he went on. "Mostly, I imagine, because she never got sent to my office. I don't even recall her ever getting a detention." He shrugged, spreading his hands regretfully. "High school. It's like anywhere else, you know? Squeaky wheel, and so on."

Then something else occurred to him. "What I do recall is that she was an excellent student. In math and science, she took college courses starting as a high school sophomore."

"Really." My internal eyebrows went up. Nobody had yet described Cindy Munson as a brainiac. "And after she graduated?"

"She went to community college, where she learned how to repair electronic devices," Macrae said definitely.

So he did remember her. See how this works? Just get them talking. "Laptops, tablets, game consoles. But now it's mostly remote controllers for drones, robots, small robotic vehicles."

Just as an aside, I'm fine with robot vehicles as long as they're only allowed around robot pedestrians. Anyway . . .

Macrae looked up at me. "I understand she had a rough patch for a while. But she turned herself around, somehow. Now she's got her own electronics repair business."

"That's great." Also fascinating, since I hadn't seen any kind of electronic equipment anywhere in her house, and no one had mentioned any business address. "What exactly did she do?"

"She fixed and sometimes fabricated the electronic elements of the devices the kids build in their robotics classes. It's really quite amazing, things they've done—with her help, one kid put together a remote-controled submarine that brings back seafloor samples, if you can imagine."

I remembered the buzzing drones zooming around behind

the gymnasium the previous day when we'd delivered the eclairs. "Let me guess, you're the faculty sponsor for the club?"

The parlor window looked out onto an autumn-blown garden and a small clear pond palisaded by cattails. He dragged his gaze back from it.

"Yes, I am. And the kids are doing great. Some of their aerial photographs are truly—"

I felt myself being led down a sidetrack, though whether it was on purpose or not I couldn't tell. "So, you'd be in touch with Cindy fairly often, then," I cut in. "She'd be fixing whatever didn't work in the robotics lab and so on, at the school. Right?"

He stopped, unused to being brought to heel so abruptly; in his world, he directed the conversations.

"Well, yes," he replied slowly, "but only professionally." A frown creased his freckled forehead. "Why, what are you—?" Then a new, even less welcome thought struck him. "Oh, now, you don't think I had anything—"

"To do with her murder?" I smiled brightly at him across the intricate inlay of the coffee table. "Of course not. I told you, it's only Ivy's welfare I'm interested in."

He got to his feet. I got up, too; that stiff velvet upholstery was itchy, and maybe it had been a mistake to try nudging him so hard. But in response he'd shown me something I hadn't expected: how fast I could unnerve him on the topic of Cindy Munson.

I moved toward the hall past a dining room crammed with more objects: another sideboard, a tabletop forest of china, silver, and cut crystal, elaborately framed paintings, a pair of finely engraved dueling pistols . . .

Macrae followed me. "The police didn't give you that idea, did they? That they suspect me? Did they ask you to come here?"

Outside, white birch trees shook yellow leaves beneath the

towering evergreens, under a fast-darkening sky. Thunder rumbled threateningly in the distance as I turned back to Macrae.

"No one from law enforcement has said one single word to me about you, not that they're in the habit of favoring me with their every thought. What do you think, I'm their confidante?"

He grumbled something in answer, and in the yard, we managed civil goodbyes. I thanked him for speaking with me, and he winced, clearly wishing he hadn't. Too late now, of course, to ask him who else I should talk to. Still, as I got into the Fiat, I thought the visit had been successful, information-wise.

For one thing he struck me as way too well-informed for someone who'd said he hardly knew Cindy Munson. And for another, this unassuming rural high school principal had a house filled to bursting with valuable antiques, and how had that happened, I wondered?

In the rearview, Macrae stood with a hand raised in half-hearted farewell, a tall, athletic-looking man with frowzy, silver-threaded red hair, standing unhappily in the doorway of a house full of treasures.

Rain drummed the car's canvas top suddenly as I started the car, and when I got back to Route 190, the skies opened. On the causeway, foamy waves overslopped the pavement, and by the time I reached Eastport and the Chocolate Moose the downspouts on the Water Street buildings were gushing like firehoses.

I sat in the car outside the Moose, waiting for the deluge to end and watching the rain sheets march whitely across the bay's racing waves. It must've been at least a minute or so of rain pounding, wind gusting, and waves heaving, plus thunder and lightning, before I noticed the car across the street, windshield fogged and engine idling, in the fish pier parking lot.

It was the old brown Chevy station wagon we'd last seen outside Cindy Munson's house: Lawson's car. A small gap opened in the clouded windshield; he must've turned the defroster fan on. Next the wipers flapped a few times, clearing the glass.

Behind it was Terry Lawson, looking through a pair of field glasses he had aimed at the Moose.

Which was how I knew who must be there.

"I'm at my wit's end for what to do," confided Bella when I'd gotten inside. "She can't seem to calm down, and nothing I try does any good."

Ivy sat at the table near the rain-streaming window, her head bent over a coloring book, not looking up.

Which explained Lawson spying from outside. I hauled my wet jacket, sodden socks, and horridly squishy-soaked shoes off and dug around for dry stuff in the coat closet, where we'd amassed a whole wardrobe of garments accidentally left here.

"She'll be fine," Bella went on quietly, "and then all of a sudden, she'll pitch a fit. Not even *about* anything, just—"

Outside it was raining again, so hard I couldn't see out through the window. Ivy went on coloring, not lifting her head.

It's about something, all right, I thought. And looking at her now, I got the oh-lord-I'm-not-up-to-this feeling that she was relying on me to find out what that something was.

And fix it. "Ivy," Ellie was saying, "wouldn't you be a lot happier at Jake's house where you can—"

"No," she said, carefully outlining a flower petal with a purple crayon. Then she regarded her work for a moment before scribbling over it in black.

"She can stay," I put in. "I'll keep an eye on her."

I put my arm around Bella's bony shoulders. Wearing her standard daytime uniform of housedress, cardigan, and sturdy black orthopedic shoes, she felt like a bundle of sticks in my careful embrace.

"In fact," I told her, "how about you go and she stays?"

Lately, I'd tried lessening her housekeeping duties while of course not reducing her pay, but the attempt had failed: Bella would no more take money for less work than she would work for no pay. She'd reluctantly agreed not to climb any more stepladders, though, which I'd taken as progress.

But now Ivy had worn her out, and she took my advice without argument, refusing my offer of a ride and only stopping to hug Ivy and accept Ellie's kiss on the cheek before grabbing her raincoat and umbrella and stepping out into the squall, now fortunately diminishing.

"So!" said Ellie, with a bright look around when Bella had gone. "Shall we get this show on the road?"

Finishing today's baking project, she meant. I didn't want to, but we absolutely had to, so we buckled down and began. The ladyfingers were already baked, but the chocolate-cherry trifles we meant to create with them had yet to be assembled and chilled so they'd be ready for delivery tonight.

Ellie got the ladyfingers from the shelf where the last ones were still cooling. We'd already stewed the fresh cherries in a mixture of sugar, cherry liqueur, and a little cornstarch; waiting in the fridge now was the cream that we would whip with instant Quick Jel so it would stay stiff for hours.

While I lined up the rest of the ingredients—vanilla extract, sugar, enough spare ladyfingers for me to nibble—Ellie wiped the butcher-block worktable and turned on some music.

Elvis belting out Chuck Berry's "Promised Land" sounded just right; I cranked the volume way up as Elvis rocked into the tune's Greyhound section and Ivy glanced up with a tiny smile.

Yeah, my kind of kid. Even the sudden tempers lined right up with things I understood. Rage, sorrow—they melted together sometimes. In me, they'd stayed that way, but maybe she still had a chance to keep them clear of one another. Or almost clear. So that she could tell the difference, anyway. "You'll blow that child's ears out," said Ellie, when I got back to the kitchen. She was covering the bottoms of a long row of cut-glass trifle dishes, rubbing chocolate ladyfinger crumbs out between her palms to distribute them evenly.

The uncrushed ones were even more delicious-looking, tender and delicate, and so full of chocolate, you should've needed a doctor's prescription for them. I hoped the class reunion people appreciated them, but then it occurred to me suddenly that they weren't who really needed them.

"Hey, Ivy! Hey, come on out here a minute!" As with most of what I'd been up to recently, I had essentially no idea what I was doing. Maybe Ivy should be left to grieve in her own way.

But I didn't think she wanted to be let alone. I hadn't. "Hey," I called again, "Ivy?" Then, I looked down at the spot right beside me and she was in it.

"What?" she queried. There were dark circles smudged under her eyes, and the fingernails that I could see were bitten past the quick.

"Try this." I held out a chocolate ladyfinger. Eyeing me, she took it, her childish front teeth piercing the just-crisp-enough wafer. Then she chewed, and I could see a little light going on in her brain, chocolate's über-reliable dopamine boost kicking in almost at once.

Better living through chemistry, folks. Behind me, Ellie went on placing ladyfingers crumbs into the dishes, but I could feel her listening.

Smiling, too. "Okay, now," I told Ivy, "how about this one?" I dragged the end of a ladyfinger through a small bowl of cherries in syrup, held it out like before, and this time she didn't hesitate.

"Good?" I said, when she'd scarfed it down, and she nodded emphatically. "And for our last trick," I intoned, pulling another ladyfinger through the cherry concoction and dolloping it with whipped cream.

Managing that one took both Ivy's hands, one holding the

luscious-looking combo by the edges and the other positioned under it to catch falling cream and cherries.

"Mm," she said through a mouthful, and that was all I'd wanted, really: a little relief for the poor kid.

Ellie poured cherries over the first layer of ladyfingers, one dish after the other. Ivy swallowed and looked up at me, biting her lower lip as if trying to decide something.

Or solve something. "C'mere," she said, crooking her finger at me as she led me through the beaded curtain to the front of the shop. Outside the front bay window, the rain had backed off; cars moved smearily in the street.

"I need to ask a question," Ivy said when we got to the front table. I couldn't see if Lawson's car was still out there.

I sat across from her. "Okay. What do you want to know?"

She clasped her small hands together on the table and took a deep breath. "Well," she began, "the thing is, I hardly knew her." Her mother, she meant, the late Cindy Munson. "I hardly ever even saw her. Not since I was little."

"Okay. Because you lived with your dad, right?"

She nodded. Here came the hard part. "So if I hardly knew her or ever even saw her— "

She slid off her chair and took a step just as I crouched, reaching out. "How come I'm so sad, then?" she sobbed. "Why?"

And for that one, I really didn't have an answer.

Seven

Three hours later, I was forty feet off the ground, high in the oversized mountain ash tree in Cindy Munson's backyard.

"Ellie," I gasped, "I'm losing my grip." My equilibrium, too. Below, Cindy's grass spun dizzyingly.

"Right," said Ellie from where she perched several branches above me. "I haven't wanted to mention it, but . . ."

"Ha," I replied, unamused, and may I just say right here that I had gotten up into the tree successfully, and I would like that feat to be recognized, too, not just my clumsier moments.

Never mind that at the moment I feared the recognition would come posthumously. Back at the shop, the chocolate-cherry trifles had been assembled, adorned with alternating stripes of chocolate glaze and freshly whipped cream, and placed in the cooler.

The longer they sat, the more cherry syrup would soak into the ladyfingers. Soaked but not soggy was what you wanted; we'd find out later whether we'd timed it right. For now, we had some time to play with, if you could call this "playing."

"Oof," said Ellie, hauling herself higher and sending yet another shower of the tree's small orange berries pelting down onto me. Also, the ash tree's branches were wet, slippery, and not especially sturdy-feeling.

"You think Ivy's okay with Bella again for a while?" Ellie asked, meanwhile swinging from one branch to another in a way I thought only happened in circuses.

"I do." After we'd finished the trifles, I'd brought Ivy back to my house and delivered her into the hands of the ever-forgiving Bella, who'd received the child tenderly. They'd be fine for the afternoon. The big question was, would I?

I'd sworn not to climb up into any more trees after tumbling so ignominiously from the last one (don't ask). Now I grabbed for the next handhold, missed it, and wound up dangling precariously by four fingers like a monkey in the jungle.

"Why couldn't we watch from some nearby roof?" I groused. It was ineffective, but it kept me from panicking. I grabbed for the handhold again and caught it.

"And get up there how?" she asked reasonably. "Levitate?"

Yeah, not a good plan. "I could break my fool neck here," I grumbled, regaining my grasp on a branch way too skinny to hold my weight.

"You could," Ellie agreed, moving away from me up the tree. "Although knowing you, I imagine you could probably break it on solid ground, too."

It's true, in the dangerous-physical-activities arena, I can just about lick peanut butter off a sharp knife, and that's as far as it goes.

And yet, here we were. "You really think somebody might be coming here tonight?" Ellie asked a minute later.

"Yup." It was 4:30 PM and nearly dark; cold, too, under an overcast sky still flickering with distant lightning. At last, I reached a branch high enough to watch from but low enough not to give me heart failure every time I looked down. Only after perching myself there did I discover the truly huge wasps' nest, like a big tan paper lantern, hanging right next to me.

"Um, Ellie?" I whispered. A single wasp clung to the nest's dark opening like a wary doorman.

Or an armed guard. The wasp slowly came alert, stretching its wings and waving its antennae curiously.

This seemed like a bad sign, and now suddenly there were two of them, communicating excitedly with those waving feelers.

It wasn't the feelers that worried me. "Oh, for heaven's sake," Ellie said from above me, "just ignore them, they're not interested in you unless you annoy them."

These looked interested, also annoyed, and more were appearing all the time, launching their yellow-and-black striped bodies like small fighter planes off the nest's entryway.

A single sting stabbed me, red-hot like a match to my forehead. An instant later another one got me just over my right eye, and a third nailed my chin.

Then, while swatting them away, I lost track of hanging on to the branch, and I was dropping, branches whipping and bopping me and smacking me in the face as I fell. Landing hard with a mouthful of those orange berries, I found they were as bitter as aspirin.

But that wasn't the worst of it. Cold, wet, bruised, and wasp-bitten, I rolled over in the grass to spit out the berries and came face-to-face with a big brown boot.

Sock in the boot, foot in the sock, et cetera . . . My gaze went on up the denim-clad leg to a beaten-up leather belt pulled tight under a prominent beer belly, past that to a plaid flannel shirt, and last of all to the bearded face.

Rain streamed down the face, which looked as surprised as I felt, and also as if it could use some soap along with that water. The heavy brow looming over me furrowed puzzledly as its owner tried making sense of my presence here and couldn't.

"Miz Tiptree?" the large, unexpected man said uncertainly, swaying a little. "What're you doing here?"

Bloodshot brown eyes squinted down at me. "Max?" I squinted back, confused. "What're you doing here?"

It was the locally well-known Max Fritz, Eastport's most prolific generator of drunk-and-disorderly complaints. He'd been one of the guys in the barroom at Brady's Brunch the other day, drinking breakfast with his soused pals.

Max was not a bad guy, just an unfortunate one. The wasps had retreated, still a few zipping around but most drifting harmlessly. Max reached out a big hand and grabbed one out of the air, and crushed it.

"Bastids," he uttered. But he looked guilty as hell about something, glancing around shiftily and clearly wishing Ellie and I would go away. Then: "Cindy let me stay here in bad weather." He stared down at his brown boots. "In good weather, I camp," he added earnestly, looking up. "Or I stay in the tunnels."

Ellie spoke up. "What, like the ones Hester Bailey wants opened? You mean they're real?"

The only tunnel I wanted was the one that led into some other reality, one where I wasn't in the house of a dead woman who was that way because somebody wanted her that way.

"So, you're sleeping rough?" I asked gently, and Max nodded, meaning he slept outdoors, in a field or wherever, mostly due to his habit of losing his temper once he got fully loaded. Max was everyone's acquaintance, but nobody's friend.

Cindy must've been an exception. He saw me thinking this. "We, uh, went to the same meetings," he explained reluctantly.

The light dawned: AA meetings, of course. "See, she even gave me a key," Fritz said, holding one up for me to inspect.

Ellie had climbed down out of the tree. Now she looked questioningly at me, at the key, and then at me again.

"I guess another short visit couldn't hurt," I said, shrugging.

Hey, it's not every day a house key just falls into your hands. The idea tickled a memory, something vague about other keys . . . But I couldn't pry it loose and I didn't have time to think about it right now.

"What if someone else shows up while we're here?" Ellie asked. Meaning, I supposed, Dylan Hudson, who was always so sure that without him we'd cluck things up royally or get clucked up, ourselves.

"Dunno," I said, as Fritz lumbered up onto the deck and opened the sliding glass door with his key. "We'll have to improvise," I said, then followed him into the familiar darkness of the late Cindy Munson's superclean living room.

Not until he switched on a lamp and the room jumped into view, however, did I know for sure that Ellie's worry about us getting caught here yet again was groundless—at least, nobody nefarious was going to arrive.

They'd already been here. Papers, manila envelopes, file folders, yanked-out drawers, ripped-open sofa cushions, books with their spines broken . . . Even the sofa had been upended and its underpinnings unpinned, springs and canvas ripped out.

"Oh, man," said Fritzy sorrowfully, rubbing his head.

"Good heavens," Ellie exhaled, staring.

"Heaven had nothing to do with this," I snapped. The carpet had been pulled up at the edges where it met the wall. An old print issue of *Popular Mechanics*—a drone hovered on its cover, I noticed—lay under a tipped-over coffee table.

The place had been ransacked, in other words, and I was guessing I knew who'd done it. "Lawson," I said. After all, he'd been lurking around here, and besides, who else?

Fritz headed downstairs, clearly wanting no part of this; I remembered the disreputable-looking blankets and pillows down there. "Somebody got in here after we did," I told Ellie when he'd gone. "Looking for something."

Which, yes, was stating the obvious—so sue me. I picked up

a tossed-aside phone bill, a crumpled flyer from the Chamber of Commerce, and a note to buy milk written in a clear, strong hand.

Cindy's handwriting, I supposed. "But whatever it was they wanted, they didn't find it. If they had, this place wouldn't be so torn apart."

Ellie nodded. "Should we talk to Fritz a little more? He was at the dinner dance the other night, you know, working as a custodian. He might've seen or heard something."

I hadn't known, but of course he had been, because that was exactly the kind of annoying business this was all turning into.

"He might've even heard something here," I said. The last thing I wanted was to visit Max Fritz at his rumpled bedside, conveniently located in a murder victim's basement.

And as it turned out, we didn't have to, because when we got downstairs to the cellar and made our way to his rickety cot, he wasn't in it, or anywhere else in the basement, either.

The Fiat's glowing dashboard made the car feel like a firelit refuge as we drove home, the heat kicking in almost at once to warm my wet feet. Outside, small wood-framed houses sent window gleams into the streaming night.

"He didn't like thinking we might ask him questions," I said, through the sound of the wipers flapping back and forth on the windshield. Pounding on the pavement, rushing in the gutters, gushing into storm drains, the rain just kept falling.

"Which way do you suppose he went?" Ellie wondered, peering out into it.

"I think we both know." Ahead, on the breakwater, the dock lamps sent rain-spangled beams into the night; across the black water on Cherry Island, the beacon flared bloodred.

Brady's Brunch on Water Street was a daytime affair; at night the Brunch sign got covered and the BERNIE'S TAP sign lit up in neon script. The old-fashioned barroom had red-leather stools, a long mahogany bar, and a vintage electric advertising sign that featured a flow of sky-blue water into a pool.

We parked at the fish pier, ran through pelting raindrops, and slid onto a pair of stools at the bar. At one end of the pine-paneled room, four big guys in gray T-shirts and blue jeans played pool and drank Allagash; at the other, a quartet of serious-looking ladies in good dresses and full makeup sipped mixed drinks through little straws.

It was that kind of place. From behind the bar, Bridget Brady smiled tiredly at us, then brought a cream soda for Ellie and a martini for me.

Which, in hindsight, might've been a mistake. One sip, and I thought I might dissolve and just ooze right off the barstool. I put the drink aside as Bridget finished wiping glasses and joined us.

"Hey, you clean up nice," I told her. Despite the long day she'd already had, she still looked lovely in a white peasant blouse and long paisley-patterned velvet skirt. Hammered brass hoops in her ears, smoky eyes, and dark lipstick the color of berries gave her a vaguely witchy appearance.

"Hah," she brushed off the compliment. "My feet feel like I'm on hot coals."

Sure, they did, because despite her youthful looks Bridget Brady's spring-chicken days were in the past. She'd inherited this place from her dad, the aforementioned Bernie—plus not much else—and she'd been trying to sell the place for years.

But no luck. I looked around: no Jax, either. The puppy was usually bouncing around in here in the evenings. No little blue dog bed or cozy crate for the animal, no water bowl . . .

Bridget saw me wondering about it. "I had to take Jax back to the lady I got him from," she said regretfully. "I couldn't give him the attention he needed."

She didn't look at me as she said it. "He's okay, though—

he's with his mom and the other pups. Happy as a clam when I last saw him," she added.

"Oh, that's too bad," I sympathized, thinking I understood. Puppies need house-training, walking, playing—all kinds of things Bridget just didn't have time for. It was easy to underestimate how much time and devotion pups took until you had one.

"Funny thing," Bridget went on, wiping down the bar's long mahogany surface with a towel. "It was Cindy who'd been taking care of him sometimes, when my hands just got too full."

"Really?" Her back was turned to me, but her face in the mirror behind the bar was expressionless. "I didn't know she—"

Cindy's yard hadn't looked like a dog run. "Yeah, I'd drop him off sometimes. Put him inside if she wasn't there right that minute, she had a baby gate to keep him in the kitchen. I paid her, of course."

That made sense. Cindy wouldn't have been living on tech repairs and school consulting alone. Like many people in this lovely but economically depressed area, she'd worn a lot of different hats to make ends meet. Even some of the fishermen had other jobs, too. And if she'd give Fritz a housekey, she'd surely trust Bridget with one. Outside it was coming down cats and dogs again. "Where does Fritz drink when he's not in here?" I changed the subject.

I hoped Fritzy wasn't still out there in the rain somewhere, after we'd scared him out of his dry bed. Bridget made a face.

"There's the Black Horse," she said, her tone expressing distaste.

The Horse had plywood floors and a bar built of scrap wood and contact paper. How it kept its liquor license was unknown. Ellie had been silently nursing her cream soda. "We could go look," she suggested reluctantly now.

The Horse was the only establishment in town where you left your wallet at home and took a shower afterward. I contemplated the rest of my martini, took a deep breath, and knocked it back. "Okay," I said.

Outside, we crossed the fish pier parking lot to the paved path that ran along the harbor. "Bridget looked tired," I said.

More than tired, actually. Wrung out. "Quarterly taxes are due," Ellie said. "Again."

True. And Bridget's were so far in arrears already, she'd never dig herself out. I knew because she'd unburdened herself to me one whole rainy afternoon when I'd sat in here and listened to her desperation, listening being all I could do. The days when I could have lent her the money were long gone.

Maybe, I thought, it really would be a good idea for Bridget to get together with Lawson again, join in on whatever schemes he cooked up to get and stay out of bankruptcy.

But that thought was for later. Here in the gloom, the backs of the Water Street buildings looked out over the boats all picked out in sharp-edged black and white by the breakwater lights.

"So what do you think?" Ellie said. Hands in pockets, we strode side by side through the damp shadows.

"I think I want to find out what Max Fritz saw or heard at Cindy's before he forgets any of it even happened," I said.

Ahead, the shadowy path opened up to a small grassy park with amphitheater-style granite-block seats for concerts and outdoor movies.

I've never been to a concert or movie that made granite-block seats worth sitting on, but never mind. Past the park, the path narrowed between another set of redbrick buildings on the left and an ancient falling-down wooden pier with a rusted-out Quonset hut perched on it, on the right.

In fading letters, the sign on the hut read C-FOOD. "Dark back here," I observed.

Pitch dark, actually, for about a dozen yards; then the path angled back up to Water Street again. "D'you suppose Fritz came this way?"

I thought I could smell the beer that had been on his breath earlier. "He could've," said Ellie. "Why?"

As if in answer, the toe of my shoe met something softly yielding, then stopped suddenly. The rest of me continued on, first sailing over what I'd stumbled upon, then flying through the air very suddenly and surprisingly, finally coming down fast toward the path's black-topped surface.

When I got up to see what I'd tripped over, I found Max Fritz lying across the path.

He was passed out cold, rain puddling in his upturned ear. "He'll catch his death," Ellie fussed, because Fritzy could be a real pain in the tail when he was sozzled but nobody wanted him getting pneumonia.

"Maybe we should call Lizzie," I said. She'd put Fritzy in what she used for a drunk tank—the coffee room at the police station was warm and dry and had a daybed in it—until he was awake again.

"I suppose the three of us could haul him up there," Ellie allowed.

Aside from everything else, Fritzy was a big man, and right now he was deadweight. "Or we could call an ambulance for him ourselves. They could bring a stretcher," she said.

"Mm." But if I took his shoulders and Ellie took his feet . . . "Let's bring him to the Moose."

Ellie looked skyward, possibly in hopes of heavenly help in warding off my crazy notions.

"Come on. We'll dry him off, caffeinate his wits out, feed him some hot food, then top it all off with a brownie and some chocolate liqueur." I put my hand over my heart. "I hereby predict he will become an absolute fountain of information." And when she still looked doubtful: "Look, if it doesn't work, at least we'll have gotten him out of the cold rain."

And without alerting Lizzie to our evening's activities, especially about me climbing all the way up into the tree; it was Lizzie who'd made me promise never to do that again.

Chilly droplets began pelting us again as we stood there. It struck me once more how dark it was back here at night. And so quiet, we might as well have been on the moon.

"Hey, Jake?" Ellie crouched by Fritzy's head. "You know that thing you said about a fountain of information?"

She looked up at me. "I don't think so."

I positioned myself at his feet. "Oh, sure he will. Just wait till that chocolate liqueur hits him. Now, you just take his shoulders, and I'll take— "

I looked at those brown boots. They'd left the beaten-up stage a long time ago and were now well into the coming-apart stage, thin gray socks showing in the worn-through places.

I did not want to touch them; the legs, either. But I had to, so I— "Jake." Ellie crooked a finger at me. "C'mere."

I let go of Fritzy's ankles. "What? Is he waking up?"

"Not exactly," Ellie said. Then I noticed the raindrops striking Fritzy's wide-open eyes. His mouth sagged open, but no breath moved in or out of it.

"Look closer," Ellie said, so I did, and finally spied the neat, dark hole just above the bridge of his nose.

"Whoa," I said, and then we just stood there in the rain with him for a minute. I hoped this wasn't the only funeral he would get. Out on the water a foghorn hooted mournfully.

"Okay," I said finally, "let's go get— "

Lizzie, I was about to say. She'd get the official "person found deceased" stuff going.

But Ellie cut me off, her eyes suddenly alarmed. "Jake, we forgot to— "

Then it hit me, too, the task we'd lost track of amid all the falling out of trees and finding dead bodies and so on.

"Trifles," I said. "We were going to deliver the chocolate-cherry trifles to the high school."

With the stewed fresh cherries, and the whipped cream in lofty peaks, and the many, many chocolate ladyfingers we'd taken so much trouble to prepare . . .

Suddenly they seemed trifling. Poor Max Fritz. His death would end up being barely noticed by most people, just as his life had been. I didn't know how he'd wound up this way or who would miss him, if anyone. And that, I thought, was the worst thing of all; it was as if he'd been dropped into the middle of the ocean and, sinking, left barely a ripple.

Half an hour later Ellie braked to a screeching halt in the brightly lit parking lot behind the high school. Rain thrummed in silvery sheets across the gleaming blacktop.

We'd gotten the call an hour earlier; the boiler was fixed and the alumni dinner was on. "You get the door, and I'll carry a tray in. Then I'll hold the door and—"

"Yup." We'd done this in a howling blizzard; now should be no sweat. Still, we were late. I grabbed a tray from the rear seat, straightened the plastic wrap on it, and eased back out of the car rear-end-first.

Half a dozen steps to the gymnasium's back door; too bad that on the first one I plunged ankle deep into a pothole full of ice-cold rainwater, and on the next into a mess that I did not want to identify—but based on certain evidence, I had dog-related suspicions.

So what could I do but step back into the ice-water and swish the shoe vigorously in it? In the process my foot froze all the way to my hip socket, but the shoe got clean; that it was soaked through made little difference by now since the other one was, too.

Right now, the whole world felt like an icy puddle. But the tray full of chocolate-cherry trifles was intact and that was the important thing. Ahead of me Ellie held the door; I slog-squished through it, then skirted around the edge of the softly lit gym, now full of candlelit tables, glinting silverware, and gleaming china.

And people, maybe forty of them, I noted. There'd be a few extra trifles, then—good. I spotted Ian Macrae, dressed to the professorial nines in black turtleneck and a brown tweed jacket with leather patches on the elbows.

"Oh, good," he said, hurrying up to me. "I was hoping you wouldn't get here too early. Things are running a little slow."

"I'm glad it worked out," I said, giving him my best "I'm a professional" smile. Once again, the Chocolate Moose lived up to its unofficial motto: *Come hell or high water!* "Looks like the night is a success."

He smiled back, then grew serious. "I'm sorry I got so excited before. I guess I've been more upset than I realized."

About this student from thirty years ago who you hardly knew, I thought. Sure, Ian. "Apology accepted," I said lightly.

We'd called Lizzie about Fritzy's condition and location, then hung up and left before she could object. Now the fragrance of old gym socks threaded faintly among the aromas of beef, chicken, or vegetarian entrées. Also, from the sound of some of the conversations floating from the tables as I'd gone by, a good deal of wine was being drunk.

Macrae took the tray I carried from me and walked with me toward the school's kitchen, but before we went in, I stopped. Near the swinging doors stood some long tables; on them, 8 x 10 glossy black-and-white reproductions of yearbook photographs lined up in alphabetical order, surrounded by other memorabilia: a football helmet, choral music sheets, a pair of cleated shoes.

Set slightly apart with white carnations and purple crepe paper tastefully surrounding it stood another yearbook photo, this one of a lively-looking teenaged girl with the kind of curly red hair that grows in ringlets.

High forehead, upturned nose, stubborn chin . . . it was Cindy Munson when her eyes were still clear and optimistic, before real life started knocking it out of her. A small bowl of yellow chrysanthemums, a burning tea candle, and a card that read NEVER FORGOTTEN stood on the table with a guest book and pen. It seemed she had been, though. No signatures were in the book.

Macrae ignored the small shrine as we pushed through into the school's Nutrition Center, which is what they call a six-burner hooded gas stove, a combination cooler/freezer, a grill the size of Montana for burgers, which is all the kids want, and a steam table for delicious foods like tuna casserole and (in season) venison-meat Sloppy Joes.

Oh, and some trash cans and stainless steel sinks, too. "Looks like Cindy might've been a private sort of person," I probed tactfully.

Macrae put the tray down. "I suppose." His eyes were baggy and tired-looking under the kitchen's fluorescent lights. "I don't really recall if she had friends. But I've overheard some pretty awful comments about her tonight," he added. "Speculating how she might've died. Haven't any of them ever learned not to speak ill of the dead?"

I began carefully unwrapping the trifles as Ellie came in and stashed the whipping cream, the large glass bowl, and the beaters for the electric mixer in the freezer.

"You think grownups don't gossip just as much as when they were high school students?" I asked Macrae. "What are you, five years old?"

I might not've been so blunt if I hadn't had a day for myself already. My feet in their squishy wet shoes were still numb with cold, and everything else just hurt for the hell of it, I guess.

Then Ellie came back in again and he brightened, taking some of the trifle dishes she carried. But it wasn't the dishes that caught my eye, it was the shoebox she was balancing them on.

I happened to know that the shoebox had sneakers in it—my sneakers. I must've left them in her car. A clean pair of socks hung half in and half out of her jacket pocket.

And that, in a nutshell, was Ellie. I made my most earnest praying gesture at her, then grabbed the dry footwear and sat down on a nearby metal folding chair to put it on.

"Have you heard anything more about the investigation?" Macrae asked us casually. "Or is it pretty much open and shut?"

Against Lawson, he meant. "Because if the police want to talk any more with any of the alumni . . ."

He waved toward the gym, where the aforementioned alumni sat enjoying a once-forbidden beer or cocktail while relishing their freedom to get up and walk out of here any damn time they pleased, wear their skirts any length they liked, and even smoke in the boy's room if they so chose.

"Right," said Ellie, laying out the paper plates, the silver cake slicer, and a stack of the really luxe white paper napkins we hoped subbed adequately for linen.

Because we were a bakery, not a laundry, that's why. "By tomorrow night the alumni'll be spread out all over the country again," she finished.

Just then behind her the double doors flew open and a teenaged girl in jeans and an Eastport High shirt rushed in and began setting paired cups and saucers on the brown plastic lunchroom trays stacked by the sink.

In the doorway behind her leaned a tall, lanky teenaged boy wearing blue jeans, a black T-shirt, and a blue denim jacket, a look of wistful adoration on his face. She didn't seem to notice him.

"Hey, Polly, thanks for your help," Macrae told her, ignoring the boy. "You and all the volunteers tonight."

Polly Harper, her stick-on name tag read. "No problem, Mr. Macrae. Anytime," she added, and if she didn't bat her long, darkly mascaraed eyelashes at him, she might as well have.

The kid in the doorway winced. “Uh, yeah,” said Macrae, looking awkward, suddenly. “Guess I’ll just get back out there to our guests, then—Oh, hi, Tommy,” he said as he passed the kid on his way out.

When he’d gone Holly Helper went on loading cups onto trays. Tommy seemed to gather his confidence, then came the rest of the way into the kitchen.

“Hi, Polly,” he said shyly, glancing at me.

I looked away; no sense making him more nervous than he already was. “Listen, I thought maybe when you’re done, I could drive you home, maybe.”

She turned and spoke kindly to him. “Thanks, Tommy, that’s really nice of you. But my mom’s coming to pick me up.”

His shoulders slumped. “Oh. Yeah, well. I guess . . .”

“Tommy,” Polly said gently. “I get it, okay? You’ve been following me around, showing up where I am, making it pretty clear how you feel about me.”

Right now, he was feeling lower than a worm, from the looks of him. But he still managed a smile. “Yeah. Guess I’m not too subtle, am I?”

She laughed. “No, you’re not. You’re a really nice guy, though, and I’m sorry I don’t— ”

He put a hand up, the smile twisting a little. “Don’t. It’s okay. I’ll stop being a pest.” He took a step back as if to demonstrate. “You ever need anything, though. Or, you know, you just want to talk . . .” He stood at attention, pantomimed a small bow. “At your service.”

Then he turned and walked out, Polly watching him go with a gentle, regretful look on her face.

Behind her, Ellie and I glanced at one another. *Not bad,* Ellie mouthed, and I agreed. Tommy might not be Polly’s cup of tea, but soon enough he’d be someone’s. Polly carried her loaded tray out. Meanwhile, I wrapped more of the deluxe napkins around more plastic cutlery, not the disposable stuff but the good kind that you wash and use again.

Ellie had already whipped the chilled cream, sugar, and vanilla together in a chilled metal bowl, and was now pulling Saran Wrap over it. "We told Lizzie we'd be right back," she reminded me.

"Yes, well, she might have to wait." Because among all these people, surely someone would have something interesting to say—Macrae had just about guaranteed it. And for once I'd come prepared: the gym's din might've prevented eavesdropping, but I'd brought along gear designed for just this situation.

Now I pulled out four plastic thingamabobs, the result of my having asked Bella for a Very Big Favor and her granting it. These gadgets were her hearing aids, the pair and the spares.

"A set for you, a set for me. Press the button on the right one for volume up, left button for down."

She eyed them doubtfully, then took a pair and fitted one in. Her eyes brightened; she put in the other. "Oh. Yes, I can see how these might be"—she adjusted them—"convenient."

They even had background-noise-reducing gadgetry in them. I put mine in, cringed, and hurriedly lowered the volume—if they're set too high you can hear yourself blink, for heaven's sake—and readied myself to serve chocolate-cherry trifles and listen for clues about murder at the very same time.

I lifted a tray. Ellie, too. "Here goes," she said.

We loaded the desserts on carts; then Ellie pushed the double doors and waited while I glanced around: coffee brewed, check. Napkins, plates . . . whoops, the extra whipped cream was back in the cooler instead of on the cart—

I spun around in a hurry, lost my balance, and landed on the hard concrete floor, pulling the folding chair over on top of me. The sound through those hearing aids was like a four-car collision. As I went down an older, heavily jewelried woman in a blond updo and bright-red wool dress stopped, then rushed in.

"Oh, lord, are you all right?" Her voice sounded like forty years of coffee and cigarettes dissolved in a glass of bourbon. She reached down a strong hand and helped me up.

"Fine, thanks." I brushed myself off. Nothing broken, which meant I'd gotten off easy . . .

Or maybe not. My red-clad rescuer's penciled brow crimped quizzically; then she smiled as if her brilliantly red mouth was a trap and a bunny rabbit had hopped in.

"Say," she said, her eyes narrowing, "aren't you one of those—?"

"Murder ladies, yes." I gave her my practiced "you got me" look; people seem to like that.

"But tonight, I'm just a caterer," I added. "Thanks again for your help, really." I moved but she stepped in front of me.

"Oh, no, you don't." Her voice was chummy, but her gray eyes glittered like rhinestones set in eyeshadow the color of plums. "I'll bet you're here to find things out, aren't you?"

The ice-cold whipped cream bowl was beginning to sweat. The woman in red was sturdily built, brassily blond, and heavily made-up: purple eyelids, pink cheeks, the danger-flag-red lips.

I put the whipped cream bowl hastily into another, larger bowl filled with ice and a little water. "That's right," I said. Why not? It was obvious that she'd already figured it out. "We're snooping into the death of Cindy Munson."

The woman's face changed, not in a nice way. "That bitch," she uttered, and I most certainly would've asked why, but just then my dratted phone rang and it was Deanna Wright, Ivy's Family Services caseworker.

"Sorry, but it's bad news," her voice came tinnily into my ear. "My supervisor can't approve temporary placement with you when there's another spot available."

"But why? And what does that mean?" Another thought hit me. "You're not coming for her tonight, are you?"

"No," said Deanna. "Tomorrow, though. I'm really sorry, Jake. The foster family is very nice, you'd like them, and I'm sure Mr. Lawson would approve. So, is noon okay with you?"

And after the foster family, then what? And what if they weren't really so nice?

"Jake? Are you still there?"

No, I wanted to say, don't call me again. "Yes," I managed. "I'm here. We'll be ready tomorrow."

I'd have thanked her for trying, but she'd hung up. I remembered the tall stack of files I'd seen piled on her car's front seat. Soon Ivy's would be one of them.

Thinking this, I wanted to hurl that damned bowlful of whipped cream against a wall. But instead, Ian Macrae came down the locker-lined hallway between the kitchen and the gymnasium, saw my face, and hurried up to me.

"Is everything okay?" Behind him, the pretty teenager who'd been in the kitchen with us peeked out from the gymnasium and spotted him, then closed the door swiftly again.

Yeah, she was bird-dogging him, as Sam would've put it. "No," I said. Seventeen hours until tomorrow noon. "Everything is not okay."

I picked up the icy metal bowls, brushed past him, and headed for the gymnasium doors. Then I gritted my teeth, slapped a smile on over them, and served that whipped cream to folks busy reliving their long-ago high school days, some happily and others less so.

They all seemed to enjoy their desserts, though, and Ellie and I enjoyed seeing the paycheck that Ian Macrae forked over at the end of the evening.

"All's well that ends well," Ellie breathed tiredly as we got into the car minutes later. Behind us, couples and groups were getting into their cars, laughing and calling out to one another.

"It didn't all end well." The rain had stopped but the streets still gleamed wetly. "And I don't only mean Fritz."

I relayed what Deanna had told me. "And now I don't know what to do," I said. "At the start, I just wanted to do Lizzie a favor."

"But 'no good deed goes unpunished?'" Ellie suggested with a quick glance at me.

I recalled Ivy's pinched little face when I first saw it. "Something like that. And now . . ." The moon peeked from between the departing clouds, shedding silvery light. "Now. I don't know," I finished.

She pulled to the curb in front of my house and I got out. Ellie leaned across the front seat toward me.

"Jake, have you thought about what you do want out of this? I mean, when all's said and done?"

I shook my head. Another headache rumbled warningly, like something heavy turning over up there. "Haven't had time."

I'd been running mostly on coffee and adrenaline, and now that our job was done, a legion of sprains, strains, scratches, bruises, and a great big lump on the front of my noggin were all suddenly competing for my attention, each in its own lousy way.

Ellie took all this in swiftly and sympathetically. "Go lie down, let Bella take care of you if she's still up."

"Good idea," I said. "Bella would love it." She would, too; fussing and clucking came naturally to her. But no way in the world was I going to wake her or anyone else if I could help it.

Ellie watched from the car until I got to the porch. In the half light, humidity made her reddish-gold hair pouf out around her face like dandelion fluff. I waved as she pulled away.

Then I went inside, changed my clothes, toweled my hair, and poured out a generous shot of Bella's cordial. The stuff was delicious, kicked like a Kentucky mule, and was said to put hair on your chest, though it hadn't yet on mine.

Fala showed up silently in the kitchen, padding in to lean against my legs. I patted her gratefully, then knocked my drink back, poured another, and stood there sipping it.

After that, I peeked into Ivy's little room where she lay sleeping, one hand on a stuffed toy skunk that the dog must've lent to her. Good luck, kiddo, I thought at her, turning away. Good luck to both of us.

Then I put the empty glass in the sink, patted Fala once more, and went out to find the annoying red-dress lady from tonight's class reunion and question her.

Gently, if possible. And if not, then not.

Eight

The lights were still on at the school when I pulled up in the parking lot and hurried inside. In the gym, the smell of an institutional dishwasher floated in the air, soapy steam with a hint of sour milk.

Custodians with brooms and wheeled bins bustled about, sweeping up dropped napkins, clear plastic cups, and general detritus. A mound of half-melted Neapolitan ice cream stood in a punchbowl surrounded by a lake of warm, flat ginger ale.

I found the tables where the yearbook photos of reunion attendees had been displayed. The photos were gone, but I found many of them in one of the wheeled bins that the cleaning crew was using.

Included was a candid high-school–era shot of the red-dress lady I'd met earlier. Wearing a cheerleader outfit, she'd been caught midjump, with her heels up behind her, pom-poms waving.

Back in the car I looked her up—Karen Hamm, the photo's caption said her name was—on my phone. Karen lived on Redoubt Hill, just on the edge of town; I fired up the Fiat, pulled out of the parking lot, and headed out Route 190, hoping she wasn't already in bed.

A left turn off the highway delivered me to the correct part of town; finding the right house, though, was a project since house numbers weren't always a guaranteed thing around here. Still, I had time—if she was already asleep, I planned to throw pebbles at her window until she woke—so I started with a slow cruise past the neighborhood's expansive two-story houses and wide, tree-shaded lawns.

Almost at once, though, I found a driveway with the name HAMM neatly lettered on a small wooden sign at the end of it. Landscaped borders edged the driveway, the parking area, and the brick-laid path from there to the house.

Inside, a few lights were still on. When I got to the front door, a small terrier-type dog was there, yapping to be let in. A Mercedes stood in the driveway; not a new one, but still.

"Yeah, me too," I said to the yapping dog. Around us on the slate-paved terrace, large and small clay-potted cacti stood in the dim unearthly-looking glow of numerous solar lamps.

Very dim; tripping over a slate paver, I knocked a clay pot to its side. In the late-night silence, the clatter sounded more like an avalanche and made the dog bark harder.

I was bent over straightening the pot when the door opened at last. The red-dress woman—brassy blond hair, makeup by the bucketful, eyelids like heavy draperies over kohl-smudged eyes—saw me and moved to close the door again.

"Come on, Barkley," she told the dog, who resembled a dust mop with eyes.

"Wait," I said as it scampered in past her and she turned to follow. She wore a maroon housecoat, gold satin slippers, and a shawl, dark purple with heavy gold thread woven into it.

"You were right about Ellie and me," I said. "But why we're snooping—it's for a little girl."

She stopped.

"Please," I said quietly, letting my hands fall to my sides.

Sometimes sincerity is just what some jerk needs to hurt you. But not this time. She stopped with her back to me, spoke without turning. "Come along, then, you might as well come in."

Her highly processed hair glinted metallically in the firelight of her small sitting room, where a burning incense cone sent sandalwood smoke coiling to the shadowy ceiling. A cat blinked sleepily at me from a window seat backed by leaded glass.

"We're looking into Cindy Munson's death," I said, once she'd sat me down by the hearth and poured tea. "If her ex-husband killed her, their daughter could end up in foster care for who knows how long."

On the way here I'd been thinking about what Ellie had asked: what did I want? For Ivy's life to return to normal, whatever that was, or for it to change utterly with me as some kind of a triumphant savior, swooping in to fix everything?

And what I came up with was that despite my strong feelings, this wasn't about me, not even a little bit. If it had been, I could have given it up.

Karen Hamm sat down and lit a cigarette. "I knew I'd be seeing you again." Her voice was gravelly, smoky, and world-weary.

"Sorry it's so late." I sipped tea as she rolled her dark-lined eyes at me, waving the burning cigarette tiredly as if to say, what did it matter?

The room was furnished with clean blond wooden furniture, tweedy fabrics, and splashes of bright, unexpected color: lime, gold, pink. A four-foot-tall oil portrait of a cat stood against one bare wall; a rooftop study of Eastport in rain, also in oil, hung on another.

"I did those," she said, seeing me notice. "But then I switched to pottery." She pointed at a collection of large, big-bellied pottery vessels glazed in dark earth tones; I noticed her muscular hands and forearms, from pottery-making, I guessed.

But I wasn't here for the arts-and-crafts tour, and she seemed to know it, tapping her cigarette briskly into a ceramic ashtray. "Okay," she said. "So you found me from the yearbook picture?"

I sat up straight. The tea was a lifesaver, strong and sweet. "Right. And what I need to know is why you called her a bitch. Cindy Munson, that is."

Karen stubbed out the cigarette, lit another. "Because she was. They cropped that yearbook picture of her, you know."

I hadn't. Over in the corner the purse-sized terrier went into a tiny little dog crate about the size of a breadbox and settled down on a washcloth-size bed.

"The decorations committee cut Terry Lawson out of that photograph," she said. "I guess maybe they thought it might make me feel bad if they didn't." She leaned back in her chair. "Which it wouldn't have," she added. "Though I don't blame them for thinking so. Terry and I had been a pair since eighth grade."

The little dog snored, a sound like a miniature match being scratched against a teensy matchbox. I kept silent, because once in a very great while I'm smart enough to shut up.

She paused, collecting her thoughts. Then: "After we graduated," Karen went on, "he meant to go to college and, after that, business school. Even back then he was determined to become a success."

"You'd be going together? I mean, that was the plan you two had?"

She nodded. "Until halfway through high school, yes. And I'd be going to nursing school."

She dragged again on the smoke and squashed it out. "I wasn't *that* stupid," she added. "The minute he laid eyes on her, it was Cindy this and Cindy that until I could've—"

She fell silent. *Killed her . . .* The words hung unspoken.

"And then what happened?" I ventured after a moment.

"They got married the day after we graduated from high school and went off together just like the two of us had planned. Well, except she picked beauty school instead of nursing."

She shrugged. The incense stick had burned out. "It lasted about as long as you'd expect," she said, and got up stiffly.

Thirty years hadn't done those high-kicking muscles and joints any favors. Crossing to the mantel over the hearth, she fetched a silver-framed picture and handed it to me.

In the photo, a youthful Lawson and a beamingly happy Karen Hamm smiled into the camera. "You were so young!" I exclaimed.

And happy, and good-looking . . . but I handed the photo back uneasily. Something suddenly didn't make sense.

"But Karen, that was thirty years ago, right? And if they divorced soon after their marriage—" Ivy was six, not twenty-six.

"I didn't say they divorced." Karen set the framed picture back on the mantel with a sharp click. "I said they didn't last. She came back here. Hung out for a while with a hard crowd, got in some trouble, straightened herself out," Karen recited.

I guessed the next part; it could hardly be any other way. "And then he came back. Lawson did."

Karen's lips tightened into a thin line. "Yup. He came back a few years ago to settle his parents' estate, sell the house and so on."

Uh-huh. "Which she got wind of," I guessed some more. "And since they were still married—" Follow the money, always. It will never let you down.

"—she wanted a cut," Karen said. "And I don't know how she did it, but the next thing you know they were back together, all lovey-dovey again."

I could probably figure out just how she did it, and from the "what's new?" look on her face I gathered Karen could, too.

"For," she added, lighting up again, "about six months." She blew out a plume of smoke, tapped ash. "That's how long it took for the little girl to be on the way, and for him to figure out that she'd made a fool of him."

"So, no love lost between them now," I said, and she tried to laugh, but ended up coughing instead while I sat there hoping that these weren't her final moments or something.

At last, she recovered. "No love at all, no. See, the thing about Terry was, he was nice until he wasn't. He could be mean."

"Like, if he thought you deserved it?" The fire on the little hearth was falling to embers; I finished my cold tea.

Her laugh grumbled raggedly in her chest as she walked me to the door. By now, somebody at home would've gotten up for a drink of water or to use the bathroom or to find a dropped binky or just to walk around thinking about something, and they'd have noticed I wasn't home.

From the door, the view into the low-ceilinged sitting room was cozy and pleasant, the hearth glow still warm. But I sensed that it was going to feel much emptier once I wasn't in it.

"There was another woman he saw a lot of, too, while he was back, but I only heard about that, I never saw them together. Or even knew who she was, come to think of it.

"Anyway, after he finally he got out of there, she really hit the skids," Karen said. "It's why he got custody of the little girl."

It was time for me to go, if I didn't want the police called out to look for me. But Karen kept saying things, as if she'd been waiting all these years just for someone to listen.

"That might've shocked some sense into her," Karen said, "him leaving again."

Maybe it had, because after that Cindy had straightened out once more, got sober and got herself into a technical field she was apparently pretty good at. Made a living at it, even.

Which reminded me. "You know, I've been in Cindy's house," I said. We were nearly to the door I'd come in through, past a room that smelled sweetly of oil paints and turpentine.

"Even down in the cellar," I added.

Her dark-lined, wrinkle-draped eyes turned sharply to me. "Have you, now?"

"And I didn't notice a workspace for electronics. Or equipment, or—" I stopped on the doorstep, turned. "Karen, why did you let me in? You must've known talking about what happened might upset you."

She met my gaze. "Cindy wanted Terry back. I know people who knew her," she put a hand up. "They told me tonight at the alumni dinner how she talked about it all the time. The other night at the dance with Lawson and Ivy you'd have thought she'd died and gone to heaven, they said."

Right. Until she got murdered. I wondered if the custody suit was just part of a grand plan, with Ivy as pawn. Suddenly the money that Lawson had hidden made more sense. But—

"I already tried telling all this to the detectives when they interviewed me," Karen said, pulling her shawl up against the night's chill. "They looked at me like I was from Mars."

I could relate. Behind me in the shadows, the Fiat waited patiently under the trees; by now, Bella would've called out the National Guard.

"I tried calling him once," she said suddenly.

Wistfully. She'd lit another cigarette, its smoke swirling up through the dim yellow porch light like a genie coming out of a bottle.

"He hung up on me," she said.

I drove home that night under a moon so bright it felt like my X-ray was being taken, and when I got there a miracle had occurred: everyone was in bed, sound asleep, and soon I was, too.

But early the next morning, Ellie and I met Lizzie Snow on the breakwater overlooking the boat basin.

I wasn't a big fan of early mornings, but dawn on the dock always felt worth getting up for: pristine, like the cool, damp air had never been breathed before. Around us, guys in oil-stained blue jeans, yellow slickers, and rubber boots hustled down the gangway, carrying army-green canvas backpacks full of lunches, phones, and spare socks.

As we started down behind them, Dylan Hudson pulled into a parking place on the breakwater and got out. Catching up to us just as we reached the wooden finger pier where Ellie's boat was tied up, he handed me a large brown paper bag that I thought smelled familiar.

"You didn't," I said, but he had: doughnuts.

I'd brought the coffee. Ellie had a lot of little creamers and sugar packets in her satchel, and the doughnuts in Dylan's bag turned out to be glazed crullers.

He selected one and bit in. "Food of the gods," he said around it, and in this of course he was absolutely correct.

"Okay," said Lizzie, getting right to the point. Meanwhile the seagulls were taking notice of the doughnuts, dipping and circling overhead. "Jake says they're coming for Ivy today."

Diesel engines grumbled to life on the fishing boats. "I think we all agree that's not good," she said.

Right, and especially me. Once she left here, she could end up with a foster family that did everything right.

Or not. Ellie spoke up. "I wouldn't mind so much, but if it turns out later that Lawson's tried and found guilty— "

"Then the way I understand it, it's likely the court will find permanent placement for her," Lizzie finished for Ellie.

Which again likely wouldn't be with us. But: "If I could just know for sure before I handed her over— "

That her dad hadn't murdered her mother, I'd have finished. That I wasn't sending her off either into uncertainty or into the care of a scheming killer.

"All right, so what's the plan?" Dylan wanted to know as he plucked another cruller from the bag.

"Well, the story is that Cindy wanted her daughter back,"

Ellie said, batting away a bold gull who'd decided that thievery could work. "And she'd straightened her life out well enough that she thought that could realistically happen."

"I wonder if that's what the cash was for," I mused aloud, the money that Lawson tried hiding. "Why he hid it, though, is another question."

I swigged coffee. "Maybe he just didn't want to leave it in the motel room."

"He could've put it in the safe in the office," Lizzie objected. "Besides, why would you start out by trying to give someone money, then kill them, instead?"

"Because they turned the money down," Dylan answered. "And killing them was your Plan B."

Huh. He was right. "So what about Fritzy, then? How would he figure into it?"

Dylan moved casually nearer to where Lizzie stood. She stepped alertly sideways before he could sling an arm around her. I wondered how late was too late to cancel wedding flowers.

Then Ellie was talking again. "Max Fritz said Cindy let him stay with her. She had a corner of her cellar fixed up, his bed and some belongings and so on."

Dylan nodded slowly. "So, he might've heard Cindy and Terry Lawson talking. Or arguing."

"Or," I pointed out, "Cindy could've argued with someone else." I told them about Karen Hamm's early romance with Lawson and how Cindy had broken it up.

Lizzie sighed. "I made a few inquiries about Lawson. Turns out his lawyer's finally here," she said. "So we'll see what he's got up his sleeve."

She ignored Dylan's smiling efforts to catch her eye. But luckily, the man loved a challenge, and when push came to shove, he knew just what to do about this one: he stepped confidently up beside her, put his arm firmly around her waist, and stood there until she relaxed.

Grudgingly, but she did it. "You again," she said.

"Yeah. Get used to it." He tightened his arm affectionately before releasing her.

"Okay," she said, stepping briskly away from him again. If I hadn't known them, I'd never have realized how madly they adored one another, even though they were always pushing away with one hand and pulling together again with the other. He was nuts about her, and she was crazy about him, too, but to see them sometimes, you'd think they hated each other's guts.

"I'm seeing the homicide people in ten minutes," she said. "I'll tell them about the Cindy and Fritz connection, and about Karen Hamm." She finished her coffee. "I wish I could say something more encouraging," she added to me.

About Ivy leaving, she meant; I'd been steeling myself for the event since my eyes opened this morning. "I swear if they have to carry her out, I might lose it," I said.

Meanwhile, I was thinking about why Lawson might want poor drunk Fritzy dead. Maybe, for instance, he found out that Fritzy had overheard him arguing with Cindy—or even threatening her. Yeah, maybe a lot of things.

"See if you can talk to some other old classmates," Lizzie suggested. "Karen might not be alone in her feelings."

"Entirely possible," I agreed. On the other hand, women who kept boyfriends' thirty-year-old photographs on their mantels might not be entirely reliable when discussing said boyfriend.

And the old boyfriend's murdered wife. "Sounds like this Hamm woman isn't in great physical shape?" Dylan inquired.

"It's hard to imagine her strangling anyone," I admitted. "She's strong enough, but it's just not her style. Or shooting them, either . . . she was more the poisoning type, I thought."

By now the sun had risen, spreading a hot-pink stain across the water. Lizzie hopped from the boat to the wooden finger pier and the rest of us followed.

Rather, the others followed, stepping easily up over the boat's rail and onto the dock. I placed my right foot carefully onto the step leading to the foredeck, grabbed the pole holding up the bimini—it's the awning over the foredeck, for you non-boaty types—and hoisted myself high enough to swing my left foot out over the rail.

But next came the hard part: letting go of the bimini pole. Also, it would be great not to fall on my face once my feet hit the dock. Doing both these things at once, however . . .

"Jake." I looked up. It was Dylan Hudson, holding a hand out to me. I grabbed it, pushed off with my foot, then stepped easily from boat rail to finger pier. Safe as houses, as Bella would've put it, and that in a nutshell was Dylan, a pain in the tailbone except when he wasn't.

He put a companionable hand on my shoulder. "So listen," he said as we walked together. "You thought any more about that break-in you had the other night?"

Criminy, that again. "Haven't had time. Why?" My midnight visitor's brief presence three nights ago had barely crossed my mind since Ivy arrived.

Dylan shrugged. "Just curious. Always lookin' out for you, kid." That smile of his should've been registered as a weapon; if you were female, you looked into it at your peril.

"Yeah, yeah," I said. "If I were you, I'd start thinking about looking out for myself. You're not exactly marrying Holly Homemaker, you know."

He'd caught sight of her waiting for us at the foot of the metal gangway. "Yeah," he sighed happily. "I do know."

"Thanks for coming out early," she told me when we reached her. "Can you believe this was the only time I had? For somebody who's not involved, they're sure keeping me busy," she grumbled.

But it was also how she kept us informed. Like a mobbed-up money guy I once knew used to say, everything's a trade-off.

Dylan tapped me on the shoulder. "Hey, one other thing. You've heard that old saying about following the money?"

The smile, again. I'd have answered, but he didn't want one, striding on ahead up the gangway, instead. It wasn't as steep as the last time I'd climbed it, but I could still see through the heavy metal mesh to the dock below.

"They don't want me getting involved," Lizzie was still griping, "but it's no problem using me for chores, paperwork, and any errands they just don't feel like doing."

"And you let them?" When climbing a gangway, keep your eyes to yourself. Put one foot in front of the other, and soon it will be all over.

One way or the other. "Ha," Lizzie said from behind me. At least that's how it sounded to me—if I looked back at her again, I'd get dizzy and that way lay disaster, so I didn't.

"You bet I let them," she said. "I make myself as helpful and cooperative as possible. How'd you think I get even as much info as I do?"

And for god's sake, I instructed myself, keep moving or you'll freeze up and not be able to move at all, and they'll end up having to pluck you off the gangway with a construction crane.

I stopped, gripping the ramp's siderails and contemplating the rest of the way up. There was a lot of it. But that wasn't what halted me in my tracks.

"It's not going to happen, is it?" I said, the truth of it washing over me like a cold shower. "He'll get off. He's got a big-city criminal attorney, and the state's got lots of theory but no real evidence."

I mean, obviously, his hair and fingerprints and so on were in the car he'd been driving. He could've picked up one of her hairs any time during the evening, then shed it at the motel.

As for motive, plenty of people had them. Karen Hamm, for instance. Opportunity? The victim was alone in a car in a dark parking lot, for heaven's sake. If you wanted to convict a guy of murder, you needed more.

Like maybe a witness. Ivy, for instance. Suddenly Lawson's zeal to get his daughter back took on a new light. Before she talked, maybe. Before she lost her fear of him enough to disobey him and tell someone what she'd seen.

I glanced back, feeling like someone had smacked me with a plank. The clue stick, maybe. Lizzie looked rueful.

"Yeah," she was saying, "I could be wrong, but I'll bet Mr. Lawson and Ivy will be leaving our jurisdiction soon. From what I'm hearing, I doubt they'll even bring a case against him."

So there it was. When the Family Services ladies showed up to take Ivy later on today, I'd most likely in effect be handing her back to her father. And the trouble was, I didn't think I could, not with all the questions I still had about him.

At the top of the ramp, there was about an eight-inch gap you had to step across to get onto the pavement. Contemplating it, I bit my lip, sucked in a breath, summoned my courage, and—

Lizzie shoved me from behind and I flew across. "Call if you need anything," she said, as I stumbled and caught myself. One thing about being clumsy, it makes life exciting.

Also, it makes great camouflage. Two or three pratfalls and a faceplant are generally enough to make people underestimate me. And when I'm snooping into murder, that's a good thing. Not that I wouldn't prefer less pain and fewer mishaps, but over the years I'd grown to accept that they'd come with the package.

"Thanks," I told Ellie, and turned toward the Fiat. She began walking away past Rosie's Hot Dogs stand, heading for the Chocolate Moose to get things ready to open for the day; Dylan was in his car.

I opened the car door. Around me the hush of dawn had given way to early-morning dockside bustle: fishermen's pickup trucks, a refrigerated box hauler, official-looking cars slowing for the Coast Guard Station's tall black iron gates.

"Hey," Lizzie called. "You two be careful, okay?" Ellie and me, she meant—she'd seen my face when she told me that Lawson would probably walk away from this. "Don't do anything stupid."

"You bet," I called back. It was 7 AM, the start of another busy day, though at the time, I had no idea how busy. Standing by the Fiat with the early-morning sun on my face and a sea breeze throwing kisses, I promised not to get myself killed or to let Ellie get killed, either, and if I had mental reservations about this, I figured that Lizzie would understand.

Hey, stuff happens.

Eastport is three miles long by seven wide, small enough so that you can usually find someone just by driving around looking for their car. I started by driving down Water Street and turning up Key Street; passing my big old house I saw nothing on fire or exploding and nobody bleeding, so I drove on to the ballfield and tennis courts, the firehouse, and the youth center, where the sign read Wednesday Night Beano.

Past that, Deep Cove Road curved sharply between apple trees and wine-colored sumac, grasses fading to pale yellow, and a culverted stream where the water had turned a wheel at one time, only the concrete slot the wheel's axle had rested in still standing.

I figured I'd start looking for Terry Lawson at this end of the island and work my way to the other end. He and I were going to have a little talk, I'd decided; I was done dancing around with him. Deep Cove on a bright autumn day, however, was nearly enough to derail my ambition.

The horseshoe beach where a small green skiff was always tied up stretched a quarter mile to the water's edge, studded with shiny wet stones and patrolled by stick-legged sea birds. Scraggly, wind-bent spruce trees scrabbled raggedly down granite ledges to the sand, and from the corner of my eye, I glimpsed a heron marching stiffly in the rocky shallows, eye cocked alertly for mussels, minnows, any cold meat, really.

But while I was glimpsing, I was thinking about Terry Lawson and money, and that made me pull out my cell phone. Hesitating, I stared at the screen; the calls I was contemplating could put me in some pretty hot water. I'd be reaching out to some people I used to know back in the city, where I was, not to put too fine a point on it, a money manager for guys who were deeply involved in a sort of family organization.

Nevertheless, I took a deep breath, held my nose, and dove into a swamp I'd left behind a lifetime ago. Punching in one memorized number after another—I hadn't even wanted to store them in my phone, but somewhere deep in my brain I'd known I'd need them someday—I asked a few questions, got a few answers, and hung up on good enough terms with my old pals to be fairly confident that none of them was coming to whack me.

By the time I ended the last call, I drove up to the high school, parked out front, and cornered Ian Macrae in his small, cluttered office.

Lawson could be mean, Karen Hamm had said, not so much when someone deserved it but when he could get away with it.

I wondered who he'd been mean to. Other than Karen herself, that is. "Did Terry Lawson get sent to your office a lot?"

Macrae eyed me levelly from behind his desk, an old metal relic with a scarred gray top resting on two file cabinets. It and the rest of his cluttered office contrasted sharply with the venerable antique pieces he lived with at home.

"I don't recall," he began, but I was already shaking my head at him.

"Sorry, bud. Not today." I happened to know that all the old school records had been put on microfilm by volunteers—likely Hetty Bailey and friends, come to think of it—sometime in the early 2000s, and he knew it, too.

So, he might as well tell me. "Yes," he said reluctantly, opening a desk drawer as if looking for something in it. "He did. Now, if that's all, I'm quite—"

I reached over and slammed the drawer shut. "It's not all. Why kinds of things did he get sent to you for?"

He was a big guy with a thick, muscular neck and bulky shoulders that mounded under his brown sport jacket, but I still saw his Adam's apple go up and down when he swallowed hard.

"Was he a troublemaker?" I probed. "Warnings, detentions, suspensions, that kind of thing?"

"Look, you can drag out the records and check for yourself, but I can't just casually violate a student's privacy because you come in and—"

"Ex-student," I reminded him, and then, because something in his face said to: "I mean, unless you have some other ongoing relationship with Mr. Lawson?"

The room's one small window looked out onto a concrete courtyard with two picnic tables and an ashtray masquerading as a potted chrysanthemum.

"All those antiques at your house," I mused aloud, watching a sparrow cock its head suspiciously at the chrysanthemum, then fly off. "A lot of them must be imported, right?"

Turning, I caught the anxious look on his face. "You bought all that legally, though, I'm sure. Paid import fees and so on."

Macrae looked stricken, perhaps recalling that some of his purchases hadn't made it onto any lists of taxable items. "Most of it belonged to my parents," he offered weakly.

I waited. He rubbed a big hand over his face. Finally: "All right. The truth is, I do remember Terry, and for a while, he was a bully, a bad one. He took a dislike to another boy—it wasn't pretty. At last, the boy's parents took him out of public school, sent him to a private academy."

"That seems pretty extreme. What did Terry do to the boy?"

Macrae grumbled but eventually spilled forth; he was right, it wasn't pretty. "Now if you could just keep it to yourself that I told you," he finished, and I promised I would with my fingers firmly crossed behind my back.

And then I went out and found Terry Lawson's old Chevy station wagon, spotting it from the end of Deep Cove Road out past the boatyard near the end of the airport runway. The car sat nearly at the top of a grassy hill on the far side of the tarmac, looking out over the beach.

Nobody was in it.

I got out of the Fiat and closed the door quietly; no one needed a heads-up. Sparrows cheeped in the low brush and scrub trees lining the road. The pointed green tops of old fir trees stood motionless in the bright air.

A grassy path led a quarter-mile down to the runway through goldenrod, purple asters, and Queen Anne's lace. Beyond the blacktop runway's end spread a swath of mown grass ending at a rocky beach.

A man sat on one of the rocks out there, gazing at the water. I started down toward him, a move that turned out not to be one of my better ideas. The flowers grew straight up, but the stems, leaves, and various root crowns all knotted together like netting at ground level; soon my feet were enmeshed.

Stinging hairs, thorns so sharp they threw sparks, and sap that oozed out of broken stems to produce instant blisters all savaged me at once. Brigades of gnats clouded the air, flying up my nose and invading my brain by way of my ear holes.

By the time I hit the beach I was hot, tired, and a walking advertisement for fast-acting allergy relief, which naturally I did not have handy. Also, a couple of red ants had invaded my pants leg and were biting an acid-hot trail up into the crease of my thigh.

And I didn't like any of those things, but I hadn't spent years as a high-level money mover for the Mob just to wuss out over some bugs and itchy weeds. I yanked the pants off promptly, never mind that Lawson had turned and was watching me, curious and beginning to be alarmed.

"Shut up," I said tightly. "Just sit there and shut up, I don't want to hear a word out of you until I tell you."

Itchy, ant-bit, and stripping in front of a stranger—any madder and I'd have burst into flames. And then I started to sneeze. Lawson got up and approached me cautiously, and shoved a handkerchief at me.

"Thanks," I muttered, taking it gracelessly. Eventually I looked up to find him eyeing me.

"What," he inquired in tones of strained patience, "do you want?"

I blew my nose again. "What's the money for? That you hid, the fifty grand."

I'd meant to start with a calm conversation, get a sense of who this guy was and what he might really be able to do in the kill-your-ex department.

I mean, not everyone can. But now, the hell with that. "And after you explain that, I want you to tell me in detail the true state of your relationship with Cindy," I added.

"Why should I?" he said. "Why should I tell you anything?"

But I'd prepared for this: my old buddies had been gabby. "You were a shooting star in the tech biz, weren't you?" Emphasis on *were.* "Brokered some funding deals for several ideas that later on were big moneymakers."

One was an app you could use to move money around. Billed as a personal banking utility, what it really did was hide funds so the feds could play whack-a-mole trying to find it. The boys in the bad families were crazy about that one.

A horsefly buzzed me menacingly; I snatched it out of the air and crushed it, surprising myself. "But things change fast," I said. "The real whiz kids are in artificial intelligence, now, and AI's not your thing."

His face said I was right. But my old pals in the city had shared a few other nuggets, too.

"You're mortgaged to the hilt, you owe money all over town, and it's rumored the Southern District of New York is looking at you for tax fraud."

Which reminded me: "How do you think your hotshot lawyer's going to feel when he finds out he's not getting paid?"

Lawyers are astonishingly expensive. There's a reason they bill by the quarter hour, and it's so their fee doesn't immediately look like they're walking off with Fort Knox. Ones who can reliably get you off a murder charge cost even more.

"You know nothing," said Lawson, "and what you think you know you've got wrong. You and that little pal of yours are a couple of village gossips playing at being detectives."

I breathed in slowly through my left nostril and out via my right until my blood quit boiling quite so vigorously. "Fine, then set me straight. It should be easy. I've got it wrong, tell me why."

No answer. He looked caught. I was right about his lawyer dropping him, and he knew it. Still, he also looked stubborn. "But why?" he demanded again

So I brought out the big guns. "Because if you don't, I'll tell Ivy about how you tied that kid to the baseball scoreboard and a red ant swarm found him. Sent the kid to the hospital."

Macrae had tried downplaying the incident, but those were the facts. There'd have been a lawsuit, but neither Lawson's family nor the school district had any money for a judgment.

A mile away across the inlet, cars and trucks moved on the causeway between Eastport and Pleasant Point. "Maybe you don't care what Ivy thinks of you," I said. "But considering your situation, I would think you'd at least want her on your side."

He thought about this for a moment while I wondered again what Ivy had or hadn't seen. "Okay," he gave in, "you're right, that's not anything she needs to know about."

The breeze stiffened and the sky was clouding over again. "But not here," he said. "I'll drive you back to your car."

All the scrapes, cuts, bug bites, and pollen-dustings I'd suffered getting here now stung maddeningly. I didn't trust him, but I was pretty sure I could handle him if he tried anything weird; besides, he'd be busy driving.

When I'd followed him down the beach and looked up at the hike I was in for just to get to his car, though, my good cheer evaporated. A thirty-foot scramble up a dry, sandy slope rising near vertically from the beach awaited me.

Next came a zigzag trail, weathered and well-furnished with loose rocks, uncertain handholds, and nests full of ground wasps: vicious, darting little guys with red-hot stingers, hair-trigger tempers, and lousy impulse control.

There'd have been guardrails and a caution sign anywhere else, but in Maine they still expect you to have brains and a self-preservation instinct. While I stood looking, Lawson began climbing; soon he was halfway to the top.

"We city guys go to gyms," he said, looking down at me. He didn't add "nyah-nyah" like some snotty middle schooler, but he might just as well have.

Grimly, I reached up and grabbed an outcropping. It crumbled in my hand. Another: this time dust and grit exploded into my face. Finally, I spat out a juicy curse word, flung my arm up as high as it would go, and grabbed a nice, solid chunk of good old-fashioned Maine granite.

And then another chunk, and another. The climb was as I expected: painful and slow. I watched for wasps floating ominously and saw none, but a horsefly chomped into my neck just below my right ear.

I slapped at it, losing my grip on the cliff. Some gym work

might be good for me, too, I reflected on the way down, or even better, a stout rope ladder.

When I looked up, Terry Lawson's face peered over the edge at me; no ladder, though. So this time I abandoned all pretense of knowing how and just hurled myself at the cliff, clawing my way up while breaking fingernails and uttering Bad Words until I hauled myself over the top.

Then I just fell down and lay there, and concentrated on breathing. "You know a lot of swear words," Lawson observed.

I opened one eye at him. "I haven't even gotten started." Then came the feeling of tiny feet skittering on my forearm; I jumped to my own feet, brushing wildly at myself while recalling the couple of centipedes I'd glimpsed during my ascent.

"Let's stop in town on the way back," I suggested when we were in the brown station wagon. We'd have to go nearly all the way in, anyway, to get to the Fiat. "We could visit the brunch place where we went last time, and talk there."

Lawson nodded, eyes on the road. He wanted brunch with me about as much as he wanted leprosy, I could tell by his face. But I got the sense that he had questions for me, too.

Or *about* me, such as, how much did I know and how much was I guessing? "Sure," he said, still looking straight ahead, "let's do that."

In tan dungarees, a gray T-shirt, and a navy blue hoodie with a legend that read ISLAND MARINE, he looked much like any other Eastport guy out to do errands or take yard trash to the dump. Only the leather loafers he wore hinted at something else.

But sitting right beside him I could hardly miss that two-hundred-dollar haircut of his, each careful strand seemingly snipped individually. Still keeping up appearances, then. But my old crime pals in the city said that's all they were.

Now we drove silently back toward town between red-studded apple orchards and the stony foundations of vanished farmhouses. Overhead a long, V-shaped flock of Canada geese arrowed south, honking. From the top of Washington Street, the Coast Guard's red-tiled roof rose into view, then the Port Authority building and the breakwater.

On Water Street, tourists took selfies with the boats and the bay. "Pull in here," I said, jerking a thumb toward the fish pier parking lot.

At midmorning the clouds had thickened over Campobello, and a thin fog lay flat on the gray, sullen-looking water. Meanwhile, the horsefly bite on my neck had stopped hurting like a bastard and begun itching the same way, which was not an improvement.

"Come on," I told Lawson when we'd gotten out of the car. The redbrick Brady Building with the tall, arched windows and massive wooden doors was showing its age, I noticed: missing mortar section here, fallen brick there. Buildings so near the water took maintenance, but this one hadn't gotten much lately.

Inside, Bridget Brady waved tiredly at us from the far end of the bar, where she stood polishing glasses. Strawlike strands poked from her usually neat-as-a-pin blond braid, and her shoulders slumped tiredly. It had been a late night once the cops got acquainted with the late Max Fritz lying right behind her building, I supposed. The deck wasn't open yet, so we took a table in the dim knotty-pine–paneled room. Bridget left the short row of morning regulars on barstools—four guys chewing the fat over shots and beers, while the TV mounted high in the corner behind the bar showed The Weather Channel—and hurried over to us.

"Hey," she greeted us briskly. I thought maybe Lawson avoided her gaze, but I couldn't be sure. When I returned from the ladies' room minus a lot of grime from my morning exertions, though, they seemed chummy enough, chatting pleasantly about something.

I slid back onto my chair. A pot of coffee, two mugs, and a pair of truly gorgeous raspberry Danish had arrived, along with a small plate of butter pats. Bridget put a sympathetic hand on Lawson's shoulder before departing.

Her friendliness seemed odd, as it had to me, earlier; Bridget wasn't one for making pals of her customers. But hey, she could've crushed on him in high school for all I knew, and I had to admit he was a decent specimen if you left out the part about him maybe killing his ex. I buttered the pastry, bit in, and washed it down with a rejuvenating swallow of fresh coffee.

Lawson picked a crumb off his own pastry, eyed it, and dropped it on his plate. "Don't fool around, do you?"

So I guess he really didn't want Ivy hearing about him torturing some kid, even long ago when he was a kid himself. I was mildly surprised; I'd been with him for over an hour, now, and he hadn't even asked about her.

But everyone's got things they don't want others knowing about, I suppose, especially their children. "So why'd you really come back to Eastport? Not for the reunion, I'm pretty sure."

Matching megamillionaires with computer nerds who need money isn't best done at small-town celebrations, usually, and from what I'd heard on the phone that morning, that's what he did for a living.

Had done, rather. The air had gone out of the business he'd been in, and so had the money.

"It wasn't so Ivy could visit with her mother," I went on. "Cindy continued to have little interest in Ivy, I'm sorry to say."

Cindy wasn't planning to take Ivy back, much less fighting to; I was sure of it from her unprepared house and the absence of any legal paperwork in her files. She might not have been using any substances anymore, but she wasn't replacing her addictions with motherhood, either.

No matter what Lawson or anyone else said about it. "At first I thought that's what the money was for, to pay her off so maybe she'd drop the idea," I said. I was doing more talking than I'd planned, but if that's what it took to get him going . . . "Now I think it must've been something else," I added.

Lawson got up abruptly. This wasn't going the way I'd hoped at all. On the other hand, I now knew what triggered him, or one thing, anyway: the money.

He stopped to speak briefly with Bridget on our way out. When he emerged to where I waited on the sidewalk for him: "I knew this would be a waste of time," he said. "I didn't have any relationship with Cindy anymore, her demand to take Ivy was real, and the money is none of your business."

Maybe he'd decided he didn't care what I told Ivy. Or not as much as he cared about the money and whatever it represented, anyway; obviously he'd meant to do something with it.

I just didn't know what. Still, it didn't mean he was guilty of anything, and now there were two other potential suspects: Karen Hamm, abandoned in favor of Cindy long ago but still feeling badly betrayed, and whoever this kid was that Lawson had tortured all those years ago.

I wondered if I could find the kid; he'd be middle-aged by now. "You don't know anything," Lawson repeated as I followed him back to his car.

"Then why not tell me?" I got in on the passenger side, thinking he meant to drive me back out to where I'd left the Fiat.

As I fastened my seat belt, Lizzie Snow drove by, giving us a long look from behind the wheel of the squad car as she passed. Then I noticed Dylan Hudson sitting on a bench in front of Wadsworth's Hardware, trying to look casual and succeeding only in resembling a hawk scrutinizing its prey.

Keeping an eye on me, both of them, and for once I didn't mind. Then when I spotted Ellie coming out of the Moose, I reached for the car's door handle to get out and talk with her.

"Stop a minute," I told Lawson, but he didn't, and that's

when I learned that the old car's inside door handle didn't work. By now we'd turned onto Washington Street and started back out to where I'd left the Fiat, earlier.

But when I reminded him—"Turn here," I said as we approached the long curve past Bay City Mobil. "Take the left onto Deep Cove Road."

He didn't.

Nine

"You don't believe a word I've said, do you?"

"Not while we're headed in the wrong direction. What's going on?" I tried the door handle again. It flopped uselessly.

"You want to know about the money so much, but you wouldn't believe anything I said about that, either, would you? So I'm going to show you something."

Lawson glanced sideways, saw the problem and the face I was making about it.

"Oh. Sorry," he said. "I bought the car when I got to town, didn't notice that until I drove it out of the guy's yard."

Buying the old car made sense: cheaper than a long-term rental, probably. The rest of it might've sounded reasonable, too, if someone else had said it, but from him—not so much.

"Just let me out." I dug my phone from my bag and punched in Lizzie's number. Time for some reinforcements.

"Wait." Lawson saw the phone and pulled the car over. "Look." He spread his hands reasonably. "I just want you to see something. You won't believe me otherwise—heck, why should you? The cops certainly don't, they think I strangled my ex-wife, possibly while my daughter watched."

I put the phone down. He wasn't reaching for my throat at least. But my Spidey-senses kept screeching a warning.

"Let me out of the car," I said. "Right now. Immediately."

"Just bear with me." He pulled back out onto the street. "Can you do that? Please. Just for a few minutes."

The pleading note in his voice was real: he sounded like a guy who was in way over his head in trouble he hadn't started. I lowered the car window and checked to make sure that at least the outside door handle worked, and it did.

"All right," I agreed grudgingly. After all, he could've killed me out at the beach if he'd wanted. Not all the little inlets and the massive boulders shouldering up out of them were visible from the causeway.

But minutes later I realized where we were going. "Cindy's house?" Alarm shot through me again—a beach was one thing, a basement another.

"Her cellar." He confirmed my fears, pulling into her driveway and shutting the car off. "That's where the things I need to show you are right now."

Um, no. There'd been nothing in the cellar. "I've already seen everything in the—"

"Wrong," he interrupted. We got out and made our way to the backyard, where he stepped onto the deck and produced a key.

My eyebrows went up. "I've had one since back when Cindy and I lived here together," he explained.

Wait a minute, my brain urged, *what's wrong with this picture?* But then we were inside, where the air smelled stale and a bar of gray light slanted between the kitchen curtains onto the floor.

Lawson glanced around briefly, then strode to the cellar door and started down. I spotted a small cast-iron skillet and grabbed it to use as a bonking tool, then followed.

The homicide team had already been here to examine Max

Fritz's few things: a battered toiletry kit, a metal box (open, empty), and the ragged jacket I'd often seen him wearing in the winter.

Lawson stood at the other end of the cellar, fiddling with something small that glinted metallically. "Okay," I said as I started toward him, "so what did you want me to see?"

"I brought you here to show you something, and I'm going to," he said

What the hell, in for a penny, and all that. If he'd wanted to try anything he'd have done it before now, it seemed to me. The steps were steeper than I recalled, though, with gloom at the foot of them. If anything went wrong there'd be a lot of them for me to climb, and in a hurry, too, probably.

Turn back now, said the voice in my head that always gives prudent advice.

Shut up, said the other voice. In a couple of hours, Ivy would be leaving forever. She might go into foster care, or—as was looking more likely, now—she might go back to her dad.

Who might still be a killer. *Can't let that happen*, I thought very clearly, ignoring the equally certain thought that I didn't want Ivy to go anywhere at all.

I started down the basement steps.

The cellar was still a bit of a shambles due to Ellie and I having had to escape from it once already. Metal shelving, cardboard boxes, suitcases that we'd tried to stack up and stand on to get to the cellar window—

"Over here," Lawson's voice came from behind the furnace, which as everyone knows is the part of the cellar most likely to hide bad surprises.

Old hinges creaked and a light snapped on back there, shining from inside a newly opened room I hadn't even known existed. Wonderingly I stepped into a bright, windowless chamber with whitewashed concrete-block walls, fluorescent lighting, a workbench with power strips and tools hung on white pegboard . . .

Tall conical air filters and a large dehumidifier unit set over a floor drain stood silently around the room. A desk with a small laptop, a phone mounted in a charger, and an open spiral-bound notebook on a green leather-edged blotter occupied the rest of the space.

Cindy did repairs here on the high schoolers' drones, robots, and other gadgets, I supposed. But it looked more like a NASA space lab to me, militarily clean and well-organized, and the electronic instruments on the workbench—screens, gauges, other items I couldn't even identify—looked expensive.

"What did she do besides fix things for the high school kids?" I asked Lawson. On the workbench lay a drone that looked like a metallic member of some alien species.

"That's what I wanted you to see. She did do repairs here." Lawson looked around almost reverently. "But you're right, this was really more of a research lab for her."

He turned to me. "Cindy was a drunk, a screwup, and not a nice person overall. But at this stuff she was a genius."

"With a certificate from a technical school?" I asked skeptically. "And how come no one else knew this about her?"

From an open padded box on the workbench I picked up a small metal-and-glass gadget about the size of my thumbnail, like a glass fuse with tiny flecks of metal suspended inside it. The thing resembled every other small electronic doodad I'd ever seen, in the sense that I knew nothing about it.

"What's this?" I asked. Lawson answered with something unintelligible about a Framm constant and the ramifications for the Bennet-Farr equation.

Or something like that. "Plain English, please," I said, and he complied: "It makes things faster. For large-volume information transfer, for instance. Much faster."

"Well, that sounds simple enough," I said, and he smiled.

"Yes. Simple, like gravity or the speed of sound." He inhaled, blew it out through pursed lips. "Before she died, I was about to offer her fifty thousand dollars for the option to have experts investigate the thing for a couple of months."

He watched my face. "All legal and aboveboard," he added. "I wasn't here to rip her off."

"Then why'd you hide the money after she died?" Hey, might as well ask, not that I was necessarily going to believe the answer. Still, it would be interesting to hear what he came up with.

"Because if they knew about it, who knows what they'd think? They'd find out I wanted more than Ivy, that I wanted something that might be worth money, a lot of money. Way more than fifty grand."

He was right. It would raise all kinds of questions, ones that could be spun a lot of different ways. That he'd made the offer, for instance, not just planned to, and she'd refused.

Motive for murder? I could see the cops thinking so. Bottom line, the money complicated a story that he wanted to look simple and straightforward.

I put the gadget down. "How'd you even know about this whatever-it-is she'd come up with?"

"She told me. And only me," he added, "after I warned her not to spread it around. People are funny, some big thing shows up and they all come out of the woodwork wanting a piece."

It sounded reasonable while he was saying it. Why not let him handle it, after all? He was already in the business of providing what she needed: money, honey. And at least he wasn't some stranger.

"I still don't see how a repair tech stumbles onto a true innovation," I said. "Plenty of people tinker around in home workshops."

Lawson nodded, purse lipped. "Right. But d'you see all those books there?" He waved at a stack of textbooks and glossy periodicals at the workbench's far end: *Annals of Multisyllabic This*, *Quarterly Report of Hopelessly Complex That*, all heavy-duty academic literature.

Unreadable by the likes of me, in other words. Lawson pointed at a framed certificate hung on the pegboard behind the bench. "Finished her master's degree last year. Most of it done online. Took high honors." He saw my expression. "What you have to understand is that Cindy really was special. Self-centered, self-destructive, a walking, talking personal disaster—but with this one interest. Or talent. Whatever it was."

He moved his hands in the air as if trying to grasp some immaterial quality. "She always could fix things. Even when we were married—a washing machine, a clock. Reverse-engineer them if she had to. Partly by reading repair manuals and partly"—he shrugged—"partly by whatever that special, weird thing was that she had in spades. Much good it did her."

Sure. Special. It all made me want to go over and pat the poor guy on the back. Or punch him in the nose—I still didn't know which.

"Sales, right?"

He squinted quizzically at me.

"You're in start-up financing now, helping bright, ambitious youngsters roll out the next big thing." My old New York contacts were well-informed. "But you started out in sales," I went on. "Making people buy what you were selling."

Like now, maybe. I pointed at the item Cindy had supposedly invented. "As for that, have you seen it work? Has anyone?"

For all I knew, it was an ordinary fuse in an unusual size, or even just a bit of junk. Still, Cindy's electronics lab was a serious-looking workplace.

"Yes," he agreed irritably, "sales. And it's a component, not a device. It works in a microprocessor's internal/external output/input—"

Or something like that. But "no can do" was the bottom line on a show-and-tell demo of Cindy's innovation, apparently.

"She had a mentor in the physics department at U. Maine," Lawson said. "Passed away recently. An old-school scientist, wrote his letters by typing them on paper, if you can imagine."

"So they discussed her work? And the letters still exist?"

"I've seen them. The originals, with his signature. They should be here somewhere."

Fascinating, and if it was true, the fifty thousand made sense—well, except for the hiding it part. And the fact that it was in cash. And that he'd been so secretive about it.

He snapped off the lights and turned to the door, sent me out ahead and closed it behind us.

"So you were going to give her the old 'sign here and all this can be yours' schtick?"

I crossed the cellar and started up the stairs.

"I told you," he said from behind me, "the money was for preliminary rights. To check the thing out, get a sense of how reliable it was and where the practical applications might be. So, it wasn't a schtick."

I was trying my best to get a read on this guy and coming up empty; sometimes I believed him, sometimes I didn't.

"Let's just get out of here," I said. So far all I'd gotten out of this visit was more confused. One thing I was sure of, though, as I headed for the sliding doors out onto the deck; if Cindy's electronic gadget turned out to be real, it just added more twists to an already complicated—

As I reached for the sliding glass door, something hit me in the head and all the lights went out.

"All right, damn it," I said, shoving myself up off the late Cindy Munson's cellar floor. Lawson must've hit me, then hauled me over and pushed me back down the stairs again.

Ouch. It would be simpler to list the parts of me that didn't hurt.

I shifted cautiously; nothing felt broken. Light coming through the cellar window said I hadn't been out cold for very long. My phone was upstairs in my bag but when I'd crawled up the cellar steps, the door at the top was locked.

As I leaned unhappily against it, the door opened suddenly, I fell through it into the upstairs hall, and Ellie caught me.

"Oh, my gosh," I exhaled. I'd been positively dreading having to climb out that cellar window again.

"I was delivering chocolate swirl coffee cakes to Myra Poundstone's card party, you know she lives right uphill from here—" I did know. From her deck, Myra could see practically the whole town. "—and I saw Lawson's car down here."

I shambled into Cindy Munson's kitchen, where she would never return to the vintage electric can opener, the linoleum countertops, or the cookie jar shaped like a smiling cat.

At the sink I ran myself a glass of water and stood there drinking it. "You didn't see Lawson leaving?"

Ellie shook her head. "No, but his car's in the driveway. He was here with you?"

I put the glass down sharply. "Yup. The car's here?" I looked out. The old brown Chevy station wagon hunkered in the driveway; no sign of Lawson, though.

"He's either taken off on foot," I said, "or he's still in the basement somewhere."

We hurried downstairs again—rather, she hurried, I limped—and found him sprawled unconscious behind the furnace.

Ellie aimed her flashlight at his face and he moaned and pushed himself upright. His features had that unmistakable "bashed-against-the-wall" look, like hamburger molded into human features. Somebody'd done a real number on this guy, as Sam would've said.

The same someone, possibly, who'd done a number on me, I

thought as I touched the new lump on my head gingerly. So, I'd judged Lawson too soon for that one, apparently; then I noticed that Cindy's workroom door stood open again.

Ignoring us, Lawson got to his feet and made his way to the workbench in there, and turned on the fluorescent lights. By their glare I saw clearly the padded box, almost like a jewelry box, that her gadget had been in half an hour ago.

But it wasn't there now.

We left Lawson's car in Cindy's driveway and rode with Ellie back to the Chocolate Moose.

"Half an hour," I said from the car's backseat. Until the ladies arrived to take Ivy, I meant; it was now 11:30.

Lawson turned questioningly. His face was impressive: I'd never seen puffing, swelling, bruising, bleeding, cuts, scrapes, punctures, and abrasions all in one place before.

I explained the custody arrangement to Lawson. "It starts today. At noon. Half," I repeated, "an hour from now.

His eyelids were puffed to the size of walnuts. "That's bad, is it?"

I regarded him, wondering if he was suffering a head injury or was merely dense. "I think Ivy going to another set of strangers while she's grieving her mom and scared about losing her dad, too"—I took a breath, controlling my temper—"yeah, I'd say that's bad," I forced myself to finish quietly.

But when I got out of the car I was still shaking, and I couldn't help it: "So, are there any other normal human emotions you'd like explained to you?"

Just for an instant, he looked like a guy who sees a train barreling toward him and can't move. Behind us, Ellie unlocked the shop and went in. "Look," he said, "I've done everything I can for Ivy. Same nanny forever, my friends adore her, our household staff loves her—"

So his money troubles hadn't hit home, yet; no wonder he

was so eager to represent a new tech find. "Wow," I said drily, "it sounds like a Broadway show. *Annie*, but without the dog."

He sighed impatiently. "It's not a perfect arrangement. But I couldn't leave her with Cindy. She was just too unstable. I couldn't risk her relapsing."

"But I thought you were so proud of her now?"

"Sure, of her work. Not her personal life. Her judgment—I heard she let vagrants sleep in her cellar, for Pete's sake."

So he knew about Fritz, or at least that someone was down there, sometimes. "Ivy seems quite devoted to you," I conceded, wishing the reverse were true, and also that we were inside the Moose, where it was warmer.

"Ivy's my daughter," he said. "I love her, and I didn't kill her mother—you've got to believe me."

I opened the shop's door, waving him in; it was a toss-up whether I died of the cold or of an acute caffeine deficiency.

"I do believe you," I said as he passed by me. About Ivy, I meant: that in his way, he loved his daughter and wanted the best for her.

Just not about much else.

Ten minutes later, I drummed up an excuse to go to the bank. We were out of change for the cash register, I said, leaving Lawson there with Ellie in charge of him.

Then I headed straight up to Lizzie Snow's office, and described recent events: Lawson and me getting clobbered, the hidden workroom at Cindy's, and the apparent theft of the thingamabob that the late electronics whiz had supposedly invented.

Lizzie leaned back in her office chair, her dark, wing-shaped left eyebrow lifted; over the couple of years she'd been in Eastport, she had learned to interpret my tone with pinpoint accuracy.

"So the alleged university mentor is dead, his letters are somewhere but currently unavailable for inspection—"

She got up and came out from behind her desk. Her lipstick was red and for dealing with evildoers today she wore black jeans, a forest-green turtleneck pullover with a black boiled-wool vest, unbuttoned, and black boots.

Plus her duty belt, of course, with the holster on it; her black leather jacket with her badge pinned to it hung behind the door.

"Have the state cops come up with anything?" I asked. She grabbed the jacket as we went out together.

"No," she said. "The homicide people are not coming up with anything." We crossed the blacktop parking lot to Water Street. "They really like Lawson for it, but there's no hard evidence." She looked at me. "I'm guessing Ivy's back home with him inside of a week, and that'll be that."

My watch read 11:45. My phone would start vibrating any second, now.

"And now this whole revolutionary invention curveball he threw at me," I said, "I don't even know what to make of it." Just the idea sounded ridiculous to me, now; only that it had come with a bonk on the head made me take it even halfway seriously.

Also, Lawson had gotten clobbered right along with me, too thoroughly to have done it to himself. By the old granite-block post office building on the corner, we waited for one of those refrigerated box trucks to make the turn, heading for the docks.

That's when I noticed Lizzie wasn't wearing her ring. "Cold feet again?" I asked. This would make the fourth time, or was it the fifth? She looked back sourly at me.

"I've gotten this far without being married. I don't see why I should have to—"

Instead of arguing with her, I tried another tack: "You don't have to."

The temperature had been dropping all morning; now the wind smelled like snow falling on salt water.

"But how about this?" I went on. "You two tie the knot, the

rest of us throw you a big party, we all have fun, and on Monday morning you can divorce him if you want to."

We crossed the street together, Lizzie thinking it over. Finally: "Huh. You know, you might have come up with something, there. That could actually—"

She no more meant to divorce Dylan Hudson than I meant to dump Wade. She just needed to be reminded that she could.

"I wish I could offer you more help with the Ivy business," she said, digging in her jacket pocket for the engagement ring and slipping it back on. The diamond Dylan had bought her looked as big as a duck's egg on her slim, red-tipped finger.

"Me, too," I agreed fervently. The Family Services folks would be getting off Route 1 right about now, heading for the causeway, Carrying Place Cove, and finally Eastport.

I wondered if they'd wait to question Ivy until she was in her new home or if they'd do it right away. In Lizzie's office, perhaps. I wondered, too, if I would get through Ivy's departure without punching anyone. That also remained to be seen.

Then Lizzie went on up the post office's granite steps, and I started back down Water Street to the Moose, where I found Ellie wrist deep in a double batch of chocolate brioche dough and Lawson gone.

Drat. He'd already told us he didn't see who hit him, but I still had questions. And since I didn't have any idea where he might've headed—to get his car, maybe?—I went back out and began walking toward Cindy's place.

In the fish pier parking lot, late-season tourists raised jacket collars and put up their parka hoods. On the benches by the mermaid statue, high school kids perched to eat lunch.

No Lawson, and after another block of peering wildly in all directions, I had to admit that he'd evaded me neatly. On the way back, I stopped in at Wadsworth's Hardware Store, whose window display featured rakes, leaf bags, bird food, black body suits printed with skeletons that glowed in the dark, and traps:

Havahart for raccoons and skunks, the original wire neck-breakers for mice and rats. Bella said a tiny shotgun would do just as well, but she was joking, I hoped.

I also thought I'd get my house key copied for Sam, who'd lost his for the third time in a few weeks just before they left for Portland—I joked he'd developed object dyslexia to go with the letters kind he'd always had—causing much outcry.

But mainly I went in meaning to invest in a few of the XXX-sized balsa-wood death machines and to ask if anyone had seen a guy like Lawson passing by the store's plateglass front window.

No one had. "Good luck with those," said the friendly clerk, handing me a small brown paper bag. I'd gotten the key copied and the death machines purchased and picked up another couple of those frog-shaped metal clickers like the one I'd given Ivy, from a box of them on the counter.

"Thanks." I pocketed my change and pulled open the door to the street.

"Watch out, though," he called after me jokingly. "You start settin' traps, you never know what you might catch."

Right, I thought glumly as the outdoor chill hit me again. I didn't know what—or who—I might catch, for the simple and sufficient reason that I still didn't know whodunnit in the Cindy Munson department. Now Lawson was AWOL, the Ivy transfer was imminent, and there was nothing I could do about any of it.

And then it hit me; the part about knowing, I mean.

Like I'd told Lizzie: I didn't have to.

Ten

"A trap," I said, pushing a dollop of chocolate chip cookie dough off the end of a teaspoon.

No Family Services people had arrived yet, Bella said when I called her. Now Ellie slid cookie sheets into the oven as fast as I could fill them with dollops.

"A trap," she repeated as she closed the oven door, "for who?"

"That," I said, as I scraped the last of the dough off the sides of the bowl, "is the beauty part."

I plopped the resulting Very Large Spoonful onto a tinfoil pie plate and stuck that into the oven, too.

"We say we know why Cindy and Fritzy died, and who killed them. We say we'll reveal the truth about their deaths at a small get-together we're arranging."

Ellie looked dubious. "But we don't know. And we don't know if anyone will even—"

"Show up?" I scrubbed my hands at the sink. "Oh, they'll show up. Macrae will be curious, he's worried about something—I can tell. And Karen Hamm will, because anything bad that happens to Lawson is catnip to her, even all these years later."

I called Bella again and asked her to bring Ivy down here. That left only my dad at home, and he never answered the door. Meanwhile, may I just say right here that I think Family Services people are the best? I know kids from awful circumstances who are alive now solely due to the child-welfare folks.

But this wasn't that, and I only meant to delay them for a little while. "Ellie's taking you and Ivy to the New Friendly restaurant for lunch," I told Bella, ignoring Ellie's gestures of protest.

The New Friendly was all the way over on the mainland; it was unlikely they'd be spotted there. "I'll only need an hour or so," I said when I'd hung up.

Ellie looked around at the projects she had going: those cookies, three loaves of chocolate swirl bread, and a bitter dark chocolate sauce for the venison roast we meant to make sometime during the upcoming deer-hunting season.

"Nothing here is going to go off the rails in that time," I said, and she agreed reluctantly, already putting the unbaked cookie dough into the cooler.

"How're you going to keep your 'little get-together' from getting mobbed, though?" she wanted to know. "If you publicly announce you're going to ID a murderer, won't everyone in town want to—?"

"No, they won't." I watched her scurry around collecting her things. "Because I'm only announcing it to people I think might've killed Cindy."

What I'd suddenly remembered was the old suspects-in-the-parlor trick, from the Agatha Christie novels Bella was so fond of. I'd have brought in Lawson's long-ago bullying victim, too, and the woman Karen Hamm said that Lawson had dated briefly before leaving Eastport for the second time.

But Karen hadn't known who the woman was, and as for the ant-bitten kid—

"Macrae told me the kid and his family moved to Bangor, and it turns out they're still there." The kid was a grown man now, of course, and not at the reunion, naturally. I'd called him on my cell phone on my way back from Wadsworth's.

"And?" Ellie turned off the heat under the chocolate sauce, took the bread out of the oven, and popped the loaves out of the pans to cool on a pair of wire racks.

"And he laughed," I said, recalling the lighthearted, not-a-bit-scarred-from-the-experience voice on the phone. "Said he barely remembered the incident, hadn't been back to Eastport since, and wasn't planning to visit anytime soon, either."

"So, like, not a suspect at all, then?" She spatulaed the last baked cookies off the last tray of them and shut the oven off.

"Not at all," I confirmed, filching one of the cookies—chocolate chip!—and biting in. Hey, snooping takes energy. "But we've still got plenty of them."

In the scenario I'd recalled, the sleuth—a charming French guy, a sweet old lady, a talking cat, you know the drill—either names the killer (who promptly grabs a hostage or fires a gun or tries to flee and is seized by the others) or tricks the killer into confessing.

Not that I had any idea how to trick anyone into anything, and I was still working on that part a few minutes later when Bella and Ivy arrived.

"Hi, honey!" Ellie smiled, crouching to greet the child.

"Hi," Ivy uttered flatly. She knew what was going on. Popping her thumb into her mouth—and how long since she'd done that? I wondered—she turned stonily away.

"Okay, just . . . keep her out of town for a while, okay?" I told Ellie. It was 11:55. "I'll call when you can come back."

"Hmph," said Bella, who was not a fan of impromptu outings. For this one, she'd pulled on a pair of blue stretch pants, black orthopedic shoes with tan pressure stockings rolled down over her ankles, and a red Christmas-themed sweatshirt, whose cartoon front depicted Grandma and the reindeer.

"You'll be fine," I assured her. She liked being out, just not going out, and Ivy might even enjoy it, or at least she'd like the french fries. But just minutes after they'd driven off down Water Street in Ellie's car, Bella and Ellie came back in looking worried.

"She jumped out at the corner of Washington Street," Ellie reported. "And that kid can really run."

Bella sank into one of the black cast-iron café chairs. "I am," she declared, "too old for this."

That's not what she says when she's badgering me to include her in something too risky or strenuous for her. But never mind.

"Which way did she go?" Half a mile from downtown Eastport and you could be in a forest or swamp where even a search party might not find you.

"Not sure." Ellie was still catching her breath, but she dragged her phone out anyway.

"Wait. Don't call Lizzie yet." I was trying to think fast, and you know how that always goes. "Why don't you go back and look for her again, first? I'll bet she's right near where you last saw her."

Ivy was a pretty brave kid, but being alone in a strange place was enough to give even me a few qualms. She'd wait for them to come back, I was betting.

Ellie nodded, putting her phone away; Bella got up. When they were gone, I got out my own phone, found Lawson's number, and punched it in.

He answered quickly, we spoke briefly. "Fifteen minutes," I said at the end, and hung up.

Then I called the others. Nobody argued much.

I told my invited guests to meet me in one of Brady's small, knotty-pine-paneled banquet rooms—Sam once said it was like eating in a casket—set off from the bar and dining area. I told them they'd be leaving their cell phones outside; I didn't need anybody texting anyone.

An accomplice, for instance—maybe someone I hadn't thought of. But there wasn't much I could do about that now, so I went across the street to set it all up with Bridget.

"Uh, sure," she said, seeming a little startled. I wasn't in the habit of throwing midday parties; *What's up?* her look asked curiously.

"I'm going to trap a rat," I said cheerfully—I really did have high hopes for this scheme of mine—then explained what I needed. Her eyes watched me speculatively as she listened, then agreed; I went off with the feeling that although this was short notice for her, it would be fine.

And at first it was. "So glad you could all be here," I said ten minutes later when everyone had arrived. In the small private side room I'd requested, two long tables stood end-to-end with chairs lined up on both sides. Coffee and tea were set up on a side table, and Bridget had said she'd be back to take drinks orders if anyone wanted one.

No one was smiling, which came as no surprise. Three of them had come because they wanted to know who'd killed Cindy and Fritzy, and one of them was here because he or she had.

I drank some of the ginger beer I'd gotten just before they arrived. The cold drink was spicy enough to scour your throat, pickle your sinuses, and make you feel that you were breathing actual fire, thus pumping up your courage.

"I know we'd all like to know who killed Cindy," I began, forgetting for the moment that I'd told each of them that I already did; stage fright, as Mika would've said, is a bitch. Maybe what I needed was more of that ginger beer, but how the heck did the sleuths in books pull this stuff off, anyway?

My mouth went on talking, apparently without reference to anything my brain might be experiencing or suggesting. "Trouble is, you all wanted her dead."

Lawson frowned, shaking his head tiredly at the notion. Karen

Hamm, her tanned, bony wrists full of bangles and bracelets and with her brassy hair sprayed into a seriously improbable-looking swirl, nodded firmly: *Correct, and I don't care who knows it.*

"I'm sorry?" Macrae drew back insulted, like someone had accused him of eating a greasy burger or something. "Just what are you suggesting? That we all got together and—?"

Beside him, young Polly Harper popped her gum irritably, twirling long strands of her dark hair in obvious boredom. None of this had anything to do with her, said her look of strained patience, and so why was she here, again?

But I wasn't so sure she had nothing to do with this. The way she'd looked at Macrae on the night of the reunion dinner had stuck with me. She was a long shot, but . . .

"So you didn't hate Cindy, huh?" I asked her. "And when you saw Mr. Macrae hanging out with her on the drone club field, that didn't make you jealous?"

Macrae tried looking surprised at this—yeah, right. "Must have been fun, though," I turned to him. "An adoring young student *and* a smart, attractive colleague—you thought of Cindy as a colleague, didn't you? Especially after she came up with her electronic whatever-it-is, some invention she was excited about?"

His brow furrowed. He was thinking so hard that you could almost smell the circuits overheating. "An invention? I've never heard about any invention of hers. Of what?"

It was a skillful deflection, but Polly was already writhing in the kind of embarrassment that only a teenaged girl can fully know, a mortified flush rising up out of her sweatshirt collar.

I turned away from her. "And you, Karen, after what you've told me, I can't help thinking you're a likely suspect, too."

"Hah!" Her bark of a laugh startled the others. "Wow, you figured that out, did you? Brilliant."

Her voice was like bourbon and ice cubes being run through a rock crusher. Her cigarettes lay before her on the table, but there was no smoking in Brady's.

"I despised them both, that's true. I've made," she added drily, "no secret of it." She tapped the pack on the table as if about to shake one out. "But if I had killed her," she went on, putting the pack down again and stretching her ring-studded hands out in front of her, "He'd be dead, too." Meaning Terry Lawson.

I got the strong sense that if she had killed Cindy, she'd have said so and been proud. But I couldn't think of a reason for her to want Max Fritz dead. I doubted, for instance, that she'd been out at Cindy's having arguments for him to overhear.

Her frank malevolence toward her long-ago romantic rival, though, was hard to ignore. She lit one of the forbidden smokes and looked around defiantly. "I think I'd like to go, now," she drawled.

The windows were all closed. Lawson coughed pointedly. Karen smiled to herself, taking another drag.

"Come on, Karen," Macrae needled, "don't you want to find out whodunnit?"

She blew smoke at him. "Nope. I don't care 'whodunnit,' as you put it. But thanks and congratulations to whoever it was, believe me."

She dropped the cigarette into what was left of her coffee. "But sure, I'll stick around. If that's what you want." Light from the closed windows glittered harshly on her rings and bracelets. "If you'll excuse me for a moment, though, I'll be at the bar. Heaven knows I need a real drink."

I turned to Macrae. He'd slid his chair away from Polly's firmly enough to send a message; she looked anywhere but at him.

"Cindy was smart," I said to Macrae. "I mean, really smart.

And you did know about this thing she'd come up with. You were the first one she told about it."

"That's not true," Macrae managed. From the far end of the table, Lawson listened the way I imagined he did to someone who had a product and a plan, and needed seed money.

"Or not the way you mean," Macrae added, shifting under Lawson's scrutiny. "We did talk about what she was working on," he admitted. "I helped her get in touch with the tech folks at the university. She got a mentor there."

Ah, yes, the conveniently dead mentor.

"And you didn't," I probed, "also develop a relationship with her? One in which you learned just how profitable this new whatever of hers could turn out to be?"

He caught my drift. "No, I did not develop any relationship with her." Beside him, Polly was trying on a series of indignant facial expressions, for his benefit, I guessed.

She was a good-looking young person; athletic, too, from the way she carried herself. Not tall enough for basketball, but soccer, maybe. She struck me as the kind of kid you'd want along on your camping trip, but I still didn't trust her. She was young and in love, and those things make you stupid—I ought to know.

"What you're suggesting is outrageous," Macrae said. "I had no relationship with her and next to no knowledge of anything in her life except the work she did for our club."

"As for you, Polly," he added, turning seriously to her. "I understand strong feelings, okay? But look, next year there'll be other students at school. And the year after that, and so on. And you'll be gone on into the rest of your whole wonderful life, where you'll forget all about me."

Okay, so maybe he was a good teacher, and he spoke to her very kindly. But the effect on Polly was merciless; her face went beet red, tears springing to her reddened eyes. I could see she just wanted to swirl directly down the nearest drain.

Silently I dug in my bag, thrust tissues across the table at her. She took them and blew, then got up, her chair scraping back with a sour screech.

"Can I go now?" she asked me imploringly, and I nodded; with a tragic glance back at Macrae, who looked as if he also wanted to vanish, she moved toward the door.

The rest sat silently. Waiting for what I might say or do next, I supposed; I'd hoped to provoke fireworks, but already this gathering of the mostly innocent had turned into a bust.

Polly opened the door, stepped out through it, then turned abruptly and came back in again. "Wait a minute," she said in tones of sudden suspicion, looking at us narrow eyed.

"You guys are going to talk about me now, aren't you?" she demanded.

Ah, the delightful center-of-the-universe delusions of youth, I'd nearly forgotten them. "If you guys are going to talk about me, I want to hear it," she said, plopping back into a chair with a defiant look on her face.

Of them all, though, I sympathized with her the most. The feelings she'd been expressing were real, I thought; about the others' I wasn't as convinced.

Outside, a bunch of seagulls started screaming about something. Probably some fish offal or bait scraps had fallen from one of the boats tied up in the boat basin a few hundred yards away, I had time to think, and the gulls were fighting over it. And then the strangest thing happened.

One pair after another, the shutters over the outsides of the windows began slamming shut—I could hear someone out there closing and latching them. Then Bridget swept in, ushering Karen Hamm ahead of her, moving wordlessly to lock the closed windows with a small key.

She'd had to replace all those windows the year before, I happened to know. They'd been so old and riddled with wood rot that they were practically falling out of their frames. Now they were made of security glass, impossible to break in through.

Or out. "What's going on?" I asked Bridget, but she didn't answer. Karen had a lowball glass of something brown in one hand and a lit cigarette between the red-tipped fingers of the other.

Polly rolled her eyes but got up and helped the older woman to a chair, where Karen sat looking around owlishly. It was not, I gathered, her first glass of the brown stuff.

"Here, now," Lawson demanded sternly of Bridget, who'd finished locking the last window. "What's all this?"

She stepped sideways, blocking him. Abruptly I remembered again what I'd been trying and failing to tell myself all along: that he could be innocent.

That someone else might've wanted Cindy Munson dead. "Hey, Bridget," I said, but she ignored me, too. Lawson got in front of her, put his hands on her shoulders to try talking to her.

She shrugged him off. "Bridget?" I tried again, and as if in reply she produced a small matte-black handgun from her apron pocket. Of course she had one behind the bar, who wouldn't? All alone here late at night, you never knew who might walk in.

I hadn't gone home for my own weapon, unfortunately: it was still locked up in my office with the equally useless camouflage jacket and black catsuit. For one thing, I might've run into the Family Services ladies, and for another, I'd known I could get help just by yelling for it out of one of these new windows.

That is, until she'd locked them.

"Bridget," Macrae tried coaxing her, "What's up?"

She looked at him. "Taxes. Lights, heat, water, license, insurance . . ."

And naturally our phones were all still outside the room in that basket on the bar's end; even Polly's, though she'd griped so hard that I thought we might have to remove it surgically.

"I've closed Brady's for the day, and I've got the awnings pulled down over the shutters," said Bridget.

The street sounds had vanished, along with the gulls' crying. In the silence, I could now hear a hissing noise, like air slowly escaping from an inner tube.

Or like a gas leak. The sound came from one of the heating grates in the floor. I crouched and sniffed: nothing, but the sound came from somewhere below me.

"Probably the cellar will have to fill up before you smell it," Bridget said.

"Are you crazy?" Macrae jumped up and leapt over the table at her, snatching for the gun. He was big and well-muscled, but he was also clumsy, and she was ready for him. The gun's barrel was at his temple in a heartbeat, whereupon he went still.

I got the sense this was a new experience for him, being overpowered; more than anything he looked surprised. Across the table, Polly huddled frightenedly beside a still befuddled Karen Hamm, who sipped mechanically at her drink while patting Polly's hand uselessly.

"It'll be okay," I told Polly, and she glanced over at me gratefully. I wished someone would say the same to me. Keeping the gun trained on Macrae, Bridget backed toward the door.

"Bridget, wait. Please." It nearly killed me, but I said it. "Just . . . tell me why you're doing this."

She paused, hand on doorknob. "You know who I am. You know what I came from. And you know, most of you"—she looked at the others, slowly around the table—"what I did to get here."

Taking Brady's/Bernie's over from her dad couldn't have been easy, especially while he was still alive and barking orders at her on how to do it. And a building on the water in Eastport is a money pit, there's no getting around it. Besides running the place, she'd taken any number of part-time jobs to finance its maintenance.

"We all know, Bridget," I agreed quietly.

She shrugged. "Now the property taxes are nearly due and so's the mortgage and the second mortgage. And my insurance just almost doubled."

Her steady hand on that gun kept me from jumping her. "I can't do it," she said. "It's not even close. So what the heck, now I'm going to let them take care of the whole thing."

"But Bridget, what's that got to do with—?" The way she held the gun said she knew how to use it, so I didn't rush her.

Karen Hamm reached for her lighter; I leaned across the table to snatch it. "Gas leak," I said, and Polly glanced around in sudden panic.

When I turned back, the door was closing behind Bridget. I heard the slide lock snick shut, and then a pair of floor bolts dropping.

Lawson and Macrae ran to the door, rattled the knob and put their shoulders to it; no dice. McRae aimed a mighty kick, then fell back clutching his knee, hopping on one foot; this was, it turned out, a steel door, not one of those cheap, hollow-core pieces of cr—I mean, junk.

"I smell gas," said Polly shakily, her eyes widening as she realized that none of the rest of us knew what to do, either.

"Don't!" I hurled myself bodily at Karen, who'd found another lighter somewhere. "Propane," I said, pointing at the floor grate.

Karen nodded ponderously. She was pie-eyed, way more under the influence than I'd realized.

"Okay," said Lawson, rubbing his hands together. "We'll pull the floor grate, one of us'll drop down there, find the shut-off valve."

The direct approach, how fearlessly efficient of him. "Oh,

just drop down there," I said. "Into a gas-filled cellar. In the dark, because God forbid you should flip a switch down there now even if you can find one."

You'd smother before you did anything, end of story.

He moved on smoothly. "Okay, how about those windows, then?"

Macrae was already investigating them. "Closed, latched, bolted, shutters, awnings," he reported. "You could get through with a chain saw, maybe. But otherwise, not so much."

The propane reek was joined by another smell: gasoline. A stream of the stuff had begun seeping in under the door. Bridget was hurrying things along, apparently. One way or another, all she needed now was a match.

Polly rested her head on her arms and sobbed into them. Macrae tugged uselessly at a window, and Lawson tried the door again, while Karen Hamm watched dourly, her heavy, dark eyelids at half-mast and her face sagging.

And oh, how I wished I didn't have to do what I was about to do next. But there was no help for it, no matter how I'd warned Lawson against it:

I got up and eased my way over to the floor grate, held down by four bolts. They wobbled loosely; I plucked them out.

Then I pulled the grate aside, took a final breath of relatively un-propaned air, and dropped down through the hole into the darkness.

The drop wasn't far; I landed on my feet. That was the last good thing for a while, though, because first, it was as dark as a tarpit down here, and second: it was really filling up with propane gas.

The hissing sound we'd all heard earlier was louder, now, and very nearby. I had maybe three minutes to do what could be done; after that I'd have to get back to the hole in the floor and suck in another breath.

I hoped. Also, pretty soon the air would be as bad up there

as it was down here. Reaching out blindly toward the hiss—no longer like air escaping from an inner tube, this was more like steam boiling from an exploded radiator—my hand found the cold propane fire-hosing out of an uncapped pipe and jerked away from it.

Cold, icy cold. I slapped my palm down onto the pipe's end anyway, but the pressure blasted my hand away—it was like trying to plug a geyser.

Above, Macrae and Lawson stomped around, trying whatever they could think of and, by the sound it, being disappointed. Polly shouted for help over and over, although if anyone could hear her cries through the locked, muffled windows, they'd have arrived already.

Just as I was about to give up and try finding my way back up there myself, a cool draft grazed my face. Smelling pungently of cold wet granite and salt water, it was a breathable draft, not propane gas.

Relieved, I turned blindly toward it, tripped over an old iron pipe in the dark, and tumbled face forward down some steps that had absolutely no reason for being there.

From above came a crash, and another; the captives I'd left up there were still trying to get out or at least get someone's attention, but with no result—

"You up there!" I shouted, "Come down, there's better—"

Air, I'd have finished, but just then glass shattered as a chair or a table above me broke a window at last. Instantly the air around me cleared almost completely, the gas now flowing away from me up to the freshly broken window like smoke rising up a chimney.

But I could pretty well guarantee that more gas was going up to the room above me than was going out that one broken pane; bottom line, I was better off, now, and they weren't.

I pushed myself up off what felt like a stone floor and felt gingerly around with my feet in the dark, leery of another sharp drop or a wall I could walk into. Carefully I put one foot forward, then the other, as the walls closed in gradually on either side of me. My breath came in anxious gasps as I inched along, not knowing where I was or if this way led out, and all around me everything was as cold as a refrigerator.

Then a deep, ominous rumble came from somewhere above me, and I froze, certain that the building was coming down on me. But then I realized: it was a car passing by on the street.

Above me. Then it hit me that this must be what Fritzy had been talking about, out at Cindy's place. And Hetty Bailey, too, with her grandfather's tales of smugglers' tunnels hacked from the granite bedrock under the street.

So maybe it wasn't just a cave some long-ago smuggler of Irish or Canadian whiskey had used for a transfer station, or a story with nothing behind it but a single deep-reaching crevice in the stone, a story that grew as it got passed on for generations.

Maybe it was real, and I was in it, and the thing about tunnels is that they go somewhere, or so I thought just moments before I walked straight into a wall.

The wall *moved,* soft fat bodies with prickly legs raining down onto my face, my neck, tumbling down my collar . . .

Well, I'm not going to describe what happened next—it's so horrid just thinking about it makes me writhe—but it involved a truly exceptional amount of hopping, swatting, shuddering, and hyperventilating.

And then there were the bites, whose sharp pain I ignored because hey, what could I do about it? Brushing the pincered, many-legged centipedes off my face and (I hoped) out of my collar, I did the sensible thing and backed off fast.

This turned out to be a wise move, as centipedes went on pouring from whatever crack they'd been packed into, the many little legs rustling, jaws clicking, filling the air with an insect stink.

But while I was retreating in horror, I noticed something else, too: A truck thundered overhead. Crumbs of moldy-smelling earth dusted down onto my face, tasting like salty gravel bits. After that came silence, but a *waiting* silence, as if everything and everyone had hit the pause button.

Then a long, low rumble began quietly, jacked up into a roar like the whole wide world was exploding, as Ivy would've put it, and ended in a concussive *boom!* that thumped my chest, boxed my ears, and knocked me down with a gut punch so hard it nearly took out my appendix.

The earth shivered and behind me a series of timbers and rafters collapsed one after the other with an agonized sound like a house being bulldozed over a cliff. Distant shouts, howling alarms, and the shrieking harmony of arriving sirens came from above.

The bell in the tower over the old granite-block post office building clanged, and the PA system at the Coast Guard station began putting out a hi-lo emergency honk that I'd never heard before. I sat down on the tunnel's damp stone floor and put my forehead on my knees.

I'd get out of here sooner or later, probably: the blast would've used up the propane, and a new gleam from behind me said the building's rear wall was now an ex-wall, right along with all the rest of them.

So maybe I could get out that way. But the others hadn't, and Ivy had lost both parents now, and that was all on me. My harebrained scheme had killed them—this had all been my own idea—so you'll have to forgive me if just for a moment, there, I didn't really care if I got out or not.

Because I'd killed them, really. Not deliberately, but . . . *I'll never stick my nose where it doesn't belong, ever again,* I resolved. Not that it changed anything. Not that it made them less dead. But then, you can't just sit there, can you? I mean you really can't. So—out of habit, mostly—I got up off the floor, blinking away thick dust stuck to my eyelashes and spitting it from between coated lips. My blast-scrambled wits said the outside was *that* way; dutifully, I trudged toward the same tiny bit of light I'd glimpsed just a few seconds earlier . . .

Wait a minute. The gleam was bigger. A lot bigger, and now a wave of warmth hit me. The building was on fire, what was left of it, anyway. I cast a final, regretful glance at what had been my exit route.

Then I looked in the other direction, into the darkness that led to I had no idea what, and that now was my only hope.

The leaping orange light blazing behind me faded as I moved down the dark low-ceilinged tunnel away from it, feeling my way along walls braced with what felt like massive timbers. But smoke drifted innocently in the air just as if it wouldn't choke me to death the very first chance it got.

The thought made my heart beat faster, and so did recalling that fires produce carbon monoxide. Hustling forward as quickly as I dared, my hands feeling blindly out in front of me, I only stopped when a stone or an old piece of lumber or something got in my way, sending me sprawling.

Okay, now, I told myself, tasting stone and very carefully not weeping with frustration—also with fear, guilt, spider-venom, and the whole miserable idea of ever getting up again to do anything, even to save my life.

Okay, now, you're going to take a minute. I nearly laughed: it looked to me as if all the remaining minutes in my life would be spent right here, underground. They'd bulldoze the ruins in spring, probably, before the tourists arrive, and that's when they'd find . . . *Stop that. Get up, dammit.*

And then: *chocolate.* Suddenly, the unmistakable smell, as penetrating as it was intoxicating, filled my head. Specifically, it was the smell of unsweetened chocolate melting with butter in a double boiler over a low flame.

Which meant it was coming from the Moose.

Suddenly I recalled the damp, low-ceilinged crawl space of our shop's basement. Other than when I checked the rat trap, that crawl space might as well not have existed, and probably that was true since the building was built.

So why did it? Exist, I mean. And that low corner had been hacked out of the granite wall using nineteenth-century tools and maybe a little dynamite here and there, so it wasn't an afterthought. Somebody had built it because they'd wanted it there.

Thinking this and sniffing hopefully at the chocolate aroma, I pushed myself to my feet. But as I got up something tickled my neck. It was a *familiar* tickle that sharpened to the tiniest of stinging sensations, then bloomed hotly into a burning coal igniting a grass fire.

Ants, I thought, clearly: the building's collapse had shaken a nest open probably, and by now, there were dozens of them on me, all thoroughly pissed off. A lit match flared behind my ear, another scorched my armpit, and a third lay a teeny-tiny red-hot branding iron on my forehead.

The worst one of all was wiggling in my pants' elastic waistband.

But it wasn't my first red-ant rodeo, so I knew the drill: I wrestled my shirt and pants off and shook them out vigorously, stomping around to kill any of the little monsters that might be preparing to swarm my ankles. Their stings were already itching like mad. By tonight, I'd be covered in cortisone cream, doped to the eyes with Benadryl, and antihistimine-sprayed until my nasal sinuses felt like they'd been hollowed out with little ice cream scoops.

But meanwhile, that tantalizing chocolate-and-butter smell grew even stronger, and now I heard music from somewhere, plus pots and pans clanging. But Ellie never clanged cookware; for one thing, this was vintage Revere Ware we're talking about, the old kind whose bottoms don't warp and whose handles don't fall off.

I felt my way around a gradual bend in the tunnel. A square of darkness outlined in light appeared ahead. After a moment my eyes translated it: a door.

Then a new smell hit me, not from the doorway ahead but sneaking up on me from behind: smoke again, and plenty of it.

Eleven

Above me, more fire trucks screamed. The fire wouldn't make it all the way up the tunnel, I was pretty sure; there was nothing in the tunnel to burn—except those big support beams . . .

Yeah, darn. And it could suck the air out of the tunnel, too. I pushed on the little door that had appeared in the darkness ahead of me. Wooden, and it didn't give, and probably no one could hear me shouting over the commotion outside.

The smoke thickened fast. I kicked the door, damaging only my toe. Maybe it was only my imagination, but it felt quite a lot warmer here, too, suddenly, despite what I'd thought about the fire not traveling far.

From behind me came a sudden scuffling sound, then a thump, a wetly unpleasant-sounding *crack!* and a cry of pain.

Whirling, I confronted a glaring flashlight beam; batting it away, I drew back to throw a punch before I saw the shape behind the flashlight. Holding the punch back, I watched the shape waver and fall with a weak, injured-sounding cry.

Faking distress is an oldie but goodie, and I wasn't buying it until I'd grabbed the flashlight and bent down to check out the mystery guest.

It was Polly Harper, and her trouble was real. The *crack!* had been her stumbling over the same scrap wood I'd tripped on and smacking her head against, I guessed, one of the tunnel's timber uprights, or possibly its granite wall.

Not so bad, then, maybe . . . but my breath caught in my throat when I spied the dark trickle of blood dribbling down her neck. Her eyes were open and she was trying to speak.

In the brightening orange light of the flames drawing nearer, making a sound like aluminum foil being crumpled—the tunnel's support timbers were ablaze, I realized—a long wooden sliver stuck daggerlike from the triangle of flesh between her neck and her shoulder.

The bleeding slowed, beginning to coagulate. Probably it had happened in the explosion. The splinter's end quivered faintly with the girl's pulse, which I most certainly did not like seeing.

"Did anyone else make it out?" I asked, trying not to let on how frightened I was for her. I'd heard enough medical stuff from my awful ex-husband, the brain surgeon, to know that a thing sticking into you might be plugging the hole, stopping blood from coming out of you, so don't pull on it.

Or let it fall out. Polly smiled weakly. I thought at first she wouldn't be able to speak. But finally: "Lawson did," she said. "That son of a bitch."

Orange light brightened ominously behind us again and the crackle of old, dry wood catching fire was like mocking laughter. Feeling around hurriedly in flickering murk, I found a hand size granite chunk and slammed it against the low wooden door I'd discovered.

The impact jolted up through my forearm, half dislocating my elbow before wrenching my shoulder and corkscrewing into my neck. But I'd rather get my shoulder broken than roasted, so I shook it off and readied myself for another whack.

Then: *Oh, the hell with it.* The only way through that door was to break it down; I'd have to find something bigger to hit it with. Something heavier . . .

But there wasn't anything heavier. I mean sure, there was one thing, but . . .

Above and behind me, what remained of the burning building groaned and popped, joists loosening and pilings leaning toward failure.

Ignoring this, I backed off from the little door about ten feet; any closer and I wouldn't have enough momentum, farther and I'd probably fall on my face before I hit the door.

"Polly, I'm breaking through. But don't worry, I'll be back for you right away."

Her eyes rolled—with skepticism, I hoped. But I was pretty sure she was losing consciousness, which was what I thought would be more pleasant right about now, too. Unfortunately, though, the heaviest thing available to hit that door with was me. So . . .

"Okay." I planted my feet, ducked down so as not to brain myself on the tunnel's low ceiling, and hurled myself forward, slamming my whole weight against that shoulder-high wooden door just as it opened.

The next thing I knew, I was leaning against the far wall of the Chocolate Moose's gloomy, gritty, wonderfully familiar old crawl space in the cellar with Ellie bent over me laughing and crying.

The rat trap lay snapped shut against the far wall of the crawl space. No rat was in it. "Ouch," I said, rubbing my temple. I really didn't think my head was going to take too many more of these hits to my frontal lobes.

"Polly," I managed, mouth sticky with dust and what little spit I had left.

Ellie found her own voice, spoke through tears. "I thought you were dead." I looked around, immensely pleased not to be.

"I was upstairs, I thought I heard something banging around down here, and—"

"Polly's back there." I waved at the dark little door that had hidden behind the heap of old bricks; I'd run full tilt into them, too. "In bad shape," I said.

Ellie pulled her phone from her pocket, then flung it down and ran up the cellar stairs. I heard the little bell over the shop door jingle as she went out.

"Ivy?" I asked when she got back moments later. "Where's Ivy?"

"EMTs are coming," Ellie said, "they were right outside."

Of course they were—a building had just exploded. "But what about—ouch."

I could sit up, move my arms, turn in all directions. But when I put weight on my foot, a bolt of hot anguish shot through my ankle.

"We need to get out of their way," she went on, taking my arm and putting it over her shoulders.

"—Ivy?" I asked again as she straightened: *yowtch.*

"Okay. You're doing great. Hang on. Almost there—"

We were not, I can assure you, almost there, nor was I doing anything even halfway approaching great. We were at the foot of the cellar steps is where we were, and there were eleven of them.

I, by contrast, had only one working foot, which meant I had to hop up those stairs, leaning on Ellie, until nearly the top. Then a large man in a yellow EMT vest reached down to haul us both the rest of the way up before charging down past us, and that whole process was a barrel of laughs, also.

At last, Ellie sat me down on one of the cast-iron café chairs at the front table. Our front bay window had survived, apparently due to a box truck that was parked out front when the blast occurred. The truck wasn't as lucky.

"But what about Ivy?" I finally burst out. Meanwhile someone had swapped my ankle joint for a red-hot coal; when more EMTs ran in and thudded downstairs, it was all I could do not to beg them for a morphine drip.

Not to mention a stiff drink, one of which Ellie brought me: that blackberry cordial again, and never more welcome.

"Ivy's at your house."

The smell of charred wood and gasoline seeped in around the front door; out in the bombed-looking street, dust clouds hung in the air, mixed with steam from the fire hoses.

"She ran straight there after she jumped out of our car."

"Huh"—I had to smile at that—"good sense of direction."

"Right. But that's not all. It seems the ladies from the Family Services Department had a little trouble getting over the causeway."

"What kind of trouble?" As long as you weren't speeding or driving on an expired sticker, getting through Pleasant Point and across the causeway was generally trouble free.

"Something about the car possibly being stolen."

"What?"

Just then the EMTs came up the stairs with Polly on a stretcher, silent and unmoving. A thick gauze pad taped to her neck hid the splinter embedded there. *Yet another casualty of my damn-fool stupid decisions*, I thought, as they hustled her out the door. Then: "Ellie, their car couldn't have been stolen."

Something else had intervened to keep the family services ladies from our door, and I had a sudden notion that I knew what.

Someone, rather. But it wasn't important right now. "Try that again," she said, gesturing at my ankle, so I put a little weight on it, and surprise, it didn't kill me. It felt like a small hungry rodent was in there, chewing steadily, but I could walk on it.

The phone behind the counter rang. "Chocolate Moose, how can we help you?" Ellie inquired pleasantly, but then her look changed to one of alarm.

"Yes. Yes, but—no. She's here, but—" Ellie brought me the handset. It was Bella, and when I'd calmed her enough to speak coherently, I learned that Bridget Brady had just been there.

She'd escaped her own arson fire as she'd intended, then gotten into her car, and driven to my house. There she'd snatched up Ivy, most likely while avoiding Fala's big sharp teeth by a hair's breadth, and sped off.

"Bella. Sit down," I said. "Ellie and I are on this, okay? We'll get her back."

"All right," Bella sniffed, sounding half-convinced. I wished I was. I got up to give the phone back to Ellie, but as I took a step, two more things happened: first, I found out that I'd been way too optimistic about that ankle. The rodent had sprouted teeth as big as Fala's, apparently, and was now biting off large chunks.

Then from outside came the huge, reverberating boom of something huge falling into the street. When the dust cleared enough to see through, what remained of the Brady Building was gone, and so, except for Bridget and possibly Polly, were two people I'd unwittingly lured to their deaths in it: Karen Hamm and Ian Macrae.

I took another step and the blinding white light I saw then was all pain, no enlightenment. But afterward, a calm, almost meditative feeling came over me.

A customer once left a wooden crutch in the shop. You'd be amazed at what people leave behind: I handed over a lady's forgotten prosthetic eye once, dropping it into her hand as if it were a hard-boiled egg. Anyway, Ellie found the crutch, and I leaned on it, with reasonable success.

Oh, no you don't, I thought, as we went out the Moose's front door—bell, jingle, et cetera. *You're not taking Ivy, I don't care what happens, you're just not.*

Dust covered everything outside: emergency vehicles *wheep-wheep*ing, smeary-faced guys in hard hats hauling hoses, and an ambulance backed up to a sheet-covered stretcher.

"Oh," said Ellie, but not at the stretcher. A large piece of building was in her car, having entered through its roof which was now almost entirely absent. Across the street, what little remained of the Brady Building smoked sullenly.

And have I mentioned that my ankle was still the equivalent of a handful of loose gravel? So maybe I could hobble, but no way could I drive the Fiat, parked unscathed right next to Ellie's thoroughly scathed vehicle.

But Ellie could. And there was a chance that Bridget might still be trying to get across the causeway, likely already jammed with first responder traffic and slowed by whatever that stolen-car business was all about.

The point was that Bridget had a head start, but not a big one. And the Fiat, for all its many quirks and annoyances, was a fast car.

A *really* fast car.

I was sitting in the Fiat's passenger seat, watching behind us as Ellie backed slowly out, when Polly Harper emerged from one of the other ambulances and started shakily toward us.

"Oh, now, that's just not possible." Ellie stopped the car and got out.

An older lady, gray-haired and wearing a spattered, rumpled white jacket over her street clothes, came out of the ambulance bay behind Polly, peering around briefly before spotting us.

"I said you're my mother," Polly uttered dully, her eyes glazed as she walked into Ellie's arms. The gray-haired woman reached us. The name tag on her white coat ended in MD.

"Which one of you's the mom?" she asked, looking at Ellie and me.

We both put our hands up. "I am," we said in unison, and the doc didn't turn a hair.

"Whatever. Okay, no concussion and the splinter missed the carotid, the jugular vein, *and* both innominate arteries, so your girl was fortunate." The doc looked kindly at Polly. "Take it easy for a day or so, come see me at the clinic for headaches, dizziness, nausea, vision troubles— "

"We'll take very good care of her," I said, putting an arm around Polly's shoulder, and for a wonder she allowed this.

"Okay," said the doc, her sharp, smart gaze lingering on me before she returned to the ambulance. I probably looked like I could use some medical attention, too.

But I didn't want any, or at least, not now. I beckoned Ellie out from behind the Fiat's steering wheel. "Get in," I told Polly, waving at the vacated driver's seat.

She looked at the car, at me, and at the car again. "You can drive, right?" I asked her. "You know how, and you're okay enough?"

The clock was ticking, Bridget and her small captive farther out of our reach with every minute that went by. If they got all the way to Route 1, we'd never catch them.

But I needed Ellie free to do things. I didn't know what things yet, but they would come up unexpectedly—they always did.

Polly nodded, biting her lip. "I know how to drive, yes. And I think I'm fine. I think I just fainted, actually."

She looked embarrassed about this. "Are you kidding?" I said. "You got out of there alive. That's amazing enough."

I wondered what Polly's real mother would say if she knew what was going on; probably nothing good. But I got the strong sense that Polly had very little adult supervision, and even if she did, I didn't have time to worry or explain. I waved toward the car again.

"Drive," I said.

It turned out she'd learned how to drive in San Francisco, where she and her parents had lived until she moved here, she told me as we drove up Washington Street. The driving school she'd attended sent her up and down steep streets, into parking spaces, starting uphill from a complete stop, and so on.

Then she told me that the driving school was her father. I congratulated him silently. She certainly had no trouble with the Fiat's stick shift. "Stay under the speed limit. We can't get pulled over," I said.

Not that she could speed up much more if she'd wanted to. Route 190 past the bank and the IGA were bumper to bumper; by now, word had gotten out that something was going on downtown, and people wanted to see what it was.

We got stopped completely as we rounded the curve by the firehouse. Polly eyed the shoulder: narrow, but there was room to get the Fiat around the line of unmoving cars ahead of us.

"You scuff this car's paint, I'll shave your head," I told her, only half joking, and in reply she hit the gas. A rooster tail of gravel spurted behind us, the tires dug in, and a hair-raising fifteen seconds later we passed the traffic culprit, a guy in an ancient Ford pickup truck, stopped for a left turn.

Polly swung back up onto the pavement and stomped on the gas, causing the guy to glance up startledly and the Fiat's engine to growl in high-RPM pleasure.

I looked over at her as she shifted smoothly again. "You didn't learn that in driving school."

She scanned the road ahead. "No. My dad was a professional driver, actually. Pete Wanamaker?" The name was familiar. "They got divorced, I ended up here with my mom." Her tone discouraged more questions. The traffic thinned out as we passed the old blanket factory and the turnoff to Quoddy Village.

"So what are you going to do if we catch up to them?" she asked finally.

We reached Perry Corners and the intersection with Route 1. There'd been no sign of Bridget so far. "I don't know," I said. "But I'll know when we find her."

"Turn left," Ellie spoke up from the backseat. "She'll stick to the smaller roads. Less chance some speed trap cop sees her go by."

True, even though by now every cop in the county was in Eastport. "Keep trying Lizzie, will you?" I said. Meanwhile, Polly followed Ellie's instruction, and soon it was all trees, all the time, on both sides of the road.

"You can pick up your speed a little out here," I said, and before the words were even out of my mouth something slammed me hard, pressing me back into the car's bucket seat. The car positively *sailed* toward Route 214, which was the shortcut to Route 9.

Polly leaned her head back onto the bucket seat's headrest, driving easily and well. And *fast* . . .

"So when you said your dad drove professionally—"

"Yeah. Race cars." She didn't take her eyes off the road, so curvy and swervy it could've been a piece of ribbon candy. "He drove the Indy 500 a few times, actually."

So that's how I'd heard of him. Ahead, a few small houses and shops appeared; then came a combination gas station and convenience store. As we approached, the mingled smells of car exhaust and unfreshened deep-fat-fryer oil perfumed the air.

But no cars were there. Next, we idled along past the concrete-block electric substation and the lumber mill, where forty-foot raw logs got turned into two-by-fours.

Somewhere nearby, a big circular saw snarled through fresh lumber. The smell was of pine needles, machine oil, and sawdust. The road curved away between a row of old maples whose yellow leaves twirled slowly down onto the blacktop.

Polly glanced over questioningly. Bridget could be miles away from us by now, and I didn't even know for sure that we were going the right direction.

I wondered what Ivy was thinking, if she was scared. The Fiat grumbled, carburetors rumbling.

So now what? Polly's expression asked.

On the other hand, if we *were* on the right track—

"Hit it," I said.

* * *

The girl jammed her foot to the floor, and we rocketed ahead. Sure enough, in the middle distance ahead of us another car soon appeared, speeding away.

"Hang back," I said. "But try to keep them in sight."

Which she did, but then the car ahead pulled over onto the gravel shoulder and stopped as if waiting for us.

"1985 Chevy Monte Carlo," she said. "That was the first year they came in maroon, and if it was much later it wouldn't have that little spoiler on the rear, see?"

"Oh," I said, suddenly doubtful. A muscle car seemed like a strange thing for Bridget to be driving right now. Or at all, actually. Polly pulled the Fiat alongside, just as the other car's rear window slid down.

"*Ooh, chickie-chickie-chickie—*"

Yeah, not Bridget. In the car were four high school kids, all boys. The one behind the wheel—I couldn't make out his face—waited until Polly had driven on past the Monte, then accelerated hard. And the Monte Carlo is not a wimpy automobile, power-wise.

Half a mile later the Fiat was screaming, the RPM needle pegged, but I swear there is no one, no one in the world more sure of his own immortality than the average teenage boy. The Fiat's speedometer read 90, now, and a lot more curves were coming up.

"Hey, you guys?" Ellie said faintly, from the rear seat.

"Uh-huh," Polly pronounced as very slowly we began pulling away from the Monte. But I could still hear the other car's engine howling as it strained to catch up, which now it was doing again, its front grill like bared teeth in the rearview mirror.

"I'm calling Lizzie," said Ellie, pulling out her phone, then hit her speed dial, waited, hung up and tried again.

"No bars," she reported finally, which meant we were so far

out in the Downeast Maine boondocks that we couldn't even get a cell connection.

Around us, the afternoon faded toward evening, the shadows turning the blueberry fields to the dark red color of old blood. The car behind us lurched forward, nudged our bumper tauntingly, veered out around us and fell back.

Hoots and cackles of young male laughter came from the Monte. Probably they were perfectly nice kids when they weren't all together in a car late at night with, maybe, a few beers inside them.

Meanwhile a bumper nudge is enough to bend the frame of a 1974 Fiat Sport Spider, and if I found one single flake of the car's apricot paint missing, I'd—

The other car pulled alongside us. "Screw this," Polly uttered, and yanked the steering wheel. The other driver swerved away, then swung back at us.

"Now he'll try to push us into the ditch," I predicted.

He did. I could make out the grin spread across the face of the little heathen in the backseat as the Monte pulled ahead, then veered sharply at us again.

This time I saw enough of the driver's face to recognize it. "Tommy?" It was the kid who'd visited Polly in the school kitchen on the night of the reunion dinner, the one who'd offered to drive her home and been turned down.

Polly let off the gas—fall back or get creamed was the deal now. The Monte veered harder, and then suddenly a bang like a firecracker smacked my eardrum.

"Are they shooting?" Ellie scanned around for bullet holes, but there weren't any; no blood was around anywhere, either, and the Monte had dropped back abruptly.

"I don't think so." Now the Monte had pulled over. The boys piled out. Smoke boiled from beneath the hood. Slowing, Polly glanced back at them in the rearview mirror.

"Bet they threw a rod," she said. "Or blew a head gasket."

Behind us the car and the boys gathered around it receded in the distance. "Right up ahead is your turnoff," I told Polly.

The shadows of big old trees lay in thick bars across the blacktop, orange late-afternoon sunlight glaring between them, *flashflashflash*. We got to the little forty-stone cemetery that marked the turnoff, the small two-hundred-year-old marble tablets still gallantly semi-upright, leaning this way and that.

Polly took the turn without slowing. The car purred along happily, just as if it hadn't very recently been revved to within millimeters of its life. Still no Bridget, though, and I hoped hard I hadn't guessed wrong about her likely route.

Then: *thunk-thunk-thunk-thunk*. "What's that?" I sat up straight, which was a mistake—I'd forgotten my ankle. It hadn't forgotten about me, though, and the yell I let out could've woken the dead in the little cemetery.

"A stick got caught under the frame, then it flipped itself out of there," said Polly.

A small groan may have escaped me. Wordlessly, Ellie dug in her bag and came up with a familiar-looking capped half-pint mason jar. The liquid in the jar looked familiar.

"Is this—?" I uncapped the jar and took a slug of the contents, and it turned out that blackberry cordial is just what you want when you've dropped a big building on your ankle. "Oh, thank you," I breathed after swallowing another dose. X-rays and surgery might loom in my future—the ankle felt way more than sprained—but for now at least I'd be too pie-eyed to worry about it.

I handed the jar back. At the top of the hill we'd just crested stood a cluster of radio towers; to their left, a long slope led into the far distance where the land met the bay. In the opposite direction, mile-high Mount Katahdin shimmered like a mirage in the fading sky.

Starting down the long, steep hill here on Route 214 reminded me that the Fiat's brakes weren't supersturdy: the car was made to go, not stop. Polly applied them, downshifted, then downshifted again.

We slowed considerably. Just not enough; it was a very steep hill. "Polly," I said, gripping the center console for dear life with one hand and the doorframe with the other.

"Yeah, yeah." She touched the brakes briefly again. "I hear you." She shifted down a third time; the resulting jolt flung me forward and nearly stalled us, but not quite. Instead, by the time we reached the stop sign at the bottom of the hill, we were barely crawling.

I pushed myself up straight in the Fiat's bucket seat once more, using just one leg this time—the blackberry cordial was good, but not that good. Crammed in behind me, Ellie tried to straighten her own legs, but with limited success.

Polly sat quietly with her hands on the steering wheel, biting her lip. "Nice driving," I said, and she managed a smile.

Sort of. A small spot of blood stained the gauze square still taped to her neck. "That thing okay?" I gestured at it.

I figured she didn't need to know her wannabe boyfriend Tommy was behind the wheel of that other car; right now, we all had more important things to think about.

"Yeah," she said, touching the gauze gingerly. Around us, the shadows of old trees deepened in the near-dusk. "Now what?"

I blew a breath out. "Beats me."

"I got nothing," Ellie agreed from the backseat.

A car went by, headed in the opposite direction. Taillights vanished over the hill. "Maybe we should go back," I said.

After all, hadn't I already done enough? Gotten people killed and a building destroyed *and* made sure that Ivy would go into foster care, the complete opposite of everything I wanted—

"We'll go back to Eastport and get Lizzie up to date on everything that's happened," I said, looking out the passenger-side window into the oncoming evening. The shadows between the trees were darkening to black, the few streetlights out here blinking hazily on. "And then we'll let the proper authorities take care of Ivy," I finished.

Like they'd taken care of me all those years ago, I added silently. Or not—it was the uncertainty that was killing me. I raised a hand, let it fall, wanting to hit something.

Wanting to turn back the clock and reverse all my stupid choices, dangerously unworkable plans, and risky—"Polly, take us back to town, now, okay?"

But Polly wasn't listening, frowning into the Fiat's rearview mirror as a car approached from behind us, coming down the hill at us pretty fast. I had time to blink before it sped around us and through the intersection.

It was Bridget's duct-taped old rattletrap Studebaker, which despite its age apparently still had a few good miles left on it. A small, white face peered frighteningly out the rear window as the car sped away.

Twelve

We shot out of the intersection behind the fast-shrinking taillights. Almost at once the road narrowed to a hilly, twisty ribbon of blacktop, crumbling at the edges and just wide enough for two cars: no shoulder, deep ditch, plenty of humps and ruts.

"We can catch up on Route 9," I said, although what we'd do then I had no idea. Right now, we were bouncing and rattling over a stretch of back road so broken and bumpy I thought parts might start falling off the Fiat as we pounded through long-unrepaired potholes.

Then suddenly the Studebaker appeared ahead of us, pulled over onto the shoulder. Polly slowed alongside: no lights, no sound, no sign of anyone.

Just the engine ticking as it cooled. Polly parked, and we got out, Ellie pulling the crutch from between the Fiat's bucket seats and handing it to me.

Crutch or no crutch, I wouldn't be chasing anyone anytime soon, but on the other hand, maybe I wouldn't need to. Two of the car's doors hung open: the driver's and the rear passenger-side. A scenario occurred to me—I lived with small children, you'll remember—and then, as if to confirm my suspicion, Bridget's angry voice came from back in the brush and trees, away from the road.

"Ivy! Ivy, you get back here, you— "

"Sounds like Bridget's day hasn't improved," I said, as a fresh pang of fear for the little girl pierced me. Having to go was a problem out here after dark; before you pulled your clothing back into place you had to make sure no centipedes, deer ticks, or tree slugs had moved into it.

As for the chance of a bear or a night-hunting coyote, I didn't even want to think about it. "Ivy!" Bridget's voice moved away; with any luck she'd get lost out there herself.

Ivy could be lost already. Any way I turned, the trees looked the same, each as toweringly tall, silent, and menacing-looking as the last. Between them grew clumped birch saplings, wild rhododendron, ferns as tall as a man . . . A dozen feet from the road you could turn around twice and become so disoriented, you'd never find your way out.

Thinking this, I leaned on my crutch and shoved my free hand disconsolately into my jacket pocket.

"Drat," said Ellie, frowning into the woods. Every so often a stray gleam of light showed back there, probably a flashlight. But between us and it lay an obstacle course of fallen branches, bramble thorns, and old cellar holes, neck-breakingly deep, with old lilac bushes still growing in front of them.

The fingers in my pocket closed around something strange-feeling. Small, round—I pressed on it: *Ribbit!*

It was the small frog-shaped clicker whose twin I'd given Ivy, keeping one for myself. Holding it, I hobbled to the road's edge, gave the crutch a shove away from me, and sat down hard on the gravel shoulder.

The plum-size gravel was sharp and pointy, and sliding down into the ditch was a treat, too, as was the climb-and-grab up the other side. Sharp-edged grasses, stabby thorns, wrist-thick vines twining like massive snakes around tree trunks the size of dump trucks . . .

Forget any decent-looking fingernails I might have been cultivating; they were long gone. But I got to the top of the ditch's other side, and there I clicked the clicker again.

Ribbit! Ribbit-ribbit! Then I waited while my ankle boomed anguish, quick-timed like my heartbeat. From the piney darkness came rustlings and scufflings, made, I hoped, by Ellie and Polly.

But nothing else, until . . . *ribbit!* Ivy's clicker was smaller and quieter than mine, coming from somewhere to my left.

Just once. Then silence. *Good girl*, I thought. Maybe she was sneaking back, first wanting to see who was clickering at her before she showed herself.

Come on, kiddo, I urged her silently, waiting.

Then, "*Ssst.*" The sound came from behind a blackberry thicket. I nodded, beckoning with both hands, and she came out, glancing around huntedly before running to me.

"Does she still have the gun? Do you know?" I hurried Ivy to the Fiat, helped her in. The child nodded, hunkering as far down into the Fiat's vestigial backseat as she could get.

"Uh-huh." Tears streamed down her face, but she was holding it together. "She pointed it at me."

By now it was full dark, and a bright white light from a boat dealership's display lot on Route 9 glowed over the trees. The lot held rows of mostly recreational boats, I recalled, plus an office and a repair shed.

Bridget's voice came from over that way, now, too, hoarse from shouting. *Yeah, yell your head off*, I thought grimly as I lowered myself gingerly in behind the Fiat's steering wheel.

I'd already resigned myself to driving with my left foot; this meant getting my bashed right ankle out of the way, a task I won't describe because it has so many swear words in it. But after a harrowing hour or two, it was done, and I looked into the rearview mirror.

"You okay?"

Ivy nodded. Her short, straight dark hair was matted and filthy, her puffy eyes red with tears, and a bruise was purpling on her right wrist where Bridget must have dragged her. But she was alert, and she didn't appear to be getting ready to upchuck or anything.

"Ivy!" Bridget's voice came from farther away as I pulled out onto the pavement. The boatyard was maybe two miles away but it sounded as if Bridget had made it at least half that distance already. And if I knew Ellie, she'd be right behind our fleeing culprit.

"Okay, now, very shortly, we're going to be stopping," I told Ivy, "and when we do, I want you to stay right here in the car, okay?"

The boatyard was a perfect place for Bridget and Lawson to meet up and scram out of here together: right on Route 9, the only fast route out of Washington County, and also very near the direct route from Eastport to Route 9.

Of course I didn't *know* they were there, or that Ellie and Polly were on the murderous pair's track, too, and would arrive there soon if they hadn't already.

But if Bridget and Lawson were joining forces somewhere to skedaddle out of town together, the boatyard was a good place to do it: lit up, but shielded from the road by the rows and rows of boats. And after all, Bridget had been heading in the boatyard's direction.

"Okay?" I repeated. Ivy nodded, her small face a pale white mask with two big ocean-green eyes peering at me from it.

"Okay," she whispered.

Moments later we reached Route 9, the fastest route from here to Bangor and the interstate beyond. Traffic was thin, just a few cars headed home late from day shifts or in early for the evening ones. I slotted myself into the west-driving flow for a minute or so, then swung into the boatyard's lit-up driveway.

Not only did I think Lawson and Bridget might be here, but Ellie knew me well enough to know I would think so. That meant she and Polly might show up here, too, any minute, even; their route here through the woods was way shorter than mine via the road.

Bright-white yard lights still blazed over the tarp-wrapped vessels trailered in rows, their bows raised on concrete blocks so the bilge water would flow out the scuppers.

"You stay," I cautioned Ivy again. Then I opened the car door, pushed the crutch out of the car, maneuvered my bad leg down off the Fiat's console, hoisted myself out, and crutched my way to the lot's edge where the lights didn't reach.

And where I did not fall down, though it was close. Dry weeds whispered in the darkness beyond the yard lights. To the west, the sun had dropped completely behind the hills, blue dusk deepening to night as the bright orb sank out of sight.

In the sudden gloom, the dozens of shiny-white-plastic-wrapped boats looked unnatural, like bloated mummies. In the silence, broken only by the hum of the distant cars, the shadows under the trailers seemed to hunker slyly.

Soft crunching on gravel sounded behind me. I whirled on the crutch as well as I could. No one . . . but the sound came again, nearer. Backing away as fast as the crutch allowed, I reached the nearest boat and dropped fast to get under it, out of sight.

Then I watched with held breath as a pair of shoes walked by the boat I crouched beneath. They were men's shoes: good tan leather, solid stitching, thick sole, plenty of tread.

Shoes I'd seen before. Lawson's.

Ivy's head popped up over the weeds growing in the gloom

at the lot's edge, because of course she'd gotten out of the car; kids always get out of the car.

"Ivy!" I whispered as loudly as I dared. But she didn't see me. *Stay there*, I thought urgently at her. If he saw her . . .

Also, by now, I was feeling a sensation that upon unhappy closer examination turned out to be agony. A huge swelling, easily the size of a grapefruit, had formed not in my ankle as I'd thought at first but in the long bone just above.

A small piece of something stuck up from the swollen place, I saw now. A bone-colored piece of *Yeah, we're not going to look at that anymore.*

Briskly I pulled my pants leg back down, scanning around for something to splint the stupid leg with, and spotted an old, clapped-out broom, its bristles curved from standing on them for a long, long time.

Pushing with my good leg and dragging myself forward with my hands—and may I just say right here that next time anyone suggests I do anything remotely resembling this activity, I'll punch them?—I reached the broom and wrapped my hands around the old wooden broomstick.

Then I shoved the broomstick handle-end-first straight down the inside of my pants leg—which right there should've earned me a gymnastics medal and possibly also a purple heart—to jam the handle end firmly into my shoe.

I'd seen a guy do this once on a boat after a line snapped and nearly took off his leg. I tied my shoelaces and some torn-lengthwise towels that I found hanging from one of the trailer struts around the splint: knee, midcalf, and under the shoe.

Getting up was tricky, to put it mildly. On the plus side, now at least the ankle didn't flop around, and I didn't hear any footsteps anymore, either.

So, I thought, as I turned to squint at the lot's weedy edge again, maybe things were looking up.

Or maybe not. Ivy's face still peered whitely at me through the dry vegetation. Irritation flicked at me—*Dammit, I told you*—before I realized: kid or no kid, she'd never have left the car in the first place without a good reason.

Or in this case maybe a bad one.

Ivy straightened and started toward me. I put a hand up: *Stop*. Her eyes widened but she did it, hustling back into her weedy hiding place.

I waved emphatically for her to stay there, caught sight of her obedient nod, and let my breath out. Crisis averted; now I just had to find Ellie and Polly, and vamoose with all three of them—Ellie, Polly, Ivy—immediately.

If they were here. A breeze rattled the plastic wrappings on the boats as I hobbled toward the Fiat. I'd drive the car farther out toward the road, I decided, then touch the horn. At the sound, Ellie and Polly would scurry out and hop in. We'd grab Ivy out of the weeds on our way, and presto! A daring escape . . .

But when I got to the car, I discovered that the plan didn't account for the broomstick in my shoe. It worked pretty well as a combination splint and crutch, but in the foot department it was like a steel rod shoved through my instep.

But screw it, I'd have to try. My hand had just grabbed the Fiat's door handle when the sound of a speeding car and the glare of headlights came from out on the road.

The car sped on past the boatyard driveway, braked with a shriek of scorched rubber, and spun around wildly into oncoming traffic. Brake lights flared, horns blared, and indistinct curses rang out distantly as the car caught traction, swung in at the boatyard, and came at me, steam billowing from its hood.

It was the car full of boys we'd left gut-busted in the road, earlier, including Polly's would-be suitor, young Tommy. "There she is!" a young male voice yelled. "Get her!"

They were just a bunch of teenagers: despite their extreme rowdiness, I wasn't afraid of them, exactly. But I knew from raising Sam that they could be unpredictable, especially in groups. So I tried the only thing that ever worked for me when dealing with my own once-wayward boy: complete honesty.

The other car skidded to a stop behind the Fiat. I stick-walked around to the driver's-side window. A perfectly pleasant, ordinary young male face—Tommy's, I saw immediately. transformed for the evening by a mask of gleeful adolescent wickedness—grinned up at me.

"Please," I said. "We need help. Can you call the cops?"

His smooth young brow furrowed. This wasn't in the script. "A little girl," I said. "She's out there—"

A groan came from under the hood of the kid's vehicle, along with a final billow of steam. Then the engine quit running with a suddenness that seemed very ominous, indeed.

"Can you," I asked the kid, "drive stick?"

The Fiat's standard transmission, I meant, and he could, I saw it in his eyes. But would he?

"Polly's here somewhere, too," I added, and that did the trick.

He got out of the car, unfolding his long, lanky form from behind the wheel while eyeing the Fiat narrowly. "What's that—like, an old Mazda?" Behind us the other boys laughed and catcalled.

"Almost," I told him, opening the driver's-side door. In the yard lights' white glare I could see he was wearing a polo shirt with a fast food joint's work badge pinned to the pocket: TOMMY.

"Get in, Tommy." He did, settling into the bucket seat and glancing doubtfully at me. "As you may already have noticed, I'm wounded in action, and I can't drive. So start it," I said.

The key was in the ignition. He put the clutch in, turned the key to the right, and gave it a little gas; the carburetor coughed and puffed black smoke out the tailpipe.

"Don't rev it in neutral, it's touchy about that," I said, once the engine was running smoothly again. I limped around to the passenger side and hauled myself in without screaming, or anyway not out loud. Buoyed by this triumph, I slammed the car door and tried not to hear my leg pieces crunching up against one another.

"Okay," I said. "Out the main driveway." My earlier plan could still work: find Ellie, Polly, and Ivy, grab them, and get the heck out of here.

Tommy let the clutch out slowly; the Fiat crept ahead. Behind us the other boys had tumbled out of their car and stood watching; the laughing and jeering had stopped.

"You think they'll stay with the car?" I said, angling my head back at the gut-busted Monte.

"I told them to wait for me. Whether they do or not"—Tommy's shoulders moved—"we'll see."

The wicked expression was gone from his face, replaced by one of intense concentration. He wasn't as confident on a stick shift as I'd hoped, but he didn't stall it or accidentally shift into reverse while moving forward.

We pulled up in front of the boatyard's Quonset-hut-style office. "Now just creep along very slowly," I said.

The graveled aisles between the rows of boats were wide enough to drive on; I squinted left and right as we prowled up and down them. Ellie and Polly had to be here somewhere by now, and with any luck Ivy was still where I'd stashed her.

Trouble was, Bridget and Lawson were almost surely still here, too, and the car crunching on gravel sounded like a giant crushing boulders in its fists. I peered past a rudder, behind an outboard engine, under a parked trailer . . .

"You're sure they didn't take off already?" I could hear Tommy starting to wonder if I was just some crazy lady babbling on about nothing, when out of the blue, something big hit the Fiat's cloth top and came through it with a sound like a wet sheet ripping.

When the sound stopped and I'd brought my arms down from in front of my face, a pair of small feet wearing red P.F. Flyers was kicking helplessly between Tommy's head and mine.

"Stuck! I'm stuck!" cried a voice from above us.

Ivy's voice. She must have climbed up onto one of the boats and jumped down when she saw the Fiat passing below. I grabbed the little legs with the bright red shoes at the ends of them and yanked her down the rest of the way into the passenger compartment.

"Ssh!" I hissed, pulling her onto my lap. I could see Tommy reassessing this whole situation, i.e., even crazier than he thought. Then Ivy shifted her weight and a bolt of lightning shot through my leg like someone had amputated it with a blowtorch.

I shrieked, Ivy jumped, and Tommy reached for the car's door handle, having sensibly decided it was time to get out of whatever this was. But first he looked at me, and I saw a thought replace the fear on his face; instead of leaving, he dug in his pants pocket and came up with two white tablets, shaggy with pocket lint.

He held them out to me; I hesitated. "Are those what I think they are?" When Ellie's husband, George, fell off a roof, he'd had pills like these for the pain, afterward.

The boy nodded, looking slightly embarrassed. "Finest kind. Outta my mom's stash."

He didn't seem at all like the kind of kid whose mom would have a stash, and I wondered too what sort of pain he'd been planning on medicating, but while I wondered I swallowed them dry.

"Thanks," I said, wincing at the aspiriny bitterness. "But let's get going again. Two women, keep your eyes peeled."

The leg now felt like a nuclear meltdown, and Ivy's elbow

kept punching me in the stomach when she moved. But my partners in crime were here somewhere, and we had to find them so that we could get out of here, ideally all still alive.

I peered out the window again, squinting into the shadows until Tommy braked too suddenly and the Fiat stalled. Twenty feet ahead of us Bridget Brady stood holding a gun out in front of her, steadying it with both hands.

"Come on, Jake, no one's going to hurt Ivy. Just send her over here, you don't want to be part of this."

She had that last thing right. The only thing I wanted to be part of right now was orthopedic surgery, especially the anesthesia. Meanwhile, Bridget held that gun like she knew how.

But the kid sitting beside me didn't know any of that, and his experience with guns was likely of the first-person-shooter-variety, where all the blood was made of pixels.

"Tommy," I said cautioningly. He'd started the car again and his face had a mulish look I remembered from Sam's teens. "Tommy, I really don't think you want to—"

Tommy popped the clutch and hit the gas and the Fiat sprang forward, snarling. Bridget's eyes widened; still aiming the gun at us she stepped back fast, slammed into the white-shrouded, jutting end of a boat trailer, and stumbled sideways.

The gun flew one way, she scrambled the other, out of the way of the oncoming Fiat. The front bumper missed her head by a few inches but pinned her blond braid to the office hut's front wall, right next to the door.

Tommy turned to me in the silence that followed. "Now what?"

"Now," I began, reaching for the passenger-side door handle. It moved just fine, but the door didn't, unfortunately. Hitting the building had bent something important. Sighing, I reached up through the haze of fresh agony that hitting the Quonset had also set off and unsnapped the convertible top's latches.

Catching on, Tommy half-stood and pushed the torn top back

down over the trunk. "Good," I said. "Now you take Ivy and run out to the road, flag someone down, and get them to call 911."

Ivy poked her head up from the car. "No," she began.

I put my face down near hers and looked into those stubborn sea-green eyes of hers. "Ivy," I said, "this is happening. No argument. You're going with Tommy so we can all get out of the mess and go home. Got it?"

It was the other thing I'd used to excellent effect on Sam: *I said it, I meant it, I'm here to represent it.*

She nodded, lips trembling, and reached up to let the boy hoist her out of the vehicle. Once they were gone, Bridget and I were going to have a little conversation. But then another voice spoke, one I'd been expecting.

Not in a good way. "Ivy," its owner said quietly. "Come to Daddy."

She was sitting on Tommy's hip. You could see it wasn't the first kid he'd carried that way—he had younger siblings, I'd have bet. I hoped he'd get to see them again.

Nothing from Bridget; maybe hitting the Quonset had knocked her out. "Come on, Ivy," Lawson coaxed, sounding about as safe and reliable as thin ice.

But Ivy just shook her head, her look the bullheaded one I was coming to recognize. "No," she whispered sadly.

His face hardened. "Ivy," he said, "if you don't come with me, I'll have to do something I don't want to do."

He'd found Bridget's gun. Now he turned it toward me. Ivy looked questioningly at me. I shook my head: *don't do it.*

"Last chance." Lawson took a step closer to me.

Like he needed one. From where he stood, he could've hit me over the head with the weapon.

"You killed her so you could steal her intellectual property," I said.

He looked impatient.

I went on: "You were convinced her innovation was real,

that it was worth big bucks, but she wouldn't take what you offered."

Lawson's eyes narrowed.

"So you found another way," I said. "For it to work, all you had to do was keep custody of Ivy—and kill Cindy."

Tommy, who had been listening carefully, spoke up. "Ivy inherits, but her dad manages her money?"

"You," I told him without turning, "have potential."

Lawson's face said I was right. It also said he was about to pull the trigger, just to shut me up. "Ivy," he said without taking his eyes off me. "Three . . . two . . ." His finger tightened.

"Go," I snapped, shoving Tommy sideways and diving hard after him. The gun's report *smacked!* against the Quonset's steel wall and bounced back, nearly deafening me.

Scrambling on my stomach toward the nearest boat-trailer combo that I could crawl under, I squinted around for Tommy and Ivy but didn't see them. What I did see was a pair of tan leather sneakers slowly strolling across the gravel toward me.

The shoes stopped. "All right, come on out of there."

I didn't. I was all out of options but nuts to him, anyway; let him drag me out. "Or I could just start firing bullets, and when your friends come running to help you, I'll get them, too," he added, the thought seeming to cheer him.

"Bite me," I said, but I began crawling grudgingly forward. I'd never have predicted that at the hour of my own death I'd be so thoroughly ticked off.

"Bastard," I muttered, dragging myself from under the trailer. Lawson stood braced with his feet planted in the gravel and his arms raised in the firing position, gripping the gun.

He'd had lessons, I guessed, probably in some fancy midtown Manhattan shooting club. Still, I was pretty sure that human targets hadn't been in the instructions.

Not lowering the weapon, he jerked his head sharply at Ivy, huddled with Tommy. "Move!" he barked. "Or I'll shoot her!"

Ivy climbed to her feet. Her face was flat, like maybe her nervous system was deciding to check itself out of all this; behind us, Bridget was waking up, snarling words so profane that even I hadn't heard some of them.

"I'm really very sorry I got you into this," I told Tommy sincerely. He looked peevishly resigned, as if he'd always known his life would end stupidly and by chance, and now here it was.

"Not as sorry as I am," he replied.

"I regret all this, too, Jake," said Lawson, while behind us a still-trapped Bridget twisted and swore. "I feel as if under other circumstances, we might've been friends."

"Yeah, me too," I replied, and then I slid that damned broomstick up out of my pants leg, whipped it around in the instant that it took him to look confused, and stabbed him in the eye with it.

With a yell of pain he staggered back, left hand clapped over his wounded eye while the gun waved in the other hand.

Tommy grabbed Ivy, hopped into the Fiat, started it, and wrenched it into reverse, then popped the clutch. Ivy screamed as the car shot backward, spinning chunks of gravel at Lawson who staggered under the onslaught, shielding his face.

But then he caught his balance, straightened, and aimed at us again. Tommy spun the wheel, let the clutch out—

Thunk. The car stalled, "*Damn it,*" uttered urgently, twisting the key, but the engine was flooded and the starter motor spun uselessly—and anyway, it was too late.

Lawson's face looming over me was a bloody mess of pain and fury. The gun barrel's end hovered inches from my face, and there was no question in my mind, now, that he was going to shoot me.

"You bastard," I said. I always had thought I'd be scared in this moment, but screw him. Just screw him, that's all. Words bubbled out of me, hot as fresh blood. "You bastard, she's just a little girl!" Then: "Run," I told Tommy. "Take her."

Lawson was distracted by another gush of blood from his injured eye socket.

But Tommy wouldn't go. "Get in," he urged me from the car, "you can—" Tommy grabbed Ivy and elbowed the car door open. Sensing movement, Lawson swung the gun toward them.

Whereupon, the hell with this sappy final moments stuff; I drew the broomstick back, readying for another stab, just as he swung back toward me again . . .

The ear-smacking *bang!* of a handgun at close range knocked me ass-over-teakettle, as Bella would've put it, and suddenly life went silent. I turned to find Tommy in the Fiat, but he was gone, and so was Ivy.

Tommy was a good kid, I thought confusedly, despite those pills he'd cadged from his mom's supply of them. Then I realized that I'd been shot in the head.

But I wasn't dead. Confused, I looked around. Maybe I was already a ghost? A person lay sprawled on the gravel nearby—not me, I noted, relieved. Well, I mean all but the top of his head, which was absent.

Then Bridget Brady, released when Tommy backed the Fiat away from the Quonset hut, staggered over to Lawson's body and picked up the gun lying by his hand.

"That'll learn ya," she said quietly to him, then put another bullet into him—I heard the gun fire, but just barely—and started toward me.

Out at the road, brake lights were flashing and vehicles were pulling over to the side; Tommy must've started flagging down cars, I thought distantly. Next, the touch of a gun barrel's cool metal end on my cheek told me that I was history.

But then the funniest thing happened: A dark red dot of light appeared suddenly in the middle of Bridget's forehead. Her face sagged, her eyes rolling up and her mouth falling open. Her hands dropped limply to her sides as she sank to her knees, then fell over, and after a few terrible moments, stopped moving.

There'd been no gunshot. I just sat there feeling brain-scrambled, not knowing what had happened or what to do, alone in a silence as big as the sky. Cars started coming up the driveway, lights flashing. Sirens, too, I supposed. I still didn't know where Polly or Ellie were. Maybe they were dead.

And maybe this was all my fault. Where, exactly, had I gotten the nerve to concern myself with anyone else's child? What business had any of it been of mine?

And screwing it all up royally, besides, I thought miserably, which is when without warning a body dropped out of the sky and landed on the gravel in front of me.

"Oof!" said the body, landing lightly on its feet. It was Ellie, and she looked to be all right.

So naturally I burst into tears. "Ugh!" Polly landed next to Ellie and straightened springily.

Just what I needed, the Walking Wallendas. Those pills of Tommy's seemed to be working, though, or anyway I could breathe without tongues of flame licking at my ankle.

Two cop cars pulled up and stopped. A state trooper with his duty weapon in hand got out of one of them.

"Don't shoot!" I yelled. "They're— "

The trooper scuttled over and ascertained that we were (a) living people and (b) not the bad guys, and that the only hazard Terry Lawson and Bridget Brady posed now was a tripping hazard.

The cop in the second car was Lizzie, looking so furious I thought she might burst into flames.

"What the hell?" she grated out at me, jumping from the car. "I mean, just what the actual— " She looked haggard. "Bella called. She couldn't reach you. Then I heard about this—this—dammit, Jake."

I told her about the three teenaged boys probably still around here somewhere, and she went off to tell the other cops not to shoot them. Then some ambulance people showed up, and unfortunately, Tommy's mom's pills didn't work very well for that.

Dylan Hudson got out of Lizzie's car and came to stand beside me while they lifted me into the ambulance's brightly lit stretcher bay. Then they were hanging an IV, applying EKG stickers and wires, and sliding a truly enormous needle into the vein in my left arm.

"Everyone's okay?" I asked him. My lips were beginning to feel thick.

He nodded. "Tommy's down by the road, puking into a ditch. I called his folks to come and get him and the others. All shook up, but they're fine." A funny smile touched his lips. "I don't think Tommy ever wants to drive a car again, though."

Whatever the EMTs were running into me through that IV had just slammed headfirst into Tommy's mom's pills: va-voom.

"Ivy's fine, too," said Dylan. "Lizzie and I will take her back to your place when she's done here."

A sharp metal clamp that was tightening around my heart let go suddenly. "But . . . Deanna? The Family Services team was on its way, they were taking Ivy to— "

"That's all on hold," he interrupted. "There's a lot to sort out, so the family court froze everything in its tracks until there's more info. No one's going anywhere for now."

Then the EMTs shooed Dylan away and closed the bay doors, and the next thing I knew I was lying on my back in a curtained emergency room treatment cubicle, feeling a lot of distant poking and prodding and hearing my heart on the cardiac monitor.

Faces ballooned and went away, sensors and alarms peeped and jangled. Something cold sluiced my leg, an X-ray machine rumbled in, and somebody said, "Wow."

Then I was watching the ceiling go by as I rolled down a

long linoleum-floored corridor, and in the following several days more things happened, many of them involving needles.

I found myself looking forward to plastic trays of instant potatoes, canned corn, and Swiss steak simmered in gravy poured cold out of gallon-sized containers, and I'd have killed for a shot of that blackberry cordial or a cup of real coffee.

They did, however, fix my ankle and force me through enough physical therapy so that I could use it again.

And after that, they did something that I liked even better: They let me out.

Thirteen

The wedding of Elizabeth Agnes Snow and Dylan Thomas Hudson took place on a chilly October morning of sleet and drizzle enlivened by blustery wind gusts that nearly blew the blushing bride off the scenic cliff edge where the service was held.

"Oh!" cried Bella, grabbing for her hat, a lavender wool number with a bright magenta rose knitted onto the brim. With it she wore a green quilted parka, thick wool gloves, and boots that would've been perfect for a stroll up Mount Katahdin.

By contrast, Lizzie perched majestically atop lipstick-red Manny Ciarcia stilettoes; in a red satin sheath, a faux ermine stole, and a red pillbox hat with a delicate red lace veil, she looked like a 1940s movie star in a *Vogue* photo shoot.

Finally, the guy who was doing the big deed arrived with the book from which he would read the vows. So there we all were looking out over Passamaquoddy Bay, south to rain-smeared Lubec, or across the wide expanse of choppy, grey-blue water to the island of Campobello.

"Do you, Elizabeth . . ." I was the matron of honor and Ellie was best woman; she stood by Dylan, whose pale, nervous face said she might soon be holding him upright.

Gathering himself, he mopped his forehead with his inside handkerchief and stuffed it away, smiling fixedly with the look of a man who is silently repeating, *I'm doing this, goddammit.*

Lizzie looked as if she was grudgingly allowing a blood sample to be taken, and could they please get it over with? Together they reminded me of that painting where the farmer and his wife stand grimly on either side of a pitchfork.

"I do," said Lizzie, sounding as if she was agreeing to be executed. She kept peeking over the cliff's edge as if comparing the merits of staying here vs. landing down there.

"You may now kiss . . ." the justice of the peace began, and that's when a gust of wind snatched Lizzie's new red hat off her head and spun it away from her.

"Hey!" she said, startled, straining on tiptoe to grab for it, and then just as her hand closed on it one of those red four-inch heels snapped like a matchstick. I saw the heel fly, bright as a blood drop, and her ankle bend sideways, her body unbalanced and too near the precipice to catch herself.

There was a moment when everyone froze, horrified. Then Dylan's hand shot out, seized Lizzie's flailing wrist, and yanked her back into his arms, wrapping them tightly around her and burying his face in her hair.

"Oh, no you don't," he said, loud enough for the rest of us to hear. "You're sticking with me."

Whereupon we all applauded; Lizzie stood still. Then she giggled and kicked off both shoes, flexing her feet in relief.

"Yes," she smiled his Dylan's face. "Yes, I am."

Then she kissed him, flinging the red hat away over the cliff where a breeze caught it and sent it sailing out across the water. When she let him go, we cheered again, and he stepped back with a look on his face that said *zowie!* and also, could he sit down, now, because his knees were going weak?

Luckily for him, the next item on the wedding-day agenda was a party with cake and champagne.

So that's where we went.

"What do you mean, simple?" the grating, gravelly voice demanded to know. "I fail to see how any of it could possibly be described as—"

Amazingly, Karen Hamm and Ian Macrae had survived gas fumes, the explosion, the fire, and the building's collapse, and had been dug out from under the only unburned beam in the Brady Building two hours later.

Now we all sat in a corner of the parlor in my big old house on Key Street while the wedding reception whirled around us. From the corner of my eye, I saw Lizzie nudge Dylan sharply at some comment he'd made, whereupon he whirled her around and kissed her again just as thoroughly as she'd kissed him earlier.

She did not, I was relieved to note, object. "It's true," I turned back to Karen, "that a lot happened."

I sat with my plaster-casted ankle stuck straight out in front of me. It burned, it itched, it crawled on its belly like a reptile. But it would be fine eventually, the doctors said.

"But everything was in service of one very specific long-term goal," I told Karen. "Cash, and lots of it."

Karen rolled her heavy-lidded, kohl-rimmed eyes, as if to say this news didn't surprise her. She wasn't smoking, just twiddling her cigarette holder between crimson-tipped arthritic fingers; I'd asked her why, and she said she'd spent three hours under a burning building and never wanted to smell smoke again in her life.

Now: "I still don't understand what the piece of hardware Cindy devised was supposed to do," I said. Something about electrons, something about metal—beyond that it was Greek to me. "But I know she and her university professor mentor thought it might be worth money," I said.

A lot of money. In an unlabeled file folder in Cindy's electronics repair shop, the police had found printed-out emails from the physics professor; his enthusiasm told me why Cindy had high hopes for the possibility, high enough to think she could support her daughter, finally, and give her a good life.

"We might never know if Cindy really wanted custody or if Lawson made that up," I said. "But she was doing well enough now that if she'd tried, I think she might've won. Too bad her invention didn't really perform the way they hoped," I added.

The state cops had sent it to the FBI, who'd sent it to a lab at NASA. The verdict: close, but no cigar. The thing worked, all right, just not for very long. After a while, the teeny-tiny wires did what all wires do when you run too much current through them for too long: they melted.

In the dining room, Bella served cake with the heirloom cake server, our only good piece of real silver.

"See, Terry was broke," I told Karen. Now that there'd been time to dig more deeply into Terry Lawson's situation, the district attorney's investigators had learned a lot. "I mean, really broke. Desperate."

The house staff he'd mentioned were getting paid out of the proceeds from second-mortgaging the house, which itself was in first-mortgage arrears. So, he needed something.

And Cindy had something. He knew because she'd told him about it, hoping for his help. "But he wasn't here to make a deal," I said.

He'd never meant to use the fifty grand he'd hidden behind the Motel East. That was just for show, a backup story, so that he could say that's what it was for if things went badly.

As they had. "He wanted it to look like he meant to pay her fair and square for rights to investigate her device, but he'd already decided on killing her."

He had to have been, first to sound out Bridget Brady on the idea and then to fine-tune the plan. Karen tipped her head cannily. "So Ivy inherits everything from her mother, and he's got Ivy, so he gets—?"

"Control of it," I said, and she nodded sagely, fumbling for a cigarette before she remembered.

Across the parlor my father held court from a bentwood wheelchair, high-backed and rattan-woven, handmade for him by a friend at the Senior Center. The polished wood gleamed in the afternoon light fading from the windows; Ivy sat leaning against one of his wheels with her arm around Fala the enormous furry German shepherd.

"Hey," said Dylan, coming up behind me. "How's it going?" He waved at my ankle; I tried to look brave. Somehow, in front of Dylan, I always wanted to.

"Yeah," he said, unfooled, and then I remembered his shoulder, which had been shot with a large caliber bullet at some time in his active-cop past and was now held together with enough wire to string a fence.

"Anyway, I wanted to tell you something I just found out."

I blinked; this was not his usual M.O.

"In Lawson's motel room," he began, and I started to feel uneasy.

He saw it. "No, no, I'm not lowering any boom on you. This is my wedding day, remember. So I'm giving you a little gift." His eyes were merry with mischief and something else. "You remember the hair?"

The one in Lawson's motel-room sink. But I hadn't told anyone about it, just left it for the crime techs.

That meant Dylan must've found it, too. That he'd been—

"It belonged to the last person who stayed there," said Dylan. "Lab sent the report back."

A small, persistent worry vanished: not only had the techs found it, but it was meaningless.

"Oh, thank you," I breathed, and he turned that smile on me.

"Always watchin' out for you, kid." He raised his glass at me and strolled away while I marveled at the number of friends and acquaintances that had come to the party; the whole town knew the happy couple, and knew how well Bella Diamond could cook for a crowd.

Even Polly Harper had come, perhaps because she knew Ian Macrae wouldn't. Once he recovered from his injuries, he'd taken a "sabbatical" to, as he'd put it in his letter to the school board, "re-evaluate his life choices."

"I came to say goodbye," Polly said when she'd spotted me and crossed the room. Her long brown hair hung straight and shiny; her face looked healthy and scrubbed. "The divorce is off and I'm going back to California with my mom." Shrugging shyly, she added, "For a while there we weren't speaking, her and me, but we've made up, sort of. And it turns out Tommy Wentworth is going to San Diego."

I was happy for her, and even happier that she hadn't bled out in a tunnel under Water Street.

Then someone touched my elbow, and when I turned it was my husband, Wade Sorenson, home at last from his voyage half-way up into the North Atlantic; he'd been delayed for a week.

"Hi. Sorry I'm late." Broad at the shoulder, narrow at the waist, face like a chunk of granite, with pale blue eyes (or gray, depending on the season)—well, I pretty much just fell off my crutch and right into his arms.

"Oh," I said. He smelled like fresh air and the lanolin hand cream that keeps skin from drying and cracking right down to the meat when people are out on the water.

Around us the room lit up suddenly with a last shaft of low sunlight. I stood letting it wash over me: *All's right with the world.*

Then his gaze found the trays and platters of food ranged out on the dining room table. Ellie and I had offered to cater this affair, but Bella had insisted and done a real Downeast Maine traditional celebration spread, complete with sheet cake, little

Wonder Bread sandwiches with the crusts cut off filled with—oh, never mind, I'll tell you about it later—and the pièce de résistance, a large cut-glass punch bowl of iced ginger ale with a melting half-gallon of Neapolitan ice cream foaming prettily in it.

Although not perhaps completely traditional: "Hey," he said, pausing his attack on the lobster-stuffed tomatoes, when he glimpsed my casted leg. "What's with the plaster?"

"Things got a little strenuous around here," I said.

Then Deanna Wright, the blond Family Services lady came over to me carrying a glass of champagne.

She handed it to me. "Here, you look like you could use this." Her spun-glass hair in the sunlight looked wheat-colored, her lipstick was Rip-Roaring Red Riot or something similar, and her smile was wide and sympathetic.

And genuine. I had to laugh; Deanna called 'em like she saw 'em, and was becoming a friend. "Am I really that bad?"

I don't know how, but she'd gotten the family court to approve Ivy's staying with us indefinitely. Now she eyed me up and down. "Honey," she told me, "I hate to say it, but you're a mile of bad road."

Yeah, the day had been hectic. I knocked the champagne back, dragged the back of my hand roughly over my lips to make Deanna laugh, and went upstairs to take her advice: hot facecloth, comb hair, general neatening—and when I got back down again, Lizzie and Dylan were preparing to leave.

She looked happy, tired, terrified: she'd done it. She'd actually gone and done it. At the door I put my arms around her. She smelled like buttercream frosting and Muguet des Bois.

"Married," she said faintly, glancing around with a hunted expression. Her dark eyes were panicky.

"Hey, look at it this way," I said, "now you'll never have to testify against him in court."

Silently, she pulled the white faux-ermine stole around herself. But she was laughing on the inside; I knew from the way her lips twitched.

And since this was exactly the talent she would need in order to be married to Dylan Hudson at all—tall, dark, oh-so-infuriating—as I watched them go off together into the long shadows, I thought she would be all right.

Later, when all the dishes had been washed and we'd made a picnic supper out of the leftover wedding feast, Sam announced that it was story time and all the children were invited.

Ivy turned to look questioningly at me. "Go on," I smiled, and she trooped out behind Sam along with Nadine and Ephraim, Fala trotting up the stairs behind her.

"I hope you don't mind," I told Wade when she'd gone. "She might be here a while." *Forever,* my heart beat out certainly.

Wade's lips pursed. "Funny, I was already thinking that," he said, and then began surrounding another smoked turkey sandwich.

I looked around the big old kitchen with the high, bare windows and beadboard wainscoting: the sink gleaming white, the hardwood floor freshly swept, and the appliances all polished to a high shine. Bella had at last given up heavy housekeeping but still claimed the kitchen as her domain; that's why it was clean enough to perform brain surgery in.

I switched off the light over the sink. Following me into the quiet parlor, Wade sank into his old leather easy chair with a sigh.

"I still don't get what Bridget's role in all this was," he said, when I'd finished bringing him up to date on recent events. "Why was she ever involved at all?"

That's what I'd wondered, too, until I realized: Lawson could've done all the rest of it alone. But somebody had to get Ivy out of the car so that she wouldn't have a ringside seat.

And so that she wouldn't be able to testify. I had a feeling that reason was more important to him than any possible injury to Ivy's psyche might have been.

"Lawson and Bridget had dated briefly in high school, and if he remembered right, she'd had money problems then the way he did now." Bridget was the girl he'd dated between Karen and Cindy, of course, and no one remembered her because by then she'd dropped out of school to work in her dad's bar."

Wade nodded, listening. "So he got in touch with her and heard her ongoing tales of woe," I said, "and finally he put it to her: would she help him?"

A thought struck him. "It was Bridget who sneaked in ahead of you and Lawson at Cindy's house, wasn't it?"

"Yup." No one could have beaten themselves up as badly as Lawson had been. But they needed him to look innocent in every way possible, and getting clobbered by a mysterious someone helped him to look like another of the victims.

Hitting him must've been satisfying for her, considering the number of times she'd done it. He had, after all, dumped her in favor of Cindy back in high school. She'd taken Cindy's gadget with her when she left, too.

And of course he'd gotten a key to Cindy's house from Bridget. She'd had one so she could put Jax inside if Cindy wasn't there.

"So bottom line, she lured Ivy away long enough for Lawson to follow Cindy out there and kill her?" asked Wade.

"Right. After that, all he had to do was say that he'd found her there dead."

"Lured her how?" Wade asked, opening his eyes.

That had been my question, too. She wouldn't have been eager to wander around in the dark. Then I heard Fala upstairs barking happily; the kids were playing with her, I guessed, instead of brushing their teeth and hopping into pajamas.

"A puppy," I said, recalling Bridget's pup, Jax. She'd still had him when Cindy died, and he'd been the sweetest little thing. "I can't think of anything likelier to attract Ivy than that little dog."

Wade got up and went to the kitchen, returning with a couple of snifters of Jameson's. "And when she heard her dad calling, she came back to the car?" he asked.

I shook my head. This was the part I didn't like thinking about. "Not exactly," I said. Ivy had tugged me aside to confide in me just before we left the house for Lizzie's wedding.

I guess she'd finally felt safe about telling me her troubles. Now I felt like I was walking around with an invisible badge of honor pinned to my chest.

"Lawson signaled Bridget with a flashlight when the deed was done. Ivy saw the light, that's how I know. Then Bridget sent Ivy back to the car, told her not to tell anyone else but her dad that she'd ever left it."

"And Ivy obeyed because?" Boat life was strenuous. But his eyes, under their bushy, blond eyebrows were lit with interest.

"Bridget said Lawson would get in trouble if Ivy didn't." I drank, savoring the whiskey's smoky flavor, like burning peat moss. "Then when she did get back to the car, she found her dad in the act of 'discovering' Cindy's body," I finished.

"Ah." Wade leaned back in his chair, swirling the whiskey in the snifter. "So now she thinks if she'd only obeyed her dad in the first place, her mom might not be— "

The look on her face when she'd said this had just about killed me. I finished the whiskey. "You got it. It turns out Lawson picked quite a few winners in the brand-new tech gadget field. But then he hit a losing streak."

"One of my old New York pals had called back with an update. Lawson had been lucky for a long time, but if he didn't come up with another new tech find real soon, now, he'd be out on his *pâté de foie gras.*

"The thing is, it worked for her." The gadget, I meant. She'd kept clear notes on her experiments, and I'd needed them translated out of High Scientese, but I doubted she'd faked them. "But not for anybody else," I finished. "Whatever the secret is, she kept it to herself."

"And now she's taken it to her grave." Wade regarded the amber liquid in his glass.

"Seems so." But I still wasn't sure. I kept thinking about Ivy's birth certificate, lost between tax records and insurance papers in Cindy's files.

Unless it wasn't lost. Unless Cindy, a clean, well-organized person now that her head was on straight, had put it there on purpose, as a (you should excuse the expression) clue.

In case a person cared to pursue it, that is, and I did, just as soon as I got back on my feet. I had no idea why Cindy might think Ivy's birth certificate would be some kind of a clue—maybe just the out-of-place-ness of it in such an otherwise well-organized setting.

Maybe some other reason, one I might even have a chance of finding out. But at this point, all I knew was that just possibly, Cindy hadn't taken her secret to the grave.

The secret, I mean, not just of how to make her whatever-it-is work at all, but to make it work properly. So that it wouldn't burn out. A secret ingredient, you might say.

Maybe Lawson even suspected she'd left out something crucial in what she wrote down, just to guard against guys like him. It could be what he'd been looking for the day he nearly caught us at her house. And then there was the blue sea-glass earring I'd lost, so carefully placed in a leaf that didn't grow there for me to find again. A leaf like an envelope, the way you'd send . . . a message? But from who, and about what?

I drained the last drops out of my glass. It would be a while before I was in good enough shape again to find out. But maybe Ivy could still end up a wealthy child, a girl who could finance her own future.

The fire blazed up a final time as Wade finished his drink, got up, and put a hand out to me. "So what about that ankle, anyway?" he asked. "What's going on with that?"

My answer was informative but profane.

"Well, winter's coming, you'll have plenty of time for rehab," he replied.

Great, I thought grumpily as the fire fell to embers with a feathery *whush*. From outside, the streetlamp's yellow glow smeared and spangled in the rain-streaked window.

Wade's voice turned serious. "Dylan said somebody got into the house while I was gone." The night when Fala woke me, he meant—with all that had happened, I'd nearly forgotten until this afternoon.

But Dylan Hudson hadn't, and he'd mentioned it to Wade, who surely wouldn't. "Oh. Well, that's a little embarrassing," I said. Although not for me exactly.

"You have to promise not to tell anyone. I know who it was—I just found out a little while ago."

His eyebrows went up but he promised. "It was Wally Bean," I said, "from across the street."

At this Wade looked as surprised as I'd felt when Wally came up to me looking guilty as hell while the wedding party was breaking up. He'd crashed the party specifically to talk to me, it turned out. He said he hoped I wouldn't be too mad.

"Seems Wally got a little confused, coming home the other night," I told Wade.

Comprehension lit Wade's eyes. "I'd given him a key. But that was—"

"A long time ago," I agreed. "To return the fly-fishing rod you lent him so he wouldn't have to leave it out on the porch, because we were all away at the time. Yes, he told me."

Even in Eastport, you didn't just leave an expensive fly rod on the porch. "But it's not about the fly rod," I said. "He didn't even have the rod with him."

It turned out that Ellie had been right. "Wally walked home from Brady's that night like he always did," I said, "sauced to the gills."

He hadn't put it quite that way, of course, but we'd both

known what he meant. "But when he got here, he got a little confused as to left versus right."

Our two houses looked nearly identical, especially at night, and Wade knew it, so he caught on right away. "Came up the steps," I said, "put a key in the lock, the key worked, and he walked right in, thinking it was his own house."

The layout inside was similar, too. But not identical. "When Fala and I found him trying to climb into one of my file cabinets, he thought he was getting into his own bed."

"Huh." Wade made a "what can you do?" face. Wally might not be the soberest fellow on the planet, but he was our neighbor and not a loud late-night music guy, a motorcycle mechanic, or a keeper of dawn-crowing roosters, and that counted for a lot.

"Doesn't explain the scratches on the back kitchen door lock," said Wade. Dylan had given him a full report, apparently.

"Yeah," I said unhappily. "It doesn't."

But just then Sam stuck his head in on his way downstairs to the kitchen. "Hey," he said, pausing, and I thought he must have overheard us.

He looked like he had when he was six and had stolen a cookie. "About that scratched lock," he said.

The penny dropped. "You forgot your house key again, didn't you? You came home late without it, didn't want to wake up the whole house . . ."

Sam glanced up embarrassedly. "Yeah."

"So you tried picking the lock?"

"Uh, yeah, that too," he admitted. "Sorry." He glanced at Wade, but Wade was busy trying not to laugh. Sam was a genius on big things like cars and washing machines, but on delicate items it was like his hands were hams.

Until now. My son, the housebreaker. I unbit my tongue. "What did you use? And did you get in?"

A flicker of triumph lit his face. "Uh. A nutpick and a thin strip of tin. And yeah, I did get in, actually."

"Great." I was not going to ask him why he'd had a nutpick handy. Instead, I waved him away. At least now I knew who should inherit those burglar tools I had tucked away up in the closet.

When Sam had gone on to fix himself another smoked turkey sandwich, Wade lifted me and deposited me into the big recliner with my pillow and blankets. I hadn't yet been able to climb the stairs to bed. The pain pill I'd taken earlier and the Jameson's I'd drunk were doing a quiet little dance in my head, which was okay by me.

Wade pulled something from his pocket. "Ellie brought this. You're to ring it if you need anything during the night."

It was the little silver bell that hung over the door at the Chocolate Moose. He set it on the side table with my mug, my phone, a clock, my book, my pills, a tube of hand cream, and some dog biscuits just in case.

"What, no clicker?" The kids had all been running around with them this evening: *ribbit! Ribbit-ribbit!* It struck me now, though, that the racket had stopped very suddenly.

Wade looked smug. "Confiscated," he said. "Every damn one of 'em. Extra children I can deal with, but there's a line even I won't cross."

Then he kissed me, chucked me under the chin, and stopped, looking thoughtful suddenly. "You know she's not going to be an easy kid, right?"

Ivy, he meant, and oh boy, did I ever. Just tonight she'd decided that baked beans were yuck, and that the penny whistle little Nadine kept tootling on to accompany the *ribbits* needed to be hidden, ideally forever. I agreed, but the resulting kerfuffle involved Ivy's repeated *nyah-nyah*ing, leading to a shoulder punch from Nadine and a lot of tears.

"Yeah. I know," I said, and when Wade had gone upstairs

and the hall light went out, I lay worrying about it for a while. But then Fala came in and sat by the recliner and whined to be let up.

It was a large chair. I patted the space beside me. The big dog leapt up happily and settled with a whuffing sigh. The last bit of log flickering on the hearth fell apart in a shower of sparks and a puff of woodsmoke; rain tapped the windows.

Then Ivy wandered drowsily in, sucking her thumb and with her blanket trailing behind her, and climbed up, too, smelling of warm milk and baby shampoo.

And to think I once said there were too many people in this house.

Strictly speaking, the recliner wasn't big enough, either, but somehow we managed, and soon we were all fast asleep.

Recipe

A chocolate-cherry trifle is a big project, but you can have a very good imitation treat that includes all the flavors and removes a lot of time and work from the process. Here to fill the bill are Chocolate-Cherry Trifle Sandwich Cookies! Like this:

Ingredients:

For the frosting:

6 ounces softened cream cheese
4 squares unsweetened baking chocolate
3 cups powdered sugar
1 tsp vanilla extract
1 tsp maraschino cherry juice

Beat the softened cream cheese and sugar together until the mixture is smooth. Melt the chocolate in a double boiler or in the microwave Add the chocolate to the sugar-cream cheese mixture and beat until the chocolate is thoroughly mixed in. Add the vanilla extract and the cherry juice and mix thoroughly again.

If the frosting is too stiff, add cherry juice; if it's too soft, add powdered sugar.

For the ladyfingers: Use vanilla wafers. Nilla wafers, chessmen cookies, and Walker's shortbread work well, depending upon how much sweetness you like, but any plain vanilla wafer will do just fine.

For the cherry component: any good commercial cherry jam. I like Smucker's, Bonne Maman, and Stonewall Kitchen.

Now assemble the sandwich cookies: Frost half the wafers with frosting, the other half with cherry jam. Press the frosting wafers to the cherry jam wafers just firmly enough to stick them together.

And voilà! You can refrigerate these to keep the frosting from slipping. Or, you know, just go ahead and make a mess . . . I won't tell!